TAKING PAINS

The stairs sprawled in front of Olivia, for whom climbing even a few steps proved a chore. She held tightly to Lord Sheldrake's arm.

"I'll not let you go," he whispered, his breath warm against her cheek. Startled, she looked up into his eyes. He stopped and stared back. Olivia was trapped by the intensity of his gaze and forgot where she was entirely.

"Ready?" he asked.

"For what?"

A smile twitched at the corners of his well-formed lips. "To ascend."

Olivia coughed and looked away. She knew she must be three shades of red with embarrassment.

"Yes, of course."

Lord Sheldrake took his time, placing each step gingerly. She did the same, keeping her eyes downcast. Once she glanced up at him through her lashes. *What a mysterious man—overbearing one moment, kind the next.* Sometimes she felt like he could see right into her soul—where she had sworn never to allow anyone. . . .

Labor
of Love

∿

JENNA MINDEL

A SIGNET BOOK

SIGNET
Published by New American Library, a division of
Penguin Putnam Inc., 375 Hudson Street,
New York, New York 10014, U.S.A.
Penguin Books Ltd, 27 Wrights Lane,
London W8 5TZ, England
Penguin Books Australia Ltd, Ringwood,
Victoria, Australia
Penguin Books Canada Ltd, 10 Alcorn Avenue,
Toronto, Ontario, Canada M4V 3B2
Penguin Books (N.Z.) Ltd, 182–190 Wairau Road,
Auckland 10, New Zealand

Penguin Books Ltd, Registered Offices:
Harmondsworth, Middlesex, England

First published by Signet, an imprint of New American Library,
a division of Penguin Putnam Inc.

First Printing, December 2001
10 9 8 7 6 5 4 3 2 1

Copyright © Jenna Mindel, 2001

 REGISTERED TRADEMARK—MARCA REGISTRADA

Printed in the United States of America

PUBLISHER'S NOTE
This is a work of fiction. Names, characters, places, and incidents either are the
product of the author's imagination or are used fictitiously, and any resemblance to
actual persons, living or dead, business establishments, events, or locales is entirely
coincidental.

BOOKS ARE AVAILABLE AT QUANTITY DISCOUNTS WHEN USED TO PROMOTE PRODUCTS OR
SERVICES. FOR INFORMATION PLEASE WRITE TO PREMIUM MARKETING DIVISION, PENGUIN
PUTNAM INC., 375 HUDSON STREET, NEW YORK, NEW YORK 10014.

I dedicate this book to my critique group.
Without your support and encouragement, I would
not have kept going. I have learned so much from you guys;
I love each one of you. Packeteers Rule!

Chapter One

Things could not be any worse. Lady Olivia Beresford shifted again on the thin cushion of her seat. She wearied of traveling these past days and tried to get comfortable in the stifling heat of the swaying coach. She rubbed her temples, but found no relief from the dull ache inside her head.

She breathed in deeply, but an uncommonly heavy heat lay in the air. Patting her forehead with a lace handkerchief, her other hand rested on the bulging swell of her belly. Again, she wondered how she was to raise the little child within her. She rested her head against the squabs and closed her eyes. There was no money left. None. Robbie, her late husband, had wasted all of it.

She looked across at her sister, who sat gazing out of the window. There would be no more funds sent to Aunt Agatha for Susannah's welfare, either. Every penny was gone.

Her insides twisted with regret. If only she had known. If only Robbie had shared the state of their finances. But what could she have done? Her husband had cared little for her company or her opinion. There were no rich relatives to take them in. There was only Aunt Agatha, her mother's sister, living on a small pension of her own.

One answer kept coming to her mind, but she had no idea how she could make it happen. She must remarry. But this time, she must marry for wealth, and wealth alone.

She swallowed her distaste at such a mercenary plan, but for the sake of her family's future, she had to do everything in her power to catch a wealthy husband. She gazed at her huge belly. No man would want her in her present condition. Perhaps, she should wait until after her child was born to pursue a wealthy match. Besides, she had not yet put off her blacks; she was still in mourning.

"Olivia, this is the place. I am sure of it!" Susannah exclaimed.

"What place?"

"Do you never listen? I was just telling you about Lord Sheldrake."

She wrinkled her features in confusion.

"Oh, do stop your woolgathering," Susannah scolded. "I told you he lives just outside of Bibury. His estate is down that pass."

Olivia leaned forward and looked out of the window. She glimpsed lush fields and a tiny stream winding its way from the lovely little town of the Cotswolds. "Indeed?" She arched a brow, unsure of the significance of Lord Shell-what-have-you's location.

"Olivia," Susannah said slowly, as if speaking to one utterly ignorant of all that was important, "he is rumored to have killed his stepfather in a furious rage."

She shook her head. "Susannah, really."

"It is completely true. Please say that we can drive past Sheldrake Hall. It sits high upon a hill, which makes it quite easy to spot from the road. Please, do say yes."

"Why on earth do you wish to see such a man's home?"

"I hear it is a veritable palace. He is rich as Croesus. And, it is not terribly out of our way and would take but a minute or two."

"I do not know," Olivia stalled. She pulled absently at her bodice, which clung to her sweat-dampened skin. A quick stop for a breath of fresh air had to be of help to her throbbing head. She looked at her sister sitting demurely across from her. Susannah's golden curls bobbed in time with the carriage's movement. She was so pretty and had grown so much since the last time they were together. She would no doubt be the toast of London if she could have a season.

Olivia experienced the familiar twist of guilt for not securing a proper future for her sister.

"I suppose it is harmless enough to stop and look," she said, giving in.

Susannah clapped her hands. "Wonderful."

Suddenly, a soft rumble of thunder sounded in the distance, but the hazy sun continued to beat in through the carriage's glass. Olivia peered out of the half-opened window to see columns of darkening clouds forming along the horizon. She smiled. It would be fun indeed to see a murderer's home with a thunderstorm to lend its own drama to the landscape. And she so needed a diversion from her gloomy thoughts.

Olivia tapped the trapdoor with her parasol. Tom Coachman opened it and with eyes squinting, looked in.

"My lady?" His gruff voice boomed.

"Tom, we wish to take a small detour."

"To Sheldrake Hall," Susannah provided.

"Yes, Sheldrake Hall," Olivia agreed.

She heard him grumble about the inclement weather and their tardiness long after she had closed the trap. She smiled at Susannah when the carriage leaned to the right, confirming he had taken the turn as she requested.

Susannah rubbed her hands together. "Is this not delicious? And so sinister. I cannot wait to tell Brownie. Perhaps we may even spy Lord Sheldrake himself."

Olivia smiled at the mention of Susannah's old nurse, who also acted as their aunt's housekeeper. "Surely a man who killed his stepfather would be in Newgate, not ensconced in the comforts of his own home."

"But he is a viscount, and Brownie told me the murder was never proven. The local constable dismissed it as an accident."

A sudden flash of lightning split the sky.

"How could Brownie possibly know it was murder?" Olivia asked.

Susannah leaned forward. "Because her sister lives here.

She and her husband are his tenants. Brownie's sister wrote that there were scandalous happenings at Sheldrake Hall, and Lord Sheldrake himself had threatened to kill his step-father on several occasions."

"Then why did the constable dismiss it as an accident?" Olivia asked.

Susannah rolled her beautiful blue eyes. "Silly goose, a viscount can easily escape the arm of the law."

"I think you and Brownie read too many novels." She winked at her sister. "When did this happen?"

"Two summers ago."

"And Brownie told you all this?"

"Yes."

Olivia laughed. Brownie, as much as Susannah, adored anything resembling a villainous scheme. The two of them read Mrs. Radcliffe's novels by the armful. She watched Susannah fondly as the girl fidgeted with excitement and kept peering out of the window. They were almost there.

Olivia tapped on the trapdoor and shouted, "Tom, do stop when we reach the Hall. We should like very much to get a good look."

Tom Coachman peeked in with a scowl. "My lady, there be a storm setting in upon us. We should be 'eading straight for the inn."

"We shall only be a moment. Do stop," Olivia said.

The trapdoor closed with a disapproving snap, but soon the carriage slowed to a stop. Susannah opened the door and stepped out.

"Move over, I cannot see." Olivia held her belly as she stooped to look out of the opened door. She tipped her head to get a better view. An enormous square building stood proud and majestic atop a rolling hill of the deepest green. The late-day sun shone through the dark clouds, casting a peachy glow on the golden bricks. She counted at least a dozen chimneys, and there had to be four floors above-ground. Herds of sheep grazed off in the pasture land, and beyond that some fields were bare with newly turned rich earth. It could have been a pastoral painting, so peaceful did the place look.

She breathed in deeply of the sweet air, but it was still almost as hot as inside the carriage. She hoped the oncoming storm would bring cooler temperatures.

"Not quite the gabled gothic you hoped for, is it?" Olivia teased her sister. "I daresay it is much too civilized a home for a madman." She stepped back into the carriage. "Come on, dear, we had best leave in order to make it to the inn before a downpour."

Susannah climbed in and sat down, a disappointed look upon her face. "It certainly is a beautiful place."

"It is that." Olivia blinked at an intense flash of lightning and tensed in anticipation of the deafening clap of thunder that then crashed around her, shaking the very ground. She heard the cracking sound of wood nearby. The horses shrieked, and suddenly the carriage jolted, sending her sewing basket tumbling to the floor. Olivia was thrown back against the squabs as spools of thread rolled under the seat, then back out again. They were moving fast, too fast.

She looked at Susannah, whose face grew pale. The carriage bounced and pitched. She reached out to her sister, gripping the edge of her seat with hands gone white around the knuckles. The carriage swerved, and Olivia fell forward onto her knees.

Wobbly and with Susannah's help, Olivia pulled herself up to grasp hold of the trapdoor. Fierce flashes of lightning surrounded them, followed by more deafening thunder.

She shouted to the coachman, "Tom, Tom Coachman!" But he could not hear her. Slapping open the trapdoor, Olivia panicked. "Susannah, Tom is gone!"

"Gone?" Susannah screamed and tried to keep from falling back down onto her seat.

A dreadful creaking sound filled the air, then a sharp crack, as though something had snapped. Olivia swayed and tried to grab hold of her sister, when suddenly the world upended itself. Something hit her head, and she fell into darkness.

Richard DeQuincy, nineteenth Viscount Sheldrake, entered the quiet kitchens. It was late, another hour or so until sunset. Damp with sweat and none too clean from a day spent overseeing the second planting, he sighed with feeling very close to contentment.

Cook set a foaming tankard of homebrew on the table before him, followed by a pitcher of the same. "A plate be ready for ye in a bit, my lord."

Sheldrake issued a grunt in response as he drained the tankard and reached to refill it. The harvest would be a good yield this year, promising a fine bonus for his tenant farmers. Too bad there would be no ball to celebrate such bounty, he thought bitterly. Sheldrake Hall had not seen the likes of a ball since Abbott died. From the grave, Abbott still managed to rob Sheldrake of the simple pleasures. Someday things would return to normal. They had to, or he feared he would lose that part of himself that knew how to enjoy life.

He set down the tankard and rose from the table. His boots clicked against the tiles as he walked to the back entrance, where the door stood open. Not even a hint of breeze stirred the still air. He wiped his sweating brow with his shirtsleeve. He was hot and his muscles ached.

Looking out, he noticed the dark clouds clustered in the sky cast an unearthly glow all around. He watched lightning fork across the horizon. A storm was coming, thank goodness, to give relief from the heat. With the planting complete, the rain could come with his blessings.

Sheldrake had liked thunderstorms since he was a child. He remembered how his father gently explained their mysteries to him when he was a frightened mite in the nursery. To help him quell his fears, his father used to sit with him, and the two of them watched the storms roll in over DeQuincy land. There was nothing held back or controlled in a thunderstorm, Sheldrake mused. If only he could let go of the tight hold he kept upon the Hall. If he could just relax and not worry about his mother and her memory. If he could finally let go . . .

"Yer supper, my lord."

Sheldrake shrugged off his self-pity and took a seat at the kitchen table. "Thank you, Cook, it looks superb."

He brandished his knife and fork with a flourish. His back ached from even that small movement. His muscles screamed in protest of his return to such hard work. It had been two years since he had taken part in any of his tenant-farming activities. It had been two long years since Abbott died.

The men were wary at first to have him join them this year. Sheldrake had prepared for the worst reactions, but he was surprised how quickly the men fell into a comfortable working silence with him. He, like his father before him, believed that working side by side with one's tenants built trust and loyalty. He thought he had lost them both, but fortunately, he was proved wrong today. It felt good to see admiration in the men's eyes. Since Belinda jilted him, he had nursed a hollow feeling that no one would ever trust him again. Perhaps now he could get on with his life and leave that part of his past behind.

Lightning brightened the kitchens, and he flinched at the explosion of thunder that followed. Some tree nearby must have been hit, he thought. He would no doubt have to check the damage tomorrow. The storm raged on as he ate in silence.

Having finished his meal, Sheldrake looked forward to a hot soak in his copper tub. As he approached the main stairs, his butler stood in the front doorway, trying to calm a very large man with a gash across his wide forehead. His clothes were coachman's livery—dripping wet.

"What is it, Simms?" Sheldrake asked, then turned to the man. "Trouble?"

"Aye, sir." The large coachman breathed heavily. "There's been an accident—a tree was struck and took me right out'a me seat. My mistress and her sister are trapped. Sir, I beg your help."

"Show me!" Sheldrake ordered.

Sheldrake wrenched open the door, and a gust of wind tore at the coat he rammed his arms into. He fished his gloves out of the pockets and forced his hands into the worn leather as he hurried along the main drive. The rain fell with great heavy drops that stung his cheeks. He could see sheets of it coming toward them, the thunder and lightning constant but softer now.

"We had better hurry," Sheldrake yelled, then gave orders to a servant to have two horses readied immediately. Once inside the stable, he instructed his groom to follow with a carriage, tools, and men.

Within minutes, he and the coachman cantered down the long winding drive that emptied onto the road. As he approached the accident, Sheldrake took in the sight of a traveling coach overturned and pinned against a group of trees, the top wheel still spinning. He could hear a young lady's voice frantically calling for help.

"Hold tight, miss, we shall have you out of there in a trice," Sheldrake yelled.

"Please, oh please hurry. My sister does not look well," the young lady cried.

He slid off his horse. He circled the equipage, testing it and finding it stable. Negotiating the axle, he climbed up onto the side. A slightly opened window faced him. The only door was on the other side, resting upon the ground. He peered into the window, then lowered the glass, but it was still too small of an opening for anyone to climb in or out.

He stuck his head completely inside. The heat from the carriage hit him like a wall. A young girl, just out of the schoolroom, knelt beside a still form. He swallowed hard against the worry building within him. "Miss, are you hurt?" he called to her.

The girl continued to cry, shaking the form that lay against the door.

"Miss!" Sheldrake said again. "Are you hurt?"

"Oh, please, you must help my sister," she pleaded with a face wet from tears.

Sheldrake's gut twisted in fear. "I will, I promise. First, we must get you out of there."

It was not yet dark, but the light of dusk had started to fade. His men had arrived with tools, so Sheldrake called for an axe. He waited for lanterns to be hung on the low branches, then ordered the girl to cover her face and protect her sister as well as he cut along the window's frame. One of his men held the window in place as he cut, keeping it from falling in. Silently, he prayed for the life of the woman inside the carriage.

The wood of the carriage splintered, but did not give way easily. He cursed the quality construction and swung the axe high, trying to hurry. Finally, the hole appeared large enough for someone to pass through. As gently as he could, he coaxed the young woman to reach up to him, but she hesitated, casting a worried look back to her sister.

The coachman leaned over Sheldrake. "Come now, Miss Susannah, grab 'old of 'is lordship's 'ands."

Sheldrake watched as Miss Susannah's eyes widened with terror. He tried to brace himself for the inevitable hysterics, but her shrieks cut through him like a knife. She thought him a monster. She had heard the rumors about him.

"No, no, Tom. He is a murderer," she gasped.

Sheldrake rolled his eyes in frustration. No one had ever truly said the words to his face, but he had heard them whispered often enough. He turned to the coachman for help. Tom Coachman looked sheepish, but scolded the girl, demanding she reach up for Sheldrake's hands. Miss Susannah showed no signs of complying.

Irritation filled him. Sheldrake elbowed the coachman out of the way. Gritting his teeth, he leaned into the hole from his midsection. "Grab hold," he growled.

Miss Susannah went stark white and looked ready to faint. Sheldrake grabbed her arms and gave a tug to keep her from falling to her knees. The coachman leaned in to help, and the two of them pulled her up and out. She slid down the side of the carriage and stumbled when she hit the ground. She struggled to stand up.

"Bloody chit," Sheldrake muttered and called for his groom. "Take her to Mrs. Boothe."

"Aye, my lord," the groom answered. He tried to carry the girl, but she forced her chin up and refused anything more than his arm to lean on. When she turned around to look back at Sheldrake, he could tell she was trying to be brave, but her fear-filled face remained pale.

Sheldrake peered back into the opening, his sympathy for Miss Susannah forgotten when faced with the task at hand. The trees shut out what light was left from the darkening sky, making it hard to see.

"Lantern!" Sheldrake ordered. The coachman was quick to obey and soon held the light close to Sheldrake's head. Carefully, Sheldrake slipped inside the carriage. The lantern lit the interior with a soft glow. He looked around and saw a limp hand peeking out from underneath a blanket. A small portmanteau lay open in the corner, its contents scattered over the still form that lay before him. Sheldrake swallowed.

He moved forward, only to step on a spool of thread. He kicked it out of the way. Stooping low, he pulled the blanket away from the woman's chin. There was a small swelling bump upon her forehead. Kneeling carefully, he reached for her neck. He hesitated slightly, then tentatively touched just under her jaw, where he found a strong pulse beating. Relief flooded through him. He pushed back a length of dusky hair that covered her eyes and nearly gasped. She was lovely. He noted that her color was good, then scanned the length of her body when his gaze connected with a belly round as newly piled hay. He swore.

"Sir, is she . . . ?" The coachman's voice faltered.

"Good God, man! This woman is heavy with child! What in the name of all that is holy are you doing driving this lady

about? Where is this woman's husband?" Sheldrake
shouted.

"Dead sir, these past six months."

A stirring sound brought Sheldrake's attention back to
the woman as she struggled to wake.

"Susannah?" the woman whispered.

"She is safe and unharmed." Sheldrake peered into eyes
of an unusually dark green. A feeling of strangeness over-
took him, as if he had seen her before, but that was impos-
sible. Surely, he would have remembered a beauty like her.
A soft moan from her interrupted his thoughts, and he asked,
"Do you think you can sit?"

"I . . . don't know." She let her eyelids close, and her
hand flew to her forehead. "Where am I?"

"Near Sheldrake Hall, ma'am. There has been an accident." She lay quiet a moment longer than he thought necessary. He hoped she hadn't fainted.

Without opening her eyes, she asked, "What was that
pounding?"

Pounding?

"I thought I heard pounding."

Sheldrake finally understood. "Yes, you did. We had to
cut through the window with an axe."

"Why not use the door?" Her voice rang deep, husky.

He smiled. "You, madam, are lying upon the door."

The woman tried to push herself up, but succeeded only
in propping herself upon her elbows. She blinked her eyes a
couple of times, then looked straight at him. Uncomfortable,
he grew conscious of his dirt. The rain, lighter now, fell
freely into the coach, and splashes hit her cheeks and nose.
He knew rivulets of rain ran down his face as well. Lamely
he asked, "Are you hurt?"

"Presently, I always hurt," she said with a groan. He
watched as she pushed herself to a sitting position. She
leaned forward, breathing heavily. Worry creased her brow
as she held her middle.

Sheldrake reached out his hand, but let it drop when her frown cleared with a slight smile.

Sounding more alert, she said, "My child moved! Oh, thank Heaven, I believe no harm has been done."

Sheldrake released a sigh of relief. Now to get her out, he thought. "Can you stand?"

"I will need your help."

"Of course." Sheldrake bent to pull her to her feet, but she did not budge. He tried again.

"No, I am sorry, but you are hurting my arm."

He stopped instantly.

"Well, that did not work." Looking thoughtful, she rubbed her arm, then added, "My good man, I believe you shall have to lift me from behind. Once I am down, I have a devilish time of it getting back up."

He blinked in surprise at her humor, even though her lower lip trembled. His gaze encountered the ball that was her belly, and he understood her difficulty. He crouched forward, half afraid to touch her. He had never helped a woman in her condition before and was not sure what to do. He reached both his hands out to her; she could decide what to do with them.

"I do apologize, but you shall have to get behind me. Place your hands beneath my arms and haul me up like any sack of grain." The woman smiled, looking embarrassed. She seemed remarkably calm in the face of such a predicament.

Sheldrake peered up through the window; the coachman looked on, his expression grim. Sheldrake crawled around her, his movements awkward. Crouching low, he pulled himself directly behind her, letting his knees straddle her back. Her warmth permeated the length of his breeches. He tried to keep his thighs from touching her, but that made matters only worse, since her bottom was in direct contact with his groin. Then her perfume caught his attention. The soft floral scent filled his nostrils. His pulse pounded in his ears. He shook his head, trying to clear it, then gently placed his hands under her arms as she had requested of him.

Because his face was very close to hers, he could not keep his rain-soaked hair from dripping water onto her cheek. Tossing back his head to get the sodden lock out of his way, his chin brushed her cheek. Incredible softness met his stubble-covered face. He felt a strong urge to run his fingers across her skin to see if it could truly be that soft.

He cleared his throat.

The woman started to speak. "Now, I will try to push myself up with my hands. You lift, and I trust my feet shall obey me and follow. Ready?" She shifted, and her movement put his hands in direct contact with two pleasantly round breasts.

Sheldrake jerked back as if he had been burned, bumping his head in the process. "No, not ready," he said through gritted teeth.

He found it difficult to breathe. Her softness surrounded him . . . skin, scent, breasts. Good Lord, what was he thinking! It had been too long since he had enjoyed a woman's company. He let out a breath he did not realize he held. "We shall go on my count of three. Ready, one, two . . . three." He lifted.

She pushed against him, and his hands slid to her waist to steady her, but they were standing. The rain had turned to a drizzle, and it settled like a mist over them. The woman leaned against his chest and held her belly with both hands.

"Madam, what is it? The child?"

"I simply need to catch my breath—a moment please."

Sheldrake gave her time as he stood with her leaning into him. He fought the urge to wrap his arms around her. She felt warm and soft, and he did not care if this moment lasted forever. He cursed himself inwardly, calling himself an idiot. He needed to figure out how to get this woman out of the carriage, not how it would feel to hold her.

Sheldrake gazed at the gaping hole that was the window. He did not like the idea of pulling her out of the carriage. He

did not want to hurt her. An idea began to form. With his
hands still resting upon the woman's waist, Sheldrake yelled
up to the coachman to throw down a thick rope.

He reached up and caught it with one hand as he shielded
the woman with his other. "I shall try to fashion a sort of
seat, then we will pull you out. It is not very far, and I will
be here steadying you from, ah, this end," Sheldrake explained when he had the rope in hand.

"Very well," she said without question.

She stood watching him as he fashioned a makeshift loop
seat with the rope. He instructed her to step into it. Again,
his hands encountered a delicate area of her person as he secured the rope in place under her bottom. Once completed,
he rubbed the stiff muscles of his neck.

"No, that will not do," Sheldrake said. Her middle
pressed against the knot in a way that must be terribly uncomfortable. Looking up through the hole, Sheldrake
scratched his head. He would hurt her if he tried pulling her
out that way. He slid the rope down the stiff skirt of her
dress.

"Here, step out of it," he said as he knelt down.

She leaned her hands upon his shoulders to steady herself. Her stomach pressed against his head, and he marveled
at the hardness of it.

"What shall you do now?" she asked.

"I have another idea." He looked up at her worried face
and gave her a smile of encouragement.

Sheldrake called for the axe. He helped the woman lean
against the other side of the carriage, out of the way. Swing-
ing the axe with caution, he slammed it against the hinges.
They bent. Again he chipped away at the wood. Finally, it
gave way and he pulled the door free to lift it through the
hole and hand it to the coachman, still watching overhead.

Without a word, Sheldrake continued to widen the opening that was the door, bringing in clumps of grass as he
went. Satisfied with his work, Sheldrake turned to her.
"There, I believe that should do."

He gave orders for his men to pull the carriage upright upon his word.

"We shall kneel here in the door's opening. When the men lift the carriage, it shall pass over us," Sheldrake explained.

A slight frown tugged her lips downward.

"Come." He held out his hand to her. "Lean into me."

She took his hand and leaned against him for support. With an arm around her back, Sheldrake helped her to kneel, then he knelt down facing her and wrapped his arms about her. She tensed, but soon relaxed against him. Her hair tickled his chin, and the soft floral scent she wore again assaulted his senses. With her belly so close against the length of him, Sheldrake felt the woman tremble.

"Do not worry, I shall keep you safe," Sheldrake murmured. He shielded her with his body and arms as much as possible. He felt her tuck her head beneath his chin.

He then gave word to his men to pull the carriage away. With a great straining sound, the carriage lifted. The woman inched closer to him, and he squeezed tighter to give her comfort. Slowly, the carriage rose over their crouched forms and away from them.

"It is all right now," he whispered into her ear. "We are free."

The rain had stopped. Olivia could not keep from trembling. She was loath to break away from the farmer's embrace, so comforting was it to be held. She looked up and peeked over his shoulder. Men were busy with securing the carriage. The team of carriage horses were tied to a clump of trees, and they nibbled distractedly at the grass. They looked so calm. Calm was something she could not claim for herself.

Tom Coachman approached them, and still she clung to the farmer who knelt with her.

"Ma'am?" the farmer asked.

"I beg your pardon, sir." Olivia flushed as she let go her tight hold.

"My lord, is she well?" Tom Coachman asked.

Olivia blinked. *My lord?*

The farmer answered him, his voice firm. He stood and helped her to her feet as well.

"I say, Lord Sheldrake, good idea with that carriage. She lifted like she were a feather." Tom Coachman chewed a length of grass.

Lord Sheldrake? The viscount! Olivia suddenly realized that her farmer was none other than the viscount who murdered his stepfather! She swayed.

Afraid, she demanded, "Where have you taken my sister?"

"She is at Sheldrake Hall, safe and sound," he answered, but he looked directly at her, as if seeing her clearly for the first time. His expression changed. He looked hard.

She watched with wide eyes as he walked toward her to stop in front of her. *Susannah at Sheldrake Hall! Alone.* Olivia's head began to pound in earnest. She held her temples with her fingers. What was she to do!

"Madam, are you all right?" Lord Sheldrake touched her elbow, offering support.

Olivia shrugged off his touch. "My lord, please, I must see my sister."

"Of course. A carriage waits. Do you need assistance?"

"I am quite capable of walking on my own," she snapped. She saw the briefest flash of something too much like hurt in his eyes. She turned and walked toward the carriage, her shoulders stiff and her head held high, and her nerves in turmoil. Never did she suspect the man who rescued her to be the viscount Susannah had described earlier. How could a man be so gentle and be a murderer?

Pulling hastily on her gown to lift it, Olivia did not watch where she stepped. She tripped on an exposed tree root. Strong arms wrapped around her in an instant. Lord Sheldrake lifted her and carried her the rest of the way.

"My lord," she gasped, "surely it is unnecessary for you to carry me so. "

"I'll not see you trip on the wet ground." His response was clipped.

She closed her eyes. She felt the utter fool. Why had he not introduced himself straightaway? He deposited her into the carriage carefully and left, but the carriage remained still. She sat there, overwhelmed. She stared out of the window and watched the men standing around the wreckage of her carriage and shuddered. She and her sister could have been killed. She rubbed her stomach and thanked God that her child continued to stir within.

She closed her eyes, forcing the knot in the pit of her stomach to unwind. She listened to the strong voice of Lord Sheldrake as he gave orders to the men. He wanted whatever could be salvaged from the carriage brought to the stables in the morning. She wondered what cousin Edmund would say if he saw the crested carriage of Adberesmere now. She laughed bitterly. It would be one less thing that he could take away from her.

She rested her head back, straining to keep her eyes open. She rubbed them, but to no avail. The grittiness ceased only if she kept them closed. And then she realized that things had just gotten considerably worse.

Chapter Two

Olivia awoke. The gentle sway of movement confirmed she was in the carriage. The luxurious butter-soft leather beneath her cheek reminded her that it belonged not to her, but to Lord Sheldrake. The scent of rain lingered, and a faint spiciness tickled her memory. Her eyes flew open. Across from where she lay, he watched her.

"Forgive me, my lord." She tried to sit up.

"No, stay." He held his hand out, gesturing for her to keep still. "We shall be at the Hall directly."

She chastised herself again for mistaking the viscount for a farmer. *What must Lord Sheldrake be thinking?* She remained lying on her side, resting her cheek upon her hands. She would sit up when she must. She need not have him close to her, trying to help. Her cheeks burned at the memory of how he had touched her.

When he had tried to help her to stand in the carriage and had accidentally encountered her breasts, Olivia thought she would laugh aloud. It would have been nothing more than embarrassing if he were only farmer; but now that she knew better, she was mortified.

He turned to look out the window, giving her a chance to study him. He did not look like a farmer now. How stupid of her to ever imagine him thus. Every trace of awkwardness toward her had vanished, leaving a distant coldness in its place. *What has Susannah gotten us into?*

She shifted when Lord Sheldrake's gaze settled upon her. His dark eyes narrowed as he openly observed her. Trapped by his gaze, Olivia stared back, until a shiver passed through her and she finally looked away. She pulled the coat, draped over her, closer in an attempt to chase away the chill that had taken hold of her. It was his coat. The fine wool rubbed her chin, and she inhaled the spicy scent he wore. It was too masculine by half and served only to chill her further.

"You are cold," he stated. "It will not be much longer, Lady Beresford."

Surprised at his use of her name, she looked up.

"Your coachman told me. I knew your late husband. A good huntsman. I offer you my condolences upon his accident."

She lay there staring like an idiot, too overcome to do otherwise. She wondered how well Lord Sheldrake knew Robbie and when they had met. And, she wondered, did Lord Sheldrake know anything about her current predicament?

In no time the carriage came to a halt. He rose from his seat and extended his hand to help her to sit up. His hands were slightly rough, but warm.

"I shall step down first, then lift you," he said.

"I am sure I can walk, my lord."

"Even so."

She moved slowly, but with his lordship's aid she managed to stand upon the first rung of the carriage step. Her muscles seemed to stiffen in the cool night air left by the storm. Mist rose from the ground, adding an eeriness she could not like. She stood there looking around the grounds, as if trying to discover the man through his surroundings. Everything was meticulously cared for—neat, tidy. It still looked sinister.

She placed her hand upon his lordship's shoulders to steady herself. Heat from his skin radiated through the lawn shirt he wore, yet it did nothing to ease the gooseflesh of her arms. She tried to step down, but her knees buckled. Lord Sheldrake swept her into his arms.

She gasped, inhaling his spicy cologne mixed with sweat,

rain, and out-of-doors. It unnerved her to be so close to him,
yet she clung to him, afraid he would drop her, so stiffly did
he hold her. He approached the main door, which opened
immediately. A worried, mid-aged woman wearing a large,
snowy white cap issued forth.

"Oh, the poor dear," the woman exclaimed. "This way,
my lord, if you please. We have a room ready for her, and
Doctor Pedley is on his way." Turning to Olivia, she continued, "Your sister is snug as a kitten before a fire, but wishes
to see you, of course. Now follow me, follow me. Simms,
out of the way! His lordship can manage, for she is truly a
small burden even in her state. Is that not so, my lord?"

"Indeed."

With Lord Sheldrake's warm body surrounding her,
Olivia managed to stop shivering. She looked at his lordship's face to gauge his reaction to such an onslaught of nervous chatter from the woman they followed. His expression
remained hard. The signs of a late-day beard around his chin
made him look all the more grim.

"Lady Beresford, this is Mrs. Boothe," Lord Sheldrake
informed her. "The housekeeper."

"Oh."

"How do you do." Mrs. Boothe bobbed a swift curtsy.
"Now careful on those stairs, my lord. Wouldn't want you to
stumble. I've chosen the green chamber, which I hope meets
with your approval. I can stay with you this night, my dear,
if you wish. A trundle has already been placed at the foot
of . . ." She coughed, then whispered genteelly, *"The bed."*

Lord Sheldrake rolled his eyes.

"Thank you." She had barely said the words when Mrs.
Boothe continued in a one-way conversation whereby
Olivia need only nod here and again in response. Lord Shel-
drake said little.

The green chamber proved to be beautiful and tastefully
decorated in shades of sage green and ivory. Olivia marveled at such exquisite style. She noticed a small sitting
room with its own fireplace. The room was fit for a queen.

"Mrs. Boothe will see to your needs." Lord Sheldrake gently lowered her to the bed. His roughened chin brushed her forehead, and Olivia looked up. Their gaze met and held. His eyes were actually blue, so deep in color that they looked almost black. His face hovered just above hers for a moment longer than necessary, then he straightened. She swallowed. He looked very much like a murderer, tall, dark, and cold.

"Thank you," she choked out from a tight throat.

His expression softened slightly as he tipped his head in acknowledgment, turned, and left.

"Here now, my lady, we must get you out of those damp clothes before you catch your death." Mrs. Boothe fussed over her like a mother hen with a new chick.

But Olivia remained transfixed, her gaze glued to the closed door Lord Sheldrake had just exited. Recovering her wits, she nodded to Mrs. Boothe and prayed that neither Susannah nor herself would catch their deaths in this murderer's home.

"Richard! Here you are. Good heavens, look at you. You wear more dirt than the road." Lady Evelyn Abbott hurried down the hall as Sheldrake reached the stairs.

"Good evening, Mother."

"Tell me, what is amiss? I was in my rooms when I heard the servants running about."

"A carriage accident. The occupants are here at the Hall."

"Well, who are they?"

"Lady Beresford of Adberesmere and her sister."

"Oh? Are they very pretty?"

"Mother, really. Lady Beresford is recently widowed and heavy with child." And positively beautiful, Sheldrake added silently.

"Goodness, no." His mother covered her mouth with her hand, her eyes wide. A few seconds later, she lowered her hand and cocked her head to the side. "What about the sister?"

"A schoolroom miss. I am awaiting Doctor Pedley, so if you will excuse me——"

"Are you not going to wash? You look the commonest of men," his mother scolded.

"Surely, the common man does not own buckskin breeches from Bond Street." Sheldrake could not quite keep a drawl from entering his voice.

"No, of course not." Lady Evelyn smoothed her silk gown. "Why you feel obliged to play in the dirt and grime I shall never understand. Even your father baffled me when he started this nonsense of working in the fields. There are plenty of men to do the work. You need not concern yourself with it."

He had heard this complaint before. "Fine then, Mother, I shall bathe quickly before Pedley shows. I will speak with you later." He bent to kiss her brow and turned to start up the stairs.

"Very well. But I do need to discuss a matter of importance with you. I have received an invitation to tea."

At hearing this, Sheldrake halted. Without turning around, he cautiously inquired, "Indeed? From whom, pray tell?"

"From Mrs. Hardcastle. She is a dear. The tea is in honor of Lady Belham. You remember Lady Belham, she is aunt to Belinda Ashton. Well, Belinda is Lady Framingham now."

Sheldrake's hands clenched in time with his jaw.

"The tea is Wednesday next," his mother finished.

"That would be a trifle awkward, would it not? I was once betrothed to marry Belinda." Sheldrake nearly spat the name.

"Yes, you were," his mother said, then added hurriedly, "but that was ages ago."

Not so long, Sheldrake thought. He closed his eyes in an attempt to block out the vision of Belinda accusing him, leaving him.

"I do not believe that Belinda will be present, so I see no reason for any awkwardness. It has been an age since I was out and about, and Mrs. Hardcastle is such a dear lady," his mother explained.

Should he deny his mother a chance to mingle with the local society after two long years? He had a habit of making excuses for her whenever she received an invitation. He tried to protect her from rumors and snubs as best he could by responding with various regrets. Perhaps the local polite society had forgotten. Other scandals had come and gone to fill their gossip plate.

But what if his mother remembered what happened that night? Sheldrake gave himself a mental shake. It was high time things returned to a semblance of what once was normal. His mother making the rounds with their neighbors was part of that. It was high time that he let go.

"Let me review the invitation, Mama, and then we can decide." He hoped it listed the other attendees.

"Very well, Richard, but I fear I shall go with or without your permission. I am your mother after all."

Dry and dressed in a warmed cotton nightdress, Olivia lay back against the pillows to await the doctor's arrival. She stopped twisting her hands only to worry the edge of the coverlet. The dull ache in her lower back, a constant companion, threatened to work its way to her neck and shoulders. A knock at the door startled her.

"That will be Doctor Pedley," Mrs. Boothe announced as she opened the door.

Olivia looked at the small man with weathered skin and squinty eyes behind round spectacles resting upon his nose. He smiled at her.

"Good evening, Lady Beresford. How are you feeling?"

"Well enough," she said.

"Good news, that. I may be old, but I've practiced as a surgeon in my youth, then as a respected physician in London before retiring here to my native village." The doctor winked.

"You are retired, then?" Her voice cracked.

"Aye, but I cannot keep away from medicine. Lord Sheldrake pays me well to care for the townspeople and his household."

"I see."

"Now then, my lady, you are in what month?"

"Tis my eighth, sir, I believe." Olivia liked the look of Doctor Pedley. He was clean and tidy, and he asked for a basin of water with soap to wash his hands. The midwife who had called upon her at Adberesmere was a gnarled, gnomelike woman with missing teeth. She practiced no such ritual of cleanliness.

"You must be very happy to soon be done with the carrying." The doctor smiled.

"I suppose." She refused to think about the upcoming birth. She would deal with that event when it came. For all she knew, it could spell her death as it had her mother when Susannah was born. Olivia had only been seven years old and scared to pieces when she heard her mother's agonizing screams. She shuddered at the memory. The panic she felt then at seven was not too different from the panic she felt now when she thought of her confinement.

The doctor must have sensed her anxiety. With a soothing voice, he said, "You are nervous, which is common when expecting your first child."

"Yes," she whispered.

"My lady, I shall give you a thorough examination to determine if there has been any damage to the babe. Try to relax. Mrs. Boothe here will hold your hand."

She felt the housekeeper grab hold of her hand and give it a squeeze. It was the longest period since her arrival that the woman had remained silent.

She looked at the ceiling in an attempt to calm herself.

"Tell me, Lady Beresford, what brings you to travel in your condition?" the doctor asked.

"My husband died, sir, and his heir requested that I leave."

"Were there no provisions made?"

"No, evidently not," she answered simply. Talking helped; she wondered if the doctor knew that.

"Where were you headed for your confinement?" Doctor Pedley asked.

"My aunt's home in Chipping Sodbury. If I can be gone tomorrow we may save her undo worry." Olivia held her breath.

"We shall see," the doctor replied.

Lord Sheldrake, bathed and comfortable in his undress, sat before a roaring fire in his study. The night air had turned decidedly cool. He was waiting for Pedley, who was not yet finished with Lady Beresford. He swished his brandy, then drank, but the smooth, sweet liquid from the finest cellars in France held no allure for him. His mind remained fixed upon a set of green eyes. Why did she seem so familiar?

He heard the sound of the door creaking open, then his butler's soft step into the room.

"Your lordship?"

"Yes, Simms?"

"The doctor wishes a word with you."

"Send him in."

Pedley took no time in entering. "Ah, Richard, how are you, lad?"

"Depends upon what news you bring me, Pedley."

"As impertinent as ever! Well, perhaps I shall give you no news until you share that brandy. I have not had real French brandy this age."

"You shall not say where you had the stuff? I need no dealings with the constable for possession of smuggled goods, even though I purchased it squarely in London."

"Pah! Half the county's gentry find something French to stash away. I am sure no magistrate will begrudge a man his drink. The war's almost done. There will be free trade with the Frogs again soon."

Sheldrake saluted his doctor friend, known since childhood, with a refilled glass. He awaited the doctor's sip, but Pedley remained quiet.

"What news have you of Lady Beresford?" Sheldrake asked.

"She cannot leave here."

"Beg pardon?"

"She must remain here throughout her confinement. She is in no condition to travel. She is skittish as a wild pony, from nerves or the accident, I cannot be sure. Either way, she cannot be moved."

"You mean to tell me that a woman about to give birth must do so here?" Sheldrake barked.

"Aye. You have the right of it." Pedley began to grin.

"Blast your eyes for enjoying this!" Sheldrake took a long pull of the brandy. A vision of Lady Beresford's brow clearing once she felt her child move within her flitted across Sheldrake's thoughts. "There's no damage to the babe, is there?" he asked with concern.

"Not that I can tell. But I would much rather be safe than sorry. There's more, lad."

"How can there possibly be more?" Sheldrake raked a hand through his still damp hair.

"The aunt," Pedley stated.

"Yes. I sent a message with their coachman, explaining their delay. I will send another about . . ."

"Not good enough, my boy," Pedley interrupted. "Lady Beresford demands her aunt be brought here as a source of comfort and to look after the sister."

Sheldrake took a swallow of his brandy. It did nothing to fortify his soul. "She told you this, did she?" His house was to be overrun by females, and he wanted no part of it. The last thing he wanted was a beautiful woman under his roof for any length of time.

"Aye, she did. Wanted me to pass the word on to you." The doctor sighed and slapped his hand upon his knee before he stood. "I best be on my way. I will stop back the day after tomorrow to see how she fares. Lady Beresford needs rest for a day or two, then she can be up and about. When she feels up to it, some very light walking but no farther than the courtyard garden. She cannot lift, she cannot imbibe spirits or spicy foods. I have left instructions with Mrs. Boothe. Oh, and do try to keep her calm. Good evening then." Pedley set down his empty glass. "I can show myself out."

"The deuce," Sheldrake muttered when the door closed. He sat swishing his brandy this way and that. "The bloody deuce."

A knock at the door roused Susannah from staring into the fire. "Come in," she called.

Mrs. Boothe peeked into the room. "I wanted to let you know that your sister is going to be just fine, miss."

Relief flooded through her, and she jumped up and ran toward the housekeeper. "Oh thank you for telling me. I've been waiting an age to hear. Can I see her?"

"Not tonight, I think. She is sleeping peacefully. I am sure you can talk with her in the morning. The babe is unharmed and all is well."

"Thank you, Mrs. Boothe."

The housekeeper nodded and shut the door with a soft click.

Susannah sighed. She walked back to the chair in front of the fireplace, but she could not sit back down. She felt pent up in this chamber long enough. She had to investigate the house since she had the chance. To spend the night at Sheldrake Hall and not to see all of it would be a dreadful waste. She had to have something more than the carriage accident to tell Brownie.

She grabbed her wrapper from the bed and twirled it about her shoulders. Quietly, she entered the hall. Candles burned brightly from the wall sconces, but all was quiet. Tiptoeing her way down the corridor, she gazed at the various tapestries and paintings upon the wall in awe. Sheldrake Hall was a grand home, grander than any she had ever been in before—even greater than Adberesmere. Lord Sheldrake was plump in funds, Susannah thought as she scanned the upstairs décor.

She continued to pad silently through the large hallway, and she noted that other hallways ventured off in other directions. There were several corridors to choose from. As she passed the main staircase, she wondered where each one led. There was only one way to find out.

Turning to her right, she walked down the closest smaller hall and glimpsed a row of doors. Curiosity got the best of her. She opened them one by one, only to find them all unused and the furniture under Holland covers. The last one, however, was completely aired and dusted as if expecting a visitor. She wondered why Mrs. Boothe had not placed her or Olivia in this room, instead of ordering the servants to ready the other rooms when she was brought to the Hall.

She stepped into the large bedchamber and noticed that it had glass doors on the other side of the room. She padded across the thick carpets to open them. She walked out onto an expanse of balcony that overlooked the gardens. She felt envy at having been placed next to Olivia's chamber with a rather common view of the main drive. She knew she was being silly. They would be here only one night.

She stepped back in and closed the doors. The room was lovely, but decorated in darker hues that were almost masculine. Looking about intently, she noticed a small writing desk set against the wall, papers and envelopes stacked upon it in a neat pile. Curious, she riffled through them and found two letters among the blank sheets.

The first letter was an interesting account of a visit to Sheldrake Hall by someone who misspelled several words, and the second was a list of items one might buy as gifts.

A sudden creak startled her, and she looked up to see Lord Sheldrake standing in the doorway. Dread spread through her to settle in the pit of her stomach, and she dropped the letters.

"My lord!" She bent down to retrieve them, but one fluttered away from her to the floor once again.

"Miss Susannah?"

"Lacey, my lord. Susannah Lacey." Flustered with fear, she curtsied rather awkwardly. "Nice to meet you, sir."

A slight smile played at the corners of his mouth. "Your chamber is at the end of north hall, I believe."

She bent again to snatch the letter that had gotten away from her. "I beg your pardon, sir. I was simply looking about. I could not quite go to sleep this early and . . ." She knocked over the wastebasket with a thud. "I am sorry."

She backed away as he walked toward her, his hand outstretched for the letter she held clutched in her hand. Realizing what he wanted, she handed it to him, then backed away against the doors to the balcony.

He looked at the paper, then crumpled it. He bent down to right the basket and dropped the crushed letter into it. He turned to her, his eyes clearly amused, not in the least angry-looking. "Nothing much in here, Miss Lacey. Perhaps you should retire for the night. It has been an exhausting day for everyone."

"Yes, my lord, sir." Susannah bobbed another curtsy and dashed out the door without looking back. She turned down the hall and realized she had gone the wrong way when she nearly collided with a lady not much taller than herself.

"Oh dear," the lady said. "You must be the young girl in the carriage accident. I am so sorry to hear about your ordeal. I am Lady Evelyn, Lord Sheldrake's mother."

Susannah let out the breath she held with a whoosh. "My name is Susannah Lacey. Thank you."

"But of course, my dear Miss Lacey." She took Susannah's hand in her own. "Are you lost? Or do you have need of anything?"

"No, er, well . . . yes, I am a bit lost. I need to find my chamber at the end of the north hall," she breathed.

"My goodness, you are turned around. Follow me, dear, and I will point you in the right direction." Lady Evelyn smiled and squeezed her hand. "And do not worry, you need not be afraid, dear, it is a big house."

Susannah suddenly relaxed. Lady Evelyn had the loveliest smile, and dressed as she was in a white billowing night-dress with matching wrap she looked like an angel. "Thank you. Thank you for helping us."

"Of course, dear, but my son is the one to be commended for the rescue. Now come along and I'll show you which way to go."

Olivia was nearly asleep when she heard a whisper from the door.

"Olivia. Are you awake?"

It was Susannah.

"I am now. Come in."

"I am sorry to wake you," Susannah said as she sat upon her bed, then bent to light the candle at her bedside. "I did not mean to disturb you, and I know you need your sleep, with traveling tomorrow and all."

"It is all right." Olivia pulled herself up to a sitting position and leaned against the pillows behind her. "Susannah, we won't be leaving tomorrow."

"Mrs. Boothe said you were well, I thought—"

"Doctor Pedley does not wish me to travel."

"Must we stay here?" Susannah's blond curls hung about her shoulders.

"Yes, until after the baby is born." Olivia plumped her pillows with her fist, hoping to dispel her frustration. Her aunt would be even less pleased; no doubt she knew Susannah's story about Lord Sheldrake as well. She leaned forward. "I have sent for Aunt Agatha. She should arrive by tomorrow evening." She patted Susannah's hand.

"But what about Lord Sheldrake?"

"He has been most kind in taking us in."

"He is a murderer." Susannah grasped her neck in a melodramatic pose.

"Shhhh! Keep your voice down." Olivia scanned the

room, but there was no sign of the housekeeper. "Mrs. Boothe will be back at any time. She plans to stay the night in my room to give me comfort, I suppose. Besides, the murder is only a rumor."

"But what if it is true?"

A chill darted down her spine to lodge itself in the pit of her stomach. Olivia did not know how to answer. She shook her head instead. "Not another word of it, Susannah. You are not to speak of such things again. The servants may hear. Lord Sheldrake has been a perfect gentleman, and nothing will happen to us, especially with Aunt Agatha present. Until she arrives, you are to stay in your room or come to mine to pass the time. Is that understood?"

"But—"

"Susannah, you must listen to me in this. I do not want you skulking about this place alone." She knew her sister's curiosity could very well land her in a coil. "Promise me."

Susannah hesitated. "I promise."

She hoped her sister would keep her promise. Susannah fidgeted with her wrapper and looked as if she positively itched to be gone. Olivia sighed. She felt too tired to make any further demands. "All right then, it is late and we both need our rest. Good night."

"Good night, Olivia. I will see you in the morning." Susannah slid off the bed and padded to the door.

"Good night, and rest well."

"I shall." Susannah quietly shut the door.

Olivia slid down under the covers. The house creaked as most do in the stillness of night. She supposed it was not such a bad thing to have the housekeeper sleep in her chamber this night. She would feel much better once her aunt arrived.

Chapter Three

Sheldrake was filling his plate a second time at the sideboard when his mother entered, dressed in flowing lilac silk.

"Good morning, Richard. Do leave some food for our guests."

"I doubt they will join us, Mother. Lady Beresford is bedridden, so a tray has been sent up for her and her sister."

"Ah yes, Miss Susannah. A charming minx," his mother said. "I met her last night. She was wandering about the halls, looking lost."

Sheldrake remained silent. She had not been lost. She had gone white as a sheet when he caught her going through some old correspondence last night. Headstrong and foolish, that one, he thought.

"What is Lady Beresford like, dear?" His mother poured herself a cup of chocolate.

"Why not meet her and find out?"

"I do not wish to tire her, and you know how I am about sickrooms. Simply cannot abide them—reminds me too much of your father's illness."

"She is not ill, Mama, she is *enceinte,*" Sheldrake pointed out. "That certainly is not a contagious condition."

His mother turned pink. "When does this aunt arrive?"

"Today."

"Perhaps she can join me for tea."

"Indeed." Sheldrake picked up his copy of the *Morning Post.* He whistled as he read the society gossip regarding a longtime friend of his who had recently wed. "Peter cut short his bridal trip."

"What, dear?"

"Peter Blessing. He married one of the Preston heiresses. They cut short their bridal trip to the surprise of the *ton* tabbies. There is a whole column here filled with speculations as to why the newlyweds left his brother's hunting lodge separately. I still cannot believe he has married."

"Why?"

"I wonder how he got the girl's father to allow such a match."

"Peter is from good family," Lady Evelyn answered.

"Yes, but he has not much else to bring to a marriage. He is a rakehell with pockets to let."

"Maybe they are in love." His mother, filled plate in hand, sat down to the table.

Sheldrake snorted in reply. "I attended the wedding, Mama. Miss Preston looked anything but pleased with the match." He would bet a bull's-eye that Peter acted less than gentlemanly in getting his betrothal. He would hear all about it soon enough. No doubt Peter was on his way to Sheldrake Hall.

"Brides can be silly on their wedding day. Peter is a wonderful boy." His mother reached across the table to take the column.

For years his friend had visited the Hall for a few weeks' respite from London's heated summers. It was an informal commitment between the two. Peter took care not to arrive on the anniversary of Abbott's death, and that was two days ago. And now he had cut short his honeymoon. He would be here soon.

Peter Blessing was the one person Sheldrake could truly talk to. He had been staying at the Hall the night Abbott died. Sheldrake regretted that his friend had been dragged into the whole mess, but he thanked God there was someone who had kept a level head that night. If not for Peter, Sheldrake may well have landed in Newgate.

*   *   *

Olivia pushed away her tray of food, most of it left untouched. She flexed her feet under the coverlet. She had slept a long and sound night's sleep despite being in a strange home haunted by rumors of scandal and murder. She watched her sister finish her meal and realized it would be difficult to keep her on a short leash when she, herself, was confined to her bed.

Susannah looked ready to be away from her, longing to explore, of that Olivia was certain. Perhaps there would be no harm, now that it was broad daylight.

"Susannah, if you please, read to me awhile before I order a bath," she said.

Her sister grabbed her book from the bed stand and opened to the page where they had left off yesterday in the carriage. " 'The villain stalked Mirabelle . . .' "

Olivia rested her head against her pillows and closed her eyes. Susannah's voice faded, and the face of Edmund, Robbie's cousin and heir, materialized in her thoughts. He wore the black suit required for a villain and played the part well. In no time, she heard his harsh words echoing in her mind.

I demand that you leave, Olivia, for the sake of my wife.

She made Edmund's wife uncomfortable as she had miscarried their child only a month previous. Olivia's condition shone as a constant reminder of their loss. She sympathized with his wife, but she found little compassion for Edmund.

The truth was that Edmund was the one uncomfortable with Olivia's presence. He was a pinch-penny and wanted nothing to do with supporting Robbie's widow and child. Edmund did not believe it was his duty since the estate was completely entailed and Robbie had left no instructions to care for his widow.

Susannah's voice invaded Olivia's visions as she continued to read from the novel.

" '. . . and Mirabelle wept for her lost love . . .' "

It had been six months since Olivia last wept. She had cried over Robbie's grave. She had almost cried again when she came upon the outstanding bills for jewels she had never been given, clothing she had never seen. It was monstrously cruel to realize that she had married a man who was so like her adulterous father.

She caressed her middle. Her baby was the result of the last chance she had given her straying husband. She anguished over her child's lost inheritance. What was left had been given away to Edmund. But even before that, it had been lost by Robbie's loose living in London.

"That is enough for now, Susannah, I am going to ring for a bath." Olivia pulled the bell rope. She had to escape from her thoughts. She had gone over the events since her husband's death far too many times.

In moments the housekeeper arrived. "Finished with your breakfast, milady?" Mrs. Boothe asked. "Oh, but you ate a bird's portion."

"I am not very hungry. What I should like above all things this morning is a bath."

"Oh, I do not know, Lady Beresford. Doctor Pedley did not say that you could."

"But he did not say that I could not. And so, if you please, I should like the water brought straightaway."

"But, my lady . . ." The housekeeper looked flustered and stopped mid-sentence.

"Really, Mrs. Boothe, I must insist." Olivia struggled with a coiling tension within her that seemed to wind tighter and tighter. Relief washed over her when the housekeeper bobbed in acknowledgment and left the room.

His mother sat in silence, finishing her toast. Sheldrake continued to peruse the paper when a scratch at the door brought his head up. Mrs. Boothe hurried in.

"Yes?" he asked.

"I was hoping for a word with her ladyship, my lord." Mrs. Boothe stood stiffly, her shoulders squared.

Sheldrake looked at his mother. She merely shrugged and said, "Go ahead, Mrs. Boothe, you may speak freely."

The housekeeper turned two shades of red, and her eyes sought the floor. "It is of a delicate nature, I am afraid."

"Truly you can trust my son. He has a hand with delicate matters." His mother took a sip of her chocolate, but he caught her smile.

"Begging your pardon, but Lady Beresford is insisting." Mrs. Boothe shifted from foot to foot.

"Go on. Is there something wrong with Lady Beresford?" Sheldrake asked too quickly as he rose from his chair.

"No sir. She . . ." The housekeeper fell silent.

"Mrs. Boothe, what is the problem?" Sheldrake asked.

"She wishes to take a bath," Mrs. Boothe blurted.

Sheldrake cast a glance at his mother, whose mouth had fallen open.

"I did not know what to do, you see," Mrs. Boothe explained. "I came to seek Lady Evelyn's advice, not wanting to offend Lady Beresford. Doctor Pedley did not advise me on bathing, you see."

"Yes, I understand your predicament." Sheldrake fingered his chin. "Tell Lady Beresford that Doctor Pedley will arrive later this evening to check on her, and she can discuss the matter with him."

"I tried sir, but she would have none of it. I fear she is in a poor mood."

Sheldrake turned to his mother. "Perhaps you would like to be introduced to Lady Beresford now, Mama?"

"Oh, my, no. Think what a poor opinion she would have of me if I go to meet her only to prevent her from taking a bath. You go, dear, as head of the house. I have faith in you to dissuade her until Pedley arrives."

Sheldrake narrowed his eyes. His mother had visibly paled. She still considered Lady Beresford ill. Was it unsafe to bathe in such a state? he wondered. Surely his mother must have some idea. Evidently not, or she would have said something more on the matter. With a sigh of resignation he said, "Lead on, Mrs. Boothe."

*   *   *

Olivia sat in her huge cotton wrapper, brushing her hair. It needed a good washing. Susannah read on about the heroine in the villain's clutches swearing to die rather than give up the secret hiding place of her lover's fortune.

At the series of taps on the door, she called out, "Come in."

Expecting a tub with buckets of steaming water, Olivia gasped in shock at the sight of Lord Sheldrake filling the doorway. She struggled to her feet and clutched at her wrapper. She watched his gaze rake her from head to toe, resting a moment on her bare feet peeping beneath the cotton wrap. She envisioned that coil of tension inside her head tighten further. She glanced at Susannah, who sat with her mouth gaping and the book dropped from her lap.

"Lord Sheldrake," Olivia whispered, dry-mouthed.

"Lady Beresford." He nodded. "I apologize for the intrusion, but there seems to be a misunderstanding."

"A misunderstanding?" she repeated. Her heart pounded in her ears. Did he overhear Susannah and her talking last night? "Susannah and I—"

"No, it has nothing to do with your sister." He cast a glance at Susannah, who looked away sheepishly.

Olivia was thrown off balance and at a complete loss to understand his presence in her bedchamber. He stood so tall and formidable among the soft flounces of the room, it was unsettling. What could he want and why was Mrs. Boothe so rosy-faced as she discreetly took a seat by the far window?

"I am here regarding the bath you have requested."

"What?" She dropped the hairbrush she held.

Lord Sheldrake stepped closer and bent to pick it up. She noticed the tops of his ears were red. He was either embarrassed or angry, and she'd guess he was a bit of both. He stood so rigidly as if he held himself in check, until he laid the brush upon her vanity with a loud clack. Her gaze stayed riveted to the hairbrush, and fear swirled about her insides.

"Mrs. Boothe is worried, and rightly so, about your taking a bath before you have spoken to Doctor Pedley."

She blinked and looked up into stormy eyes of darkest blue.

"Doctor Pedley left no word regarding a bath," Lord Sheldrake started slowly, as if speaking to an idiot. "I must insist you wait until he arrives and take the matter up with him."

The tense coil inside her finally snapped. She had just about had her fill of overbearing men, and she would be ordered about no longer. Of all the insufferable arrogance! How dare he bully her so. Had she not been bullied enough by Edmund, by Robbie, by her father? This was beyond the pale, to have him standing in her bedchamber, and Lord or no, she would tell him so.

"Lord Sheldrake." She took a deep breath and stepped away from the vanity and her abused brush. "I have taken baths regularly all my life including the last eight months of it. I assure you there is no harm, and besides it is no concern of yours."

"I think you should reconsider. A carriage accident casts a different light upon what was acceptable these past eight months and now. Do you not agree?"

She took a step closer toward him. "I do not, sir. If the doctor thought it a danger, he would have expressly said so as he did with various foods and drink that I need to avoid."

"Perhaps he assumed you would have sense enough not to chance it." His voice rose slightly.

"Oh!" She could not believe her ears. She clenched her fists so tight, her fingernails threatened to pierce the palms of her hands.

"Now, madam." Lord Sheldrake took a step closer to her.

She had to force herself not to look away from his furious gaze that bore into her from a good head length above her.

"You are a guest in my home, and in so being are placed under my protection. Therefore, I make it my concern. I cannot allow you to jeopardize your health or that of the babe you carry. We shall await Doctor Pedley's advice."

Olivia opened her mouth to protest, but nothing came out. He stood so close to her that she could smell the spicy scent he wore. She backed away, and her backside connected with the vanity, knocking her hairbrush to the floor.

"Please, Lady Beresford." He spoke more softly. "You require rest, but here you stand, up from your bed, already against the doctor's orders."

"I tell you I feel fine, and there is no reason to coddle me." She swallowed hard, fighting the tightness in her throat that threatened to choke her.

"There is every reason. You require much from your host, madam. You demand your aunt, a bath, and you have been here less than a day. I can see now how it was that you should travel in such a state. Foolhardy, most foolhardy."

She bit back a sob. "You know nothing of the reason why I travel, sirrah!" Her voice was hoarse with emotion.

"Perhaps you care to enlighten me?" His eyelids rested low.

Did she disgust him then? No wonder, she thought, with her lank hair and her fat belly sticking out. She shuddered against another sob, but did not let it escape. She looked huge and ugly, she knew. Her eyes began to burn, and she fought against the swell of tears that threatened to reveal her distress. One broke free and found its way down her cheek to her utter shame.

"I was ordered to leave Adberesmere," she whispered, then lifted her chin, daring him to question her further. She heard Mrs. Boothe cluck in sympathy from across the room.

"God's teeth, by whom?" he asked.

"Robbie's cousin and heir." She sniffed. More tears escaped, but she dashed them away with the back of her hand.

She heard Lord Sheldrake curse under his breath, an oath of some sort before he asked, "He surely has made provision for you, some stipend?"

"No, it is all gone. There is nothing left—the estate is completely entailed and mortgaged to the hilt." Olivia hung her head. She could not bear his look of pity. Ashamed of the situation, she turned away from him.

Susannah rushed to her side and wrapped her arms about her shoulders. She wore a fierce and protective expression. "I think that is enough, Lord Sheldrake. My sister is upset." Susannah's voice softened when she added, "Perhaps you should leave now."

Olivia tried to rally, but felt the utter fool. All this fuss over her wanting a bath. "Lord Sheldrake, I shall await a bath until I speak to Doctor Pedley." She heard his release of breath. "But." She faced him.

"But what, Lady Beresford?" He sounded tired or bored, she could not tell.

"I must insist upon washing my hair."

"Mrs. Boothe, see to the hair washing. Lady Beresford, I beg your forgiveness for upsetting you." He turned and bowed to Susannah as well. "And, I humbly beg your pardon, Miss Lacey."

Lord Sheldrake bent gracefully to pick up the hairbrush. He offered it to Olivia with his hand outstretched as though it were a peace offering. "Now if you will excuse me?"

"By all means," Olivia answered.

With a nod, he was gone.

She slumped against her sister. "I cannot believe I stood up to him in such a manner."

"You were very brave," Susannah said as she brushed back a lock of Olivia's hair from her forehead. "I am sorry I did not say something earlier. I was simply shocked by the whole thing."

"Susannah, you surprise me more and more. You are truly growing up! You were splendid." She gave her sister a hug. "Now, help me with my hair."

Olivia breathed deeply with a sense of satisfaction. She had not totally given over as she had done so many times with Robbie. But then, she had done everything to keep Robbie near her, trying as she could to make him love her again. She had always been afraid to anger him for fear he would never come home.

A soft smiled curved her lips as Mrs. Boothe fetched the warm water and pails needed for a thorough hair washing. As Susannah picked up her book and began to read where she had left off, Olivia decided then and there she would not be bullied ever again.

Sheldrake closed the door to his study. He did not wish to be disturbed, especially by his mother wanting to know the details of his bath encounter with Lady Beresford. He had bungled it royally.

He was supposed to keep her calm, and what must he do but engage her in an argument, insult her, then reduce her to tears! He *was* a monster. Her tears were his undoing. For some reason, he was very close to allowing the bath, just to please her.

She was beautiful even when she cried. He did not think women could be anything other than messy, sniveling weepers, but she cursed her tears with a stubborn lift of her chin even though her bottom lip trembled. He raked a hand through his hair.

To be thrown out of her home and in her condition screamed foul! It was nothing less than a crime. He took up his quill, dipped it in ink, and dashed off a note to his solicitor. He would check the conditions of Beresford's will, by God, and see what could be done.

Sheldrake twirled the pen between his fingers. He had to admit Lady Beresford showed she had pluck. He had to give her credit for that. She managed to get the last word and her hair washed.

He scribbled another note—this one to Pedley asking him to come as quickly as possible. He owed it to Lady Beresford to have the bathing matter settled as soon as possible. A vision of her lush form in a tub of soapy water rose before his eyes. He shook his head to clear the mental picture when he heard a light knock at the door.

"May I come in?" his mother asked.

"Of course." Sheldrake sat back in his chair as his mother took a seat in front of his desk.

"How did it go?"

"Terribly. I am afraid that I did not handle the situation very well." Sheldrake busied himself stacking papers and putting away his opened correspondence.

"I am sure you did fine, dear."

"What is it that you needed, Mother?" He had no intention of giving her the sordid details, and quickly changed the subject. She obviously had other matters on her mind, as she followed his lead.

"Since our guests will be with us for some time . . ." She hesitated slightly before adding, "I thought it would be polite of me to extend the invitation to Mrs. Hardcastle's tea to this aunt and perhaps Miss Susannah. You do still have the invitation?"

"Yes, I have it here." He pulled it out of his pile of letters requiring a response. "But you will have to take the matter up with their aunt, I think. She should arrive today."

"Very well, I will." His mother narrowed her gaze toward him. "Are you not going to send my regrets?"

"Not this time, Mama."

"Very well. I do believe our Miss Susannah could use some society polish. She is close to the age of having a season. A beautiful child, she will no doubt do well."

"No doubt." Sheldrake guessed that there were no funds for a season, unless this aunt proved to be well off.

"And perhaps we could open the Hall for an entertainment of sorts. By all rights, we should be thinking of our harvest ball. It has been an age since we have had one."

"Mama," he started. He got up from his desk to file some ledgers upon a shelf. "You know how I feel about that."

"I have put off my blacks a year ago, dear. I think it is time we join local society again. It may even do you some good. You are growing far too serious."

"Serious, huh." Sheldrake turned and looked at his

mother closely. There was no hint of her remembering anything about Abbott's death. It had not been fair to keep her
away from her friends and neighbors. He had curtailed his
dealings with the local gentry and nobility, but those were
choices he had made for himself. He was not yet ready to so-
cialize, but his mother seemed to be. "I shall consider your
suggestion."

"About the ball?"

"About everything. Now, what would you suggest we do
with three ladies over the next month or so?"

His mother leaned back in her chair with a smile. "Just
leave that to me."

A scratch at the door brought the butler, Simms, an-
nouncing Pedley. Sheldrake sighed with relief at the sight of
him.

"Lady Evelyn." The doctor bowed over her hand. "You
look radiant today. You are feeling well, I trust."

"Yes, of course. I shall leave you two to your discussion
of Lady Beresford." Lady Evelyn winked at her son before
leaving.

Sheldrake gestured for Pedley to sit down. "Would you
care for tea?"

"No, I plan to stay only a few moments, since I was pass-
ing by; checking on the Matthew's boy don't you know."
Pedley held up a folded piece of paper in his hand. "Your
footman gave me this when I arrived. This note from you
states that it is an urgent matter but not an emergency. What
is amiss?" Pedley leaned back and crossed his legs. He had
a bit of a lopsided smirk on his face.

Sheldrake took his seat behind his desk again. A soft
summer breeze blew through the opened window, and he
wondered how he could explain the situation to Pedley without looking like a fool. "She wanted a bath."

"What's that?" The doctor tilted his head.

"Lady Beresford called for a bath, and I did not know if
you would approve, so I sent for you." He looked about his
desk for the quill pen.

"You knew I'd be stopping by this evening, so why the note?" Pedley asked, again with that smirk.

"She was adamant, and I am afraid that I may have upset her with my refusal. I owe it to her to get the matter settled straightaway." How ridiculous it all sounded.

"I see." The doctor scratched his chin as if deep in thought.

"Is there any harm?" Sheldrake asked finally.

Pedley slapped his hands upon his knees and stood. "No, I don't believe there is. But I will stop in and visit with Lady Beresford nonetheless, and then I need not return later."

Sheldrake stood as well.

"How is your mother?" Pedley bent to retrieve his bag and headed for the door.

"She wants to return to her rounds among local society. What do you think?"

"It has been two years. But many know the stories about you, Sheldrake. If she heard something, it may jiggle her memory, but then again it might not. She has buried what happened deep inside of her, son."

"I know."

"Take it slow. Most people have forgotten all about it. I think she is right to want to return to her old life. It is a good sign."

"Very well. Thank you, Pedley, thank you for coming." He shook the doctor's hand.

"Anytime, my boy."

Sheldrake walked the doctor out to be escorted by Mrs. Boothe to Lady Beresford's chamber. *Perhaps these guests would prove to be the diversion Mother needed to keep her content at home.*

Chapter Four

Olivia leaned back against the copper tub, finally surrounded in warm scented water. Her now dry but freshly washed hair was bundled up in a towel to keep it from getting wet. Her belly stuck out too far to remain under the soapy waves so she rested her hands upon it.

She reflected how amused the good doctor had appeared when he arrived, well before he was expected, to grant her his permission to bathe. He had winked at her when he explained that Lord Sheldrake had sent a note for him to come to the Hall without delay. Olivia knew that she owed her host her gratitude. After all the fuss, she had gotten what she truly wanted.

She could not help but soften her opinion of Lord Sheldrake when she found out that he had sent for Doctor Pedley. Perhaps he was not the stiff, cold man he seemed. No, of course he could not be. When she had mistaken him for a farmer when he rescued her, she thought him the gentlest of men. It was not until he realized that she knew who he was that a veil of aristocratic coolness had taken the place of his previous warmth.

She sloshed water as she reached for a cloth and lavender soap. Working up a good lather, she sighed with pleasure as the tangy scent assaulted her nose. The heat worked wonders in helping her to relax.

Settling back against the metal rim of the tub, she recalled how highly Doctor Pedley had spoken of Lord Sheldrake; praised him, in fact. How odd considering the doctor must know about the rumors. He certainly did not seem like one to condone murder. Unless, of course, the good doctor helped in disguising the cause of death to keep Lord Sheldrake out of Newgate. Perhaps Doctor Pedley pronounced the stepfather's death an accident. They may be partners of a sort. He did say that Lord Sheldrake pays him handsomely to care for the village. *Heavens!*

Olivia banished such thoughts. She would only drive herself to distraction thinking such things. Besides, she was anxious to leave her bedchamber. Doctor Pedley had given her permission to go downstairs as long as she did not overly exert herself. She could learn more about her host when she moved about the Hall freely.

The water eventually grew tepid, so Olivia placed her hands on the sides of the tub to get up. Water spilled its way over the edge, and she worried that she had soaked the floor. She looked up as Mrs. Boothe entered the dressing room with a stack of towels and a young maid in tow.

"Tsk, my lady, here let us help you." The housekeeper reached out her hand to aid her and the maid stood ready with a towel. "This here is Bonnie. She'll be maid to you. I shall be back in a moment to take care of the tub, my dear."

"Good afternoon, Bonnie." Olivia nodded as the girl wrapped the towel around her.

The maid curtsied.

Dry and dressed, Olivia sat at the vanity while Bonnie brushed her hair until it shone. "Would you like me to fix it up pretty?" the young maid asked.

"Please do." Olivia stared at her own reflection in the mirror. Her cheeks glowed rosy, and she looked the very picture of health. Too bad she could not keep the lines of worry between her brow from marring her image. They appeared more often than not since Robbie's death.

"My ma taught me aplenty 'afore she left for Lunnon."

"Did she?" Olivia looked away from her reflection to concentrate on the petite maid, whose reflected gaze she connected with through the mirror.

"She used to wait on Lady Evelyn and fix her hair, but then she was let go."

"Oh?" She knew it was ill-bred to gossip with the servants about their employers, but she thought it best to know everything she could about the inhabitants of the Hall. "And is Lady Evelyn so hard to please?"

"Oh, no. His lordship let her off to work for his friend in Lunnon to find her a situation. My ma was too much of a reminder of the accident. I hopes to join her when's I can."

A bolt of keen interest shot through Olivia. She held her tongue a moment, trying not to appear too eager and asked, "What accident, pray tell?"

"With you not from around here, you wouldn't know. The night Mr. Abbott died sent everyone in an uproar and my ma to Lunnon."

"How dreadful." She wanted desperately to ask how Mr. Abbott had died, but Mrs. Boothe bustled in to oversee the removal of the copper tub. Bonnie turned her attention to various ribbons laid out on the vanity.

"I think this should do." Bonnie chose a ribbon of deepest rose to weave through Olivia's hair. "There, ma'am, I'm done."

She stood, smoothing the black folds of her bombazine mourning dress. "Thank you, Bonnie, but the black one would have suited me fine."

"But no one could see that, ma'am, yer hair is that dark."

She smiled at the maid as Bonnie put the extra towels and soap away on the shelf of the small dressing room.

"Lord Sheldrake will be up in a moment to escort you downstairs," Mrs. Boothe called as she ushered the maid out the door.

Olivia swallowed, her throat turned dry of a sudden. The tick of the clock on the wall blared in the quiet room as she waited. She fiddled with a tiny fray on the sleeve of her gown. What would she say to him? Their last parting had been somewhat awkward.

She paced the room until she stood in front of the window and rested her head against the cool pane. Bonnie said Mr. Abbot's death had been an accident. Perhaps that was the truth of it, and gabble-grinders had turned it into a murderous tale. It was outside of enough to be stranded in a strange home during one's confinement, but even worse with a lord rumored to be a murderer.

Too bad, she thought as she fingered the fine silk curtains. He obviously was a wealthy man. One who, she believed, was unattached. He was exactly what she needed, and she was forced to remain under his roof! She doubted a better opportunity would ever present itself again.

She grimaced. How could she think of *him* as an eligible husband? Had he truly killed his stepfather, he was a violent man. She did not want the likes of him near her child, let alone have guardianship of the babe. But, if it had been an accident, Lord Sheldrake could very well prove to be the answer to her dilemma. But could she garner an offer from him? She looked down to her bulging middle and almost laughed aloud. It was enough to make a cat laugh, she thought.

A knock at the door interrupted her thoughts. She turned, and the smile died from her lips.

"My lady?" Lord Sheldrake stood at her doorway, a grim expression on his face. "I believe it is much too early for you to be up from your bed."

Another scold! "I appreciate your concern sir, but the doctor did give his approval." She stepped forward, then hesitated when Lord Sheldrake offered his arm.

"Foolhardy, I think."

She placed a nervous hand upon his sleeve. He was a handsome man, she had to admit. A slight tremor ran through her at the thought of him courting her. She quickly corrected herself. She would be the one doing the courting, of that she could be certain. He appeared to have no such soft thoughts in mind as he stiffly escorted her from the room. Besides, she had much to learn about him before she could possibly entertain him as a possible husband-to-be.

She cleared her throat to cover the awkward silence that had settled between them. "My lord, I must apologize for the inconvenience we are to you."

"It is I, ma'am, who must apologize to you. For this morning."

Olivia peered up at him, surprised. His gaze sought hers, then he quickly looked straight ahead.

"You were only doing what you thought was best at the time. I accept your apology, sir, and for sending Doctor Pedley to me, I thank you."

"You are generous with your forgiveness, Lady Beresford."

They walked slowly. She cast a quick glance backwards, and the toe of her slipper caught in the edge of the carpet and she stumbled. Lord Sheldrake's arm was around her in a trice to steady her.

"You push your recovery," he snapped.

"I simply caught my foot on my hem perhaps." Must he be so quick with his disapproval of her, she thought.

As they reached the top of the stairs, Lord Sheldrake pulled her closer to his side.

"Really, sir!" she gasped. "There is no need to hold me so."

"Ah, but there is. Would you have me see you *catch your foot* down my stairs?"

"Well." Olivia shut her lips tight. They had had this discussion before at the carriage accident with the same dose of sarcasm. He had insisted he carry her, and her objections had not swayed him.

The stairs sprawled directly in front of them. She did not recall them being quite so steep on the way up last evening. But then his nearness made her nervous. She wrapped her arm about Lord Sheldrake's back for support and held tight.

"I'll not let you go," he whispered, his breath warm against her cheek.

Startled, she looked up into his eyes. He stopped and

stared back. She was trapped by the intensity of his gaze and forgot where she was entirely.

"Ready?" he asked.

"For what?"

A smile hovered at the corners of his well-formed lips. "To descend."

She coughed and looked away. She knew she must be three shades of red with embarrassment. "Yes, of course. Proceed."

He took his time, placing each step slowly, one foot at a time. Olivia did the same, keeping her eyes downcast. After a day abed, her steps were not as firm as they should be, and she was soon glad to lean upon Lord Sheldrake for support.

She inhaled the masculine scent he wore, only this time it was clean and fresh as though he had just applied it. A sudden vision of him standing shirtless as he went about his toilette flitted through her mind with unquestionable vividness. Shocked by the flush of heat such a thought brought to her face and body, Olivia prayed that Lord Sheldrake would not notice, and she leaned even closer. *No,* she thought, *that would not do.* She dared not cuddle up to such a man, reeling as she was from visions of him. That would be disaster.

It had been ages since she enjoyed the sight of her late husband's nakedness. As the years passed, he had turned soft from his life of dissipation. It was not so with Lord Sheldrake. She could feel the firm length of him, feel the strength of his arm that draped itself with such confidence around her. Finally, they reached the bottom of the stairs, but they did not move forward.

"You may let me go now, my lord," she said, slightly breathless.

"Yes, of course." He dropped his arm from her.

Her body seemed to protest as she felt the warmth of being close to him fade. She tried to understand her reaction to him and why, but it was simple really. He was a handsome man paying her a shred of attention—something her hus-

band barely gave her during their last few years of marriage.
She was simply starved.

She scolded herself for being a fool. She wanted to enter
a platonic, mutually respecting marriage of wealth for her
child. She wanted nothing to do with longing for attention or
soft feelings. Such things only lead to heartache, and she
simply could not bear any more of that in this lifetime.

"Have you caught your breath?" he asked.

"Yes, thank you."

"Then come, the drawing room is not very far." They
walked in silence, her hand resting lightly upon his arm.
When they entered the sun-washed parlor, she stopped to
marvel at the room. A veritable wall of windows faced her,
and she could easily spy the extensive gardens in full bloom
beyond.

"How lovely," she whispered. "You have an enormous
selection of rhododendrons."

He smiled fully at her, and the effect was devastating.
"You enjoy flowering bushes, madam?"

"Oh yes, but roses are my favorites. Where did you find
so many colors of plants?" She had never seen such variety.

"During my grand tour I brought back many plants and
propagated them here. They do seem to flourish."

He escorted her to a prime spot to view the gardens, but
she merely watched him as he plumped the pillows of a
puffy-looking chaise.

"I hope you will be comfortable here." His voice sounded
light, but there seemed to be an underlying message. She
may have been reading into his comment far more than he
could ever have intended, but she hoped that he truly wished
her to be at ease in his home.

"Yes, this will be fine." She neared the chair's edge and
sat, then sank into the depths of it as if it were a feather bed.
Lord Sheldrake bent to offer his assistance.

"Here," he said briskly as he knelt down to help her
swing her legs up onto the chaise. He moved awkwardly,

touching her briefly, which reminded her of the carriage accident.

"Thank you," she said as she smoothed the folds of her skirt and tried to breathe evenly.

"Can I offer you some books to while away the afternoon?" He was still crouched at her feet.

"Yes, I should like that very much. Thank you."

"Ah, Richard, if you will, introduce me to our guest." A woman entered with a rustle of silk, followed by Susannah.

Lord Sheldrake straightened and pulled at the ends of his waistcoat. "Mama, may I introduce Lady Beresford to you." Sheldrake turned to Olivia. "My mother, Lady Evelyn Abbott."

She reached to shake the fingers extended to her by Lady Evelyn, and together they chimed, "Nice to meet you."

Lady Evelyn laughed—a silvery tinkle that must have been practiced over and over to achieve such a pleasing effect. "La, but we shall get on famously. I have heard it said that if two people speak the same words at the same time, they are destined to be friends."

"I do hope so." Olivia smiled.

"Well now, Richard . . ."

As Lady Evelyn spoke to her son about some business with the gardener, Olivia tried to overcome her surprise. She glanced at Susannah, who appeared to take Lady Evelyn's appearance in stride. Lord Sheldrake's mother was not at all what she expected. Her very attire bespoke not the comfortable country matron, but rather a sensuous society beauty past her first flush of youth and possibly her second, so hard was it to tell the woman's age. The deep russet silk she wore hugged every curve of her slender form. Olivia had expected the mother of a rumored murderer to be a faded, sorry sort of creature in deep despair, not a vibrant woman.

Lady Evelyn turned to her and asked, "Are you well today, Lady Beresford?"

"Yes, much better, I thank you." She realized she was

staring. "I beg your pardon, but you seem much too young to be Lord Sheldrake's mother."

"Oh, but you are a dear!" Lady Evelyn laughed again. "I was very young when I married Richard's father. He wanted an heir straightaway, and so he received one nigh ten months after our marriage."

Olivia glanced at Lord Sheldrake, who stood waiting. She noticed that he looked tense. He also appeared hesitant to leave.

"Richard, you need not hover so. We three ladies shall get along famously without your help. Off with you so we can have a comfortable coze." Lady Evelyn waved an exquisitely mittened hand in dismissal of her son.

"Ladies, your servant." Lord Sheldrake bowed and left, but not before casting a look backward at the three of them.

Lady Evelyn called out to him to order tea for them just before he exited the room, then turned to Olivia. "Lady Beresford, your sister tells me you are recently widowed. I am truly sorry for your loss."

"Thank you." Dare she say the same and offer her condolences on the death of Mr. Abbott? But that was two years before. "I do hope Susannah has not been a nuisance. I expected her to stay in her chamber until I was up and about." Olivia gave her sister a pointed look.

"Oh my, no. It was nice to have someone to talk to on my walk through the gardens. Your sister graciously gave me company."

"Thank you," Susannah said, then turned to Olivia. "Lady Evelyn gave me a tour. They have the most beautiful ballroom. The biggest ever!"

"And sorely out of use," Lady Evelyn said. "But we had a marvelous time planning a make-believe ball did we not, Susannah?"

"We certainly did!"

Lady Evelyn appeared fond of her sister, and Susannah obviously adored the older woman. They chatted amiably as if they had known each other for much longer than a day.

Olivia leaned back, relieved they were not an unwanted burden for their hostess.

A knock at the door brought a footman with a stack of books as promised by Lord Sheldrake, and Mrs. Boothe with the tea cart.

Lady Evelyn scanned the collection of books. "I simply adore novels, but Richard teases me so when I read them."

"What does he like to read?" Susannah asked defensively.

"Oh, agricultural manuals mainly," Lady Evelyn answered.

"Rather dry material," Olivia said.

"Dull as dirt, more like," Lady Evelyn amended with a laugh. "He has done very well for himself. Richard inherited at a very young age, and I think he is overwhelmed with living up to his father's image and reputation. My first husband, Richard's father, was a traditional sort; he farmed the way his father did and his grandfather before him. I am glad to see my son using unconventional methods. What ever they are I have no idea, but they work. We have had excellent yields!"

Lady Evelyn's pride in her son rang clear and strong. Olivia silently sipped her tea and watched as Lady Evelyn retrieved her workbasket and pulled out a silken mass of tangled cranberry thread. She called to Susannah to help, and the two sat with their heads together working on the mess.

Olivia looked out the window. "Your gardens are divine, Lady Evelyn. I have never before seen such variety."

"Do you appreciate flowers, Lady Beresford?"

"Please, call me Olivia. Yes, I love puttering about in my rose garden. I was just beginning to cross wild strains with some hot house varieties when . . ." Olivia stopped. *When Robbie died.* It was not so long ago, and yet so much had changed since then. She knew her roses were gone from her, too. Edmund would never permit wild rose bushes to remain in what he had called a "mess of brambles."

"You shall have to speak to our gardener then. I never did have a taste for it. Richard keeps him on his toes, but he tends to prefer the bushes to actual flowers. He has the De-Quincy streak of practicality, I fear."

The afternoon passed pleasantly. Olivia found that she liked Lady Evelyn very well indeed. She listened to the older woman's gossip of the *ton,* but found it very confusing, having never experienced a season. Susannah, on the other hand, listened with rapt attention to every detail as if her life depended on such knowledge.

Susannah deserved a gay season filled with parties and dancing and all the glittering things Lady Evelyn described. And she was of an age where that day was not too far off. Olivia remained determined that somehow she would remarry. It was the only way to provide for her family.

And Lord Sheldrake presented the only possible candidate. If she could prove him innocent, if only in her own mind, she could then safely pursue him. Olivia wrinkled her nose in distress. She had never pursued a man before and was not sure how to go on. But her child's future depended upon her success. Considering this morning's argument over her bath, she knew Lord Sheldrake proved to be a challenge. But he was not ignorant of her at least. He did send for Doctor Pedley.

The butler then entered the drawing room and announced the arrival of Aunt Agatha.

The familiar sturdy-figured woman bore down upon them, a deep frown on her face. "Olivia, Susannah, I worried so! I came as soon as I received the message." Her aunt rushed to place a hand upon Olivia's brow. "How are you?"

"I am well, truly," she answered and proceeded with the introductions. When the proprieties were observed, she turned to her aunt. "Perhaps you would like to rest? I myself plan to lie down before dinner. Come, Aunt Agatha, and help me to my room." She could barely wait to ask her aunt what she knew about Sheldrake Hall and its occupants.

"Yes, of course, Olivia, do rest. I shall have Mrs. Boothe

show you both to your aunt's chamber." Lady Evelyn pulled the bell rope.

"Thank you dearly, Lady Evelyn," Aunt Agatha said. She then turned toward Susannah and said, "Susannah, come to my room when you have finished helping Lady Evelyn."

Susannah nodded.

After leaving the room, Mrs. Boothe showed them to a chamber across the hall from Olivia's. Olivia waited until the housekeeper left and her aunt sat down upon the bed before saying a word. Two trunks lay open, their contents unpacked and put away. Only a personal valise was left untouched. Everything at Sheldrake Hall seemed to be handled with utmost efficiency.

After a deep breath, Olivia blurted, "Aunt, you must tell me all you know about this place."

"I know that I cannot like it that you must remain here." Her aunt removed her hat. "I only know what Brownie says. She was in a pet to be left behind and sends you her love."

"Aunt, please, tell me what you know."

"Two years ago, Mr. Abbott, Lady Evelyn's husband, died of a gunshot wound," Aunt Agatha began.

"Do you know where he was shot?"

"No. We live too far away to hear everything. Brownie's sister lives here, though. Her husband is one of Lord Sheldrake's tenant farmers, and quite happy to be so, I might add."

"Yes, go on," Olivia urged.

"For a time, Brownie received news regularly about Sheldrake Hall but then it began to diminish. She has not heard anything about Lord Sheldrake this age."

"Aunt Agatha, tell me from the beginning," Olivia prodded.

"Yes, of course. It all started the year Lord Sheldrake traveled abroad. A man by the name of Abbott wooed Lady Evelyn. Brownie said her sister was horrified that Lady Evelyn gave the man any attention at all. He was known to be a terrible libertine." Aunt Agatha lowered her voice. "There were parties and the such as Sheldrake Hall had never seen. Then Lady Evelyn up and married the scoundrel, and when her son returned it looked like there would be hell to pay." Aunt Agatha took a deep breath. "Pardon my language."

"Yes, continue." Olivia leaned closer to her aunt.

"Well, things settled somewhat. Then all of a sudden, Abbott ends up dead. It was accounted an accident. Mr. Abbott's gun went off while he was cleaning it. The funny thing is that Mr. Abbott was not much of a sportsman."

"Oh, my." Olivia let out a deep sigh.

"Brownie's sister was heartily glad that Mr. Abbott was 'put out of everyone's misery' as she had written it. I surmise that he was not in the least liked, and no one cried at his funeral. Lady Evelyn was not even in attendance."

"How dreadful." She wished it were different. She could not help but feel terribly disappointed in what her aunt had to tell her.

"That it was. There was such scandal before Abbott even died. I do not think anyone was surprised." Her aunt stood and placed her bonnet on the armoire's top shelf. She turned and faced Olivia. "I think you should stay clear of Lord Sheldrake."

"He is our host."

"Yes, and supposedly a fine man. But there have been scandalous happenings in this Hall, and you need not ruin your reputation. It is bad enough that we are here, but I suppose with Lady Evelyn in residence and with me present to play chaperone, we should not fare too badly."

"Is it that bad?"

"Most likely not. It was, after all, two years ago. But rumors are rumors and they linger. I would just as soon not become entangled with them."

Olivia nodded in agreement. "Well, Aunt Agatha, I suppose I had best go and rest so you can finish unpacking. I shall see you at dinner." She rose to leave.

"Are you sure you are well, child?" her aunt asked with concern.

"I am fine, but simply tired." Olivia gave her aunt another hug with a kiss upon her forehead, then she headed for her room.

Once there, she lay upon the bed. She could not keep from thinking about her aunt's words. More than ever, she wished to know what truly had happened. She would rest easier if she knew. She rubbed her belly and felt the stirrings of her babe as it kicked. Fear gripped her. The birthing time was not far off, she knew.

She closed her eyes, fighting against the memory of her mother's death that lit up her mind as if she were a frightened seven-year-old child again. Chewing her lip, Olivia remembered her mother calling out to her father as he stormed across the parlor and out the door. Her mother had clutched her belly, then heavy with Susannah, and screamed. But her father had not returned.

She had to rush to the midwife for help when her mother's time came. It was a horrible thing to witness. She had bathed her mother's forehead with a cool cloth in an attempt to soothe her, but her mother's screams tore the night and Olivia could do little to ease her pain. After naming her sister, her mother choked a hoarse good-bye, then drifted into death's final sleep.

Olivia opened her eyes. Dear heaven, she thought, if that were to happen to her, there would be no hope for her child's future. If she bore a son, he would be the rightful heir, and she feared Edmund would demand to raise the boy.

She shuddered. She must know more about Lord Sheldrake, find out what manner of man he was and woo him quickly. Part of that would be to uncover the truth behind the rumors of Abbott's death. She closed her eyes, forcing herself to calm down and rest. She dare not be impulsive. She had to act wisely, with a cool head and a detached heart, for her child's sake.

Finally, Susannah thought as she took a turn away from the formal gardens and into the field beyond. She needed to walk and get some sort of exercise. Olivia, Aunt Agatha, and Lady Evelyn were all resting before dinner, and Lord Sheldrake was nowhere in sight. It was the perfect time to escape the confines of the Hall.

She tipped her face up to feel the warmth of the sun upon her skin and walked forward, daring herself not to look where she stepped. A silly game, but one she played often. She did not diminish her pace, and so far she had not run into anything, nor had she tripped.

Humming a tune, Susannah kept walking and enjoyed the peace. She wasn't quite so scared to stay at Sheldrake Hall; not with Aunt Agatha there and certainly not after getting to know Lady Evelyn. She was so beautiful and so full of charm, Susannah hoped she could be as elegant someday.

"Pardon me."

A deep voice startled her, and she looked down quickly, which made her a bit dizzy. Staggering backward, she shook her head to clear it.

"I did not mean to startle you." A man atop his horse smiled down at her. "At least, there is nothing wrong with your neck as I first feared."

"A game," she said. "I like to see how long I can walk without looking where I step."

"Ah, I see." The man slid off his horse. "And are you very good at it?" He was rather tall, very pleasant-looking, and younger that she had first thought.

"Not very. I usually fall down."

The man laughed. "I imagine that would be the way of it."

"But I did not fall today," Susannah informed him.

"Bravo. Do you live near here?"

She turned her head in the direction of the Hall and realized she had walked a considerable distance. "I am staying at Sheldrake Hall. My name is Susannah Lacey." She bobbed a curtsy.

"Miss Lacey." He bowed. "A pleasure to meet you. I am Captain Winston Jeffries, home on furlough."

"From the war?" Susannah's curiosity was truly piqued. "Are you fighting with Wellington against the French?"

"Yes, but it is far too nice a day to speak of such horrors to a pretty young lady like yourself."

She pulled a face. "Do *you* live near here?" She walked toward his horse and patted its nose.

"No, but a dear friend of mine does." He looked away and coughed, as if suddenly uncomfortable. "He is recuperating from a dreadful wound." Captain Jeffries held his horse's bridle as she scratched the animal's ears.

"A beautiful mare, sir. Is she yours?" she asked, trying to lighten the heaviness that had settled over the man. She knew she should not be conversing at length with a stranger, but something in the man's eyes made her stay.

"She is. Her name is Luna."

"After the moon—how clever of you since she has such a ghostly appearance."

A silence settled between them, and Susannah continued to stroke Luna's mane and neck. "Well, I suppose I should be getting back," she said, but made no movement to leave.

"Yes, no doubt you should." He did not move either.

She sensed a sadness in the captain. She could not simply walk away from him when he was obviously hurting. "Captain," she asked, "how long do you have before you must return to the war?"

He turned toward her and narrowed his eyes as he gazed upon her. "A week."

"You do not wish to go, do you?"

Surprise registered in his expression. "No. You are a perceptive child."

She pushed aside her irritation at being called a child and forged ahead. "Are you afraid?" They had started walking, and Luna followed slowly behind them, stopping every so often to munch the grass.

"Of course I am—war is not a pleasant experience," he said. "But I am sure you would much rather talk of something else. A party perhaps? Will there be a grand party at this Hall where you are staying?"

"I do not think so. Have you never heard the rumors about Lord Sheldrake?"

"No, I haven't." He smiled, and she thought him the most handsome man she had ever seen.

Susannah looked about to ensure that no one could possibly hear her. "Well, please be prepared for a shock when I tell you that he is rumored to have killed his stepfather in a violent rage."

Captain Jeffries looked convincingly shocked and placed his hand upon his heart. "Surely you jest."

She giggled and swatted him. "I am serious."

"Have you met this villain?"

"I have," she said. "But he is very much a gentleman, and so I cannot imagine him doing such a deed. My aunt's housekeeper says the stepfather got what he deserved."

"I see. Perhaps he is a hero then."

"I shouldn't go that far."

"My dear Miss Lacey, I am sure that if this gentleman did commit such a heinous crime, he would have been locked up. The father of the friend I am staying with is the local constable here. If anyone knew the situation in its entirety, it would be him."

"And has he never said a word against Lord Sheldrake then?"

"No, in fact I believe I have heard him praise the man, now that you mention his name." The captain looked at his watch and said, "I truly must return, and I am sure you will be missed should I keep you any longer." He whistled and Luna trotted up next to him.

She watched him mount, wishing they could talk more, but he was right, she would be missed. "Do you ride here often?" She kicked at the ground.

"Every day."

"May I see you again?"

"Miss Lacey, as much as I have enjoyed your company, I am sure it is not appropriate."

"Oh, pooh," she said. "You will be leaving shortly, and I need to take walks. If I am here tomorrow at the same time, might you be riding in this field?"

He looked up at the sky and sighed. "Miss Lacey, I just might."

Susannah smiled and waved as he took off at a canter across the field. No matter what she had to do to get back, she would definitely be in this very field tomorrow.

Chapter Five

Olivia paced back and forth in her chamber. She had searched her sister's room. She had asked Mrs. Boothe if she had seen her sister, and she checked on Aunt Agatha, who still slept. No Susannah. A thread of worry gnawed its way into a strip of fear. She needed to find her sister. She had already walked the gardens, which may have been too much for her. Her legs and lower back ached. But she had not thoroughly searched the Hall.

She hesitated at the door of her chamber. She might run into Lord Sheldrake. What would she tell him? Susannah could be into any sort of mischief. She was a young girl who considered napping before dinner a bore. She had to find her and fast, before Aunt Agatha became aware of her disappearance and threw the household into an uproar. She was not up to a lecture from her aunt, whether directed at herself or Susannah—it mattered not.

Slipping quietly down the north hallway, she started opening doors. Most of the rooms looked unused, the furniture covered, the curtains drawn. She turned down the west hallway, and again, no sign of Susannah. She took her time descending the main stairs only to find Lord Sheldrake waiting at the bottom. She tried to compose her features, but no doubt she failed. He stood looking concerned.

"Lady Beresford, is there anything amiss?"

"Nothing really." She remained on the last step, which put her at eye level with him.

"Mrs. Boothe told me that you were looking for your sister. How long have you been at it?"

She sighed. She should have known that the housekeeper would have told her lord and master. He certainly kept a strong hold on the comings and goings of the Hall. "For at least an hour or more."

"And where have you looked?" His expression betrayed nothing but kind concern, and yet he seemed tense as he waited.

"Well, I have searched the rooms upstairs and the gardens to no avail."

"That is too much strain for you, I think," he said and held out his arm to her. "Come and sit down; you have overexerted yourself." She took his arm and stepped down from the last stair. He ushered her into the drawing room, still drenched in late afternoon sunshine. "Why did you not come find me? I could have helped you."

Why, indeed, she thought. Because she was not the least comfortable in his presence, and she feared what snooping Susannah may be engaged in once found. She certainly did not wish to arouse his lordship's anger if her sister lingered where she had no business to be. She looked down. "I did not wish to trouble you, my lord. I fear our presence here is enough of an inconvenience to you."

He actually looked a bit sheepish at her statement. But it was true. She felt bad for making such a fuss about her bath, and now Susannah had come up missing.

"Nonsense," he said gruffly.

She could tell he was fibbing horribly, but she appreciated his effort. He helped her to sit down, but he remained standing, gazing thoughtfully out of the windows.

"She could simply be out for a walk," Lord Sheldrake finally said.

"Is that safe?"

He turned and looked at her, surprised. "Of course it is. I own a considerable amount of land here, Lady Beresford.

The people who work it are good people. Your sister will
come to no harm."

"Lord Sheldrake, that may be true, but in my experience,
bad people are everywhere."

His eyes narrowed, and she worried that perhaps she had
insulted him. But he merely nodded. "I will saddle my horse
and scout the grounds."

"Thank you," she said in earnest. "Oh, and Lord Sheldrake?"

"Yes."

"Please do not mention anything to my aunt. I shall handle the situation with Susannah."

"Of course."

Once he left, she pulled herself out of the chair. She may
as well search the rest of the Hall.

Sheldrake swung himself into the saddle. He knew the
chit was just nosing about somewhere, but he would not
make light of Lady Beresford's worry for her sister. He
could not help but dwell on her remark that bad people were
everywhere. He did not want to believe that about his estate,
but to be safe he would look about for himself. She had
sounded so cynical when she had said the words that he
could not help but wonder what had brought her to such an
untrusting view.

He trotted away from the stables toward the fields beyond the gardens when he saw Susannah. The girl held a
bouquet of wildflowers, and her bonnet dangled from her
other hand. She hummed as she skipped along. She started
when she saw him coming toward her and dropped her hat.
Bending down to pick it up, she nearly tripped.

"Your sister is beside herself with worry," he said.
"Where have you been?"

Miss Susannah's eyes looked round as saucers, and Sheldrake felt a bit guilty for speaking so harshly. "I apologize if
I frightened you, but do you not think it wise to leave someone a note?"

She nodded her head. "I went for a walk." She turned and pointed. "In that field. I sat for a bit and must have lost track of time. I humbly beg your pardon." She curtsied awkwardly.

The stallion pawed at the ground, anxious to be off, but Sheldrake held him tightly. "No harm has been done. And it is Lady Beresford to whom you owe an apology. You must understand that in her condition she cannot be upset."

Again the girl nodded, and tears shimmered in her eyes. Guilt seared his gut. "There now, there's no need for that. I will have a word with your sister. As a guest here, you needn't feel you have to be locked up in the house all day. I have a good stable with some gentle mounts. You do ride?"

A smile formed at the girl's lips. "Yes, sir, I do. Very well, too."

He smiled in spite of himself. "In future, you will leave a note and have a groom accompany you, is that clear?"

"Perfectly," she said, but her eyes had clouded over at the mention of a groom. He wondered what she had been up to, but decided to let it rest for now. He would be sure to keep his eye on Miss Susannah Lacey.

Sheldrake walked the drawing room floor, waiting. When the ladies finally entered, he halted his steps as Lady Beresford stood in the doorway, a vision of beauty in dark gray. It took him a moment to recover his wits. He knew his appreciation was apparent when she awarded him a soft smile, her cheeks pink.

Against his better judgment, without so much as a word to anyone else, he went to her. "Lady Beresford, all is well with your sister and aunt, I trust?" He sounded too polite!

"Yes, and I thank you, my lord." She lowered her thick lashes.

It was a simple action, the demure flutter of eyelashes. Sheldrake had seen it done a dozen times by a dozen women, yet never had he watched with such interest. She seemed totally unaffected about her looks. It was a natural movement, not the contrived coquettishness that Belinda had practiced.

"I promised Miss Susannah that I would have a word with you about her activities. She is free to make use of my stables."

She looked up to him. "She told me. Again, I must thank you. Susannah talked of nothing else, and she has promised to let me know of her whereabouts at all times."

"And one of my grooms will accompany her. Will that make you rest easier?"

"Indeed it would."

He noted that her smile was natural, and came easily. Another difference between the fair Lady Beresford and his one-time betrothed. Belinda's smile often times resembled a sneer.

The butler cleared his throat to announce dinner, and Sheldrake left off with his mental comparison of Lady Beresford to Belinda. The small party gathered around and waited for him to lead them to the dining room, so he held out his arm to Lady Beresford.

He noticed her hesitation and cursed inwardly. He had never gotten used to the wariness people displayed in his presence. Perhaps it was just as well that she was fearful of him. But deep down, he longed to put her at ease.

"Did you find any books of interest from the volumes I selected?" he asked as they walked the short distance to the dining room.

"Yes, my lord. How fortunate of you to have chosen Byron's latest work, as I have yet to read it."

"You enjoy Byron then?" Sheldrake knew most women admired the poet, so it was elementary in choosing it for her.

"Yes, but I think him rather, oh, how shall I say it . . ."

"Fast?"

"No, not precisely that."

Entering the dining room, Sheldrake helped her to her chair. His mother had arranged the seating to place Lady Beresford to his right and a vacant spot to his left. It appeared a trifle obvious, and he cast his mother a questioning look. She smiled back at him and sat down at the other end of a shortened table between the aunt and sister.

"Pray continue, Lady Beresford. How do you find Byron?" Sheldrake took his seat.

"I find him completely indecorous."

"That is a strong way of putting it, though probably truthful."

"Oh dear, are you an acquaintance of Lord Byron? I meant no offense." She twisted her napkin.

He chided himself for being so forthright. She would think him clumsy in the social graces. Who was he trying to fool—he was clumsy. He had never given a fig for grace, social or otherwise. He need not worry about it now. Perhaps if he drew her out in conversation, she would relax a bit and not fidget so. "No, I do not know Lord Byron, nor have I met him. I do find him intriguing though."

"Do you, my lord, how so?"

"He is a man of our time gaining world attention. I pay attention to the columns about him as most do, I suppose. By the by, you need not 'my lord' me all night. Sheldrake will do."

She looked taken aback for a moment, then said she would try to remember to call him thus. He watched her take a deep breath before adding, "Since I am to remain in your home for an extended visit, you must call me Olivia, my . . . I mean, Sheldrake."

He nodded. A servant brought in a tureen of soup, and he focused his attention on the pouring of wine for him and lemonade for Olivia. Her name echoed through his mind. *Olivia*—it had a bewitching sound. He cast a glance sideways to watch her as she took a sip from her drink. Her hair was swept up into a loose twist with parts of it falling down her back. The scarf she wore lay pulled to the side and fastened at her shoulder with a large opal brooch. It slipped when she set down her glass. The heaviness of the jeweled pin brought the ends of the fabric toward her breasts. He caught a glimpse of heavenly cleavage, and a shot of desire ripped through him.

She turned to him. He looked up fast, but she knew where his gaze had been and she turned that delightful shade of pink again. He watched, fascinated as she returned the brooch to its original position. She patted it as if daring it to move again. He took a healthy pull of his wine.

She turned her attention back to him and asked, "Sir, you have not really answered my question. How does Lord Byron intrigue you?"

He thought a moment—why did he like the sniveling poet? "Byron seems to have a disregard for the strictures of society. He goes about his way as if he is somehow above it all."

"And you admire him for that?" she asked, her eyes wide.

"Admire is too strong a word, but yes, in a way let us say I commend him for his attempts to throw the rules of the *ton* back in their faces." He watched her eyebrows furrow with disapproval. Before she commented on his remark, the first course was served *en famille,* and she busied herself with filling her plate.

Sheldrake thought about his own temptations to throw the proprieties to the wind when he had dealt with Abbott. Abbott gained no admiration from him, even though the scoundrel had flouted the rules of polite society. Abbott made a mockery of all that was proper and decent and did so in an evil manner. He found no courage in that.

"I could not like a society with no code of proper behavior." She took a bite of ham. She swallowed, then added, "Pandemonium would surely result."

"True, and yet there is much hypocrisy to be found that I cannot help but cheer for the one who throws such double standards back at those governing society."

"Well said, I am sure. But alas, I have no dealings with the *ton.* I had no season."

"How did you meet Beresford?" he blurted.

She shifted in her seat, then took a sip of lemonade. He

was sure he had muddled it. It would cause her pain to remember her husband, and he certainly did not wish to console a watering pot.

"Truly, it is hard to remember." She laughed suddenly before saying, "I had known Robbie since I was a child. He and his family summered with friends whose estate bordered my aunt's cottage. Robbie and I were young and fancied ourselves in love. His parents did not approve, but eventually they gave over, and so we were married. I was only eighteen."

"You must have visited your aunt often growing up." He settled a forkful of food into his mouth.

"I was raised by my aunt, sir. My sister, too."

This time he detected her discomfort. A war seemed to be playing out upon her expression. Something deep within him stirred. He knew the strange struggle to appear normal when someone hit upon a wound unexpectedly. He had no doubt looked the very same way when anyone spoke of Belinda.

Without thought, he reached out and covered her hand with his own and squeezed gently. She jumped and turned those great green pools for eyes upon him. Odd, he thought, that bloody feeling of familiarity overcame him, and he pulled his hand back.

Olivia's heart pounded, and her hand tingled where he had touched it. She took a sip of lemonade, but it did little to settle her nerves. Why would Sheldrake offer such a gesture of comfort? The idea that he could sense her sadness made her more than a little worried.

She glanced up at him through her lashes. What a mysterious man—overbearing one moment, then giving unsolicited kindness the next. She did not like the way he looked at her either. Sometimes she felt he could see right into her soul—a place she swore never to allow entry to anyone.

"How did you spend your afternoon, Susannah?" Lady Evelyn asked.

Olivia's heart pumped. She had not mentioned anything

about Susannah's absence or Lord Sheldrake's offer of the stables to their aunt.

"I took a walk about the gardens." Her sister looked at her for a clue as to how far to go on.

"Your gardens are lovely," Aunt Agatha added, and Olivia felt herself relax as the ladies moved on to another topic.

She knew she was being overly sensitive, but she did not wish Aunt Agatha to refuse Lord Sheldrake's kind offer to Susannah. Her sister needed the exercise, she needed to enjoy whatever she could while they were here. Of that, Olivia was determined. His lordship had shown consideration that she would not allow Aunt Agatha to throw back in his face with a refusal.

Throughout the rest of the meal she remained constantly aware of him. Even though she conversed with the rest of the table where she could, when he picked up his fork, or took a drink, or wiped his mouth with his napkin, she noticed his every movement.

His hands, browned from the sun, lay in dark contrast to the whiteness of the table linen. Occasionally, his fingers tapped softly. The quiet rhythm distracted her, tempting her gaze to dwell upon his flesh. She looked away, shaken at the thought of those tanned fingers drumming along her skin.

But were those hands truly capable of murder? She suddenly looked up, startled at the vision of Lord Sheldrake choking the life out of his stepfather.

"What is it?" he asked.

She shook her head to clear it. "Nothing, nothing at all."

He did not appear satisfied with her statement, and he leaned back in his chair. She had to know what happened the night this Abbott fellow died. Was it truly an accident? She could not believe how much she hoped that it was.

"Well, ladies." Lady Evelyn stood. "Shall we retire to the drawing room and let my son enjoy his port?"

He stood to help Olivia to her feet. She pushed back the chair as best she could and gave him her hand. Try as she might, she could not get up. Tired and full, she could not budge. The chair had no arm rests to push herself up from, and her leg had fallen asleep. She sat there, stuck in the dining room chair!

"Let's see, how shall we best do this?" he whispered.

Ashamed, she knew her cheeks had reddened. She looked away in time to see Aunt Agatha bearing down on them with a protective gleam in her eye.

"Here, my lord, let me," Aunt Agatha said as she took hold of Olivia's arm and pulled her up, quite hard in fact.

She looked up sharply at her aunt, but the deed was done; she was out of the chair. A hundred needles assaulted her foot. She stamped it twice. Turning to Sheldrake, she needed to apologize. "It would appear that a woman in my state is not suited for your dining chairs, my lord. I beg your pardon."

"None needed. I am sorry for your distress."

"Please," Olivia said, then stopped. Her aunt practically pulled her from him.

Once in the hallway, she turned on her aunt. "Really, you could have been more discreet about getting me out of the room."

"Me! Olivia, what the devil were the two of you carrying on about, your heads together and you pink as any debutante?"

"Byron, Aunt. We were speaking of Lord Byron's works."

"Well, inappropriate subject matter to be sure. You had best keep a level head and keep your distance from that man. He is too handsome by half and will no doubt turn your head."

"He is our host," she hissed. "To not speak to him would be rude."

"Nonetheless, I shall not stand by and watch you cast sheep's eyes at him."

"I did no such thing!"

"What is the matter?" Susannah had come up behind them.

"Nothing," Olivia answered, her nerves raw. She stomped her way to the drawing room, her foot still tingling.

Lady Evelyn asked Susannah to play the pianoforte. Her aunt sat next to their hostess, and the two settled into a game of pique. Since Olivia declined to join in a game of cards, she sat looking out the windows. The setting sun cast a golden glow upon the gardens, and she wanted to be out there among the flowers in peace.

She rose from her chair. "Aunt, I believe I shall take some air and then retire for the night. Lady Evelyn, I bid you good evening."

"Rest well, Olivia," Lady Evelyn answered.

Aunt Agatha nodded as she played her card.

Olivia sighed with relief that her aunt was more interested in the game than in her announcement to walk in the garden. She opened the glass doors and felt a welcome rush of cool evening air upon her face. She took a turn around a small section of rosebushes, and the heady perfume calmed her.

Mentally, she cataloged each bloom. Lord Sheldrake did not have an extensive choice in roses, but what he did have were positively lovely. Red blossoms grew side by side with pink ones and yellows. They had been planted close together and drew strength from one another, their colors intermixing. She rubbed her middle, in hopes of quelling the movement within. The babe was most active after meals.

Walking farther, she came upon a prettily wrought iron bench that sat atop a slight hill that overlooked the small lake. A pair of swans glided across the still water, casting shimmering ripples of gold behind them. She sat down and pondered her aunt's harsh words about her interaction with Lord Sheldrake. Surely, she did not appear taken with him. But he did affect her. She could not deny how attractive she found him. And after this evening, she began to consider him as not totally unaware of her. That was good. But she wished she did not find him quite so physically pleasing. Such delight in his looks could only lead to complications.

Sheldrake was all that a titled lord should be—handsome, polite, and rich, yet underneath she sensed an emptiness in him that called to her. She did not want to feel sorry for him; she did not want to feel anything for him at all!

Yet, if she could prove him innocent of Abbott's death, she would rest far more easy as would her aunt, she was sure. Even if she did prove him innocent, she doubted her aunt would approve of her plan to pursue him.

Dearest Aunt Agatha. Olivia had a penchant for opposing her aunt since she was a child. She had learned her sums when her aunt said she would never grasp arithmetic. She had married Robbie when her aunt said his parents would never allow it. She was inclined to prove her wrong about Sheldrake as well.

"Olivia?"

Startled, she turned to see Lord Sheldrake standing by the tree. He had a warm wrap in his hands.

"It is turning cool. I thought you may want this." He walked forward and held out the shawl.

"Thank you." Olivia had not shivered until she heard his voice. She took the shawl from him and wrapped it about her shoulders. "This is very peaceful. You have a lovely home."

"Thank you. I often come out to watch the sun set."

"Oh! I do not wish to intrude." She tried to get up.

"No, stay. Had I wished to be alone, I'd not have come."

She moved down the bench as he sat beside her. To her annoyance, her insides flip-flopped.

"How are you feeling this evening?" he asked.

"I am very well, thank you." She looked down at the ends of the shawl he had given her. She worried the fringed edges as they sat in silence. She dare not ask the question weighing most heavy in her mind. *Did you kill your stepfather?*

"When did you go to live with your aunt?" he asked. He

sat staring out toward the lake, his legs stretched out before him and crossed at the ankles.

"When I was seven."

"And your sister?"

"She was a new baby. My mother died in childbirth," she explained woodenly.

"But your father, was he not alive?" he asked, then quickly added, "I beg your pardon; I have no right to ask you these things."

"My father was away, sir," she fibbed. How could she tell him that her father was thrown out of England? That he, the mighty Mr. Charles Lacey, was a low ne'er-do-well who left his wife to die and children to fend for themselves because of his dallying with married ladies and duels with their angry husbands!

"He was away your whole life?" Sheldrake asked

"My whole life," she answered sharply, uncomfortable with the conversation.

"Again, I beg your pardon. I merely thought . . . never mind. Here, ask me something and we shall call it even."

"Is the rumor about you true?" The words were out of her mouth before she could catch them.

Shock registered on his face. She could not believe she had asked such a thing and wished she could disappear. She held her breath, waiting for his reply.

"Depends upon which rumor." His eyes narrowed.

She was not about to balk now. Gathering her courage, she said slowly, "The one where you murdered your step-father in a rage."

She could not tear her gaze from his face. His eyes closed briefly. She thought the very grass awaited his reply, so still was the world around them.

"Do have a care in listening to rumors," he said.

Olivia's eyes widened. The anger in his voice rang clear as a bell. He did not like her question, and so the discussion was over. Sheldrake stood and offered her his hand. She did not know if she should take it. He must have noticed her hesitation as he let his arm drop to his side, and with a curt nod he left her.

She sat there stunned. She had asked him, but he did not tell her. What she had expected, she did not know. Considering the attraction she felt toward him, she had hoped he would have told her it was all a bit of fluff and nonsense. But he hadn't. He had been angry with her for asking such a question. And rightly so, perhaps.

Sheldrake walked away from her and into the drawing room. His mother and Olivia's aunt were deep in a card game, and neither paid him much attention. Susannah seemed lost in her music as she played with a dreamy, far-off look. He took a seat, closed his eyes, and listened to the incredible music she made.

Olivia had heard the bloody rumors! But of course, he already knew she had, just by the way she had became fearful of him when she learned who he was after the carriage accident. But to have the question asked of him in such a way. What was worse was that he desperately wanted to tell her that they were not true! He wanted to assure her that he was an honorable man. He wanted to kiss her, for pity's sake! But he could not do any of those things.

"Are you sleeping, dear?" His mother's voice permeated his thoughts.

"No, Mama, I am not." He opened his eyes. "I am listening to Miss Lacey's skill at the pianoforte."

"She plays divinely," Lady Evelyn said, then to the aunt she asked, "Who does she take lesson's from, dear?"

"She has long since stopped with her lessons, but I think because she loves it so, she continues to improve."

Sheldrake nodded and turned to look out the window. Dusk was settling, but Olivia had left the bench. He wondered what she could possibly be thinking and decided he should not want to know. He stood with a sigh. "Ladies, I do believe I shall retire for the evening. I bid you all a good night."

"Good night, dear," Lady Evelyn crooned.

The aunt merely nodded, and Susannah waved. Well, at least he had won their youngest guest over. With that thought, he left the room and headed toward his rooms. Halfway up the stairs, he realized that he would not fall asleep directly. There had to be a book he could read to keep him from his thoughts, so he turned and made his way to the library. Once inside, he found Olivia there.

"Lord Sheldrake," Olivia said when he entered, "I hope you do not mind, but your mother told me I might find another book to read here. I was not in the mood for Byron tonight."

"Are you anticipating a difficult time falling asleep?" He knew he was. But he was satisfied somehow when her cheeks colored and she looked away.

An awkward silence settled between them, and he was sorry for it, but it could not be helped. He'd be addled if he was going to tell a woman he met less than two days ago what had happened to Abbott. He walked over to the shelves she perused and offered his help. "What are you in the mood for?"

Her gazed flew to his, and he realized his question could be construed as inappropriate. "What I meant was . . ." he stammered, then turned to read the bindings of the books. He selected a book of poetry. "Here, this is a rather soothing selection."

Did he have to rub her nose in the fact that she would indeed spend a night fretting about what she had asked him? Olivia wondered, deciding the man was insufferable. "Perhaps you could lend me a book on agriculture, my lord. Your mother said that you read those constantly. Surely, that would put me to sleep."

He looked surprised at her sarcasm, but then he smiled and Olivia knew she had never seen a more handsome man. He definitely needed to smile more often.

"You think agriculture a dull subject, do you?"

She looked him straight in the eye, the tension of rumors

gone and replaced by a flirtatious anxiety that was completely new to her. "Dull as dirt," she said.

"You obviously need an education in the excitement of making things grow." Then he looked down at her belly bulging between them, and started to laugh. "But I guess you already know about that."

She was smiling, too, and felt they had made peace with each other, for now at least. "Lord Sheldrake—"

"Please, call me Sheldrake, remember?" His voice was soft, almost caressing.

"Sheldrake then." She backed up when she realized they were standing close, much too close. "I actually have experience making other things grow."

He cocked an eyebrow. "Such as?"

"I dabbled in raising roses. I was experimenting with crossing a hot house variety and some wild rosebushes when Robbie's heir and cousin moved into Adberesmere." Her lightheartedness suddenly left her at the reminder of her situation.

"And you were not able to see the results, were you." His voice had softened, and the compassionate look in his eyes told her he understood.

She ran her fingers down the books on the shelves, not looking into his eyes that seemed to know more about what she was feeling than she did. "I am afraid the wild roses will have to go—far too unruly for Edmund."

When he did not speak, she noticed that his fist was clenched, and she looked up at him, trying to make the subject matter pleasant again. "But I have my aunt's roses to work with when I return there."

"And does she have the greenhouse varieties you will need?"

"No, mainly just wild ones."

"Then I suggest that I offer you some of the varieties I have to start with. I am interested in what you can create with these strains."

"That is most generous of you, my lord," she whispered.

It sounded too much like a future for them, a future she found that she truly wanted and looked forward to.

Turning to another shelf, she said over her shoulder, "My goal is to create a hardier plant with a longer blooming time."

"A very practical idea, but what of the fragrance?"

"Fragrance, my lord?" She turned to face him.

"In my humble opinion, the only thing worth the trouble of roses is their fragrance."

She smiled and knew he was not trying to be forward at all. He truly wanted to discuss roses! "But I favor the sheer beauty of them; the fragrance is an added bonus, depending on the variety, of course."

"I have no wild rose bushes here," he said with a slight frown.

"I noticed that." Were they speaking only of roses? She gazed at the bookshelves again, suddenly feeling awkward. But then she turned and faced him. "I am sure you could find them somewhere if you wished to transplant them into your gardens. They would complement your rhododendrons."

He looked at her, and she gazed back at him longer than what could be considered appropriate. She felt a stirring in her belly and absently stroked her side to quell the soft kicking of her babe. With considerable daring she asked him, "May I have one of your agriculture books to read? I should like to learn more about it."

She held her breath as she saw admiration in his gaze. If she wanted to woo him, she had evidently done a good job with this subject, even though she had done poorly with the subject of rumors.

"Of course you may." He reached toward the top shelf and pulled out the thinnest volume there. Still, it was a rather thick book. "This explains what I have been trying to do here. But truly, if it bores you, I can choose something else."

"I am hoping to fall asleep quickly, remember?"

He nodded and laughed and she felt as though they had forged a sort of connection.

"Let me escort you up the stairs." He held out his arm to her.

"I am perfectly able to—"

"Please. You have no doubt had a tiring day. I want to help you; besides I can carry your book."

"But are you not going to choose one for yourself?" Surely he had come to the library seeking something to read.

"It doesn't matter. I do not believe it will make the least bit of difference for me."

Was he anticipating trouble sleeping as well, or did he sleep like the dead regardless? She shivered at the analogy. She had to find out what happened to Abbott.

Chapter Six

Olivia woke to the smell of chocolate and the sound of Mrs. Boothe's humming as she opened the curtains. Early morning light poured into the room. Olivia yawned, then asked, "What time is it?"

"Seven-thirty, milady," Mrs. Boothe answered. "There is a full spread served in the breakfast room at eight o'clock, or I can have a tray sent up."

"The breakfast room shall be fine." She sat up and the book Sheldrake had given her fell to the floor with a thump. She smiled. She truly had fallen asleep while reading it. She would have to tell him.

She swung her legs over the side of the bed and asked the housekeeper to send for Bonnie. She sat for a moment, rubbing her eyes. Surprisingly, she had not been overly plagued by Sheldrake's response to her blurted question last night. She had found the farming techniques described in the book somewhat interesting, but in no time she had fallen asleep.

She sat a moment longer remembering the set-down Sheldrake had given her for asking him about the truth of the rumor she had heard. He did not bother to protest his innocence; in fact his indignant refusal to address the matter seemed more of a sign of innocence than any denials he could have made. Even so, she wanted to know for sure.

She sighed deeply and forced herself up off the bed. Moving slowly, she unraveled the long braid of her hair. Perhaps breakfast with him would reveal more clues. She instructed Bonnie to hurry when she arrived, as she did not wish to be late for breakfast. Brushed, dressed, and looking forward to seeing her host, she made her way to the stairs. She heard male voices—laughing.

Carefully, she descended and stopped near the bottom to watch Sheldrake embrace a gentleman who had just arrived. The man was of shorter stature and a thicker build than Sheldrake, but it was apparent that they knew each other well. She did not wish to interrupt them, so she quietly took the rest of the stairs, but it was too late. He saw her.

"Olivia." Sheldrake turned toward her and held out his hand. "Come, you must meet my friend."

She placed her hand in his and was led forward.

"Lady Beresford, may I present Mr. Peter Blessing. Peter, this is Lady Beresford. She, along with her sister and aunt, are guests."

Olivia's eyes widened with embarrassment as Mr. Blessing bowed before her and took her hand to place his lips upon her knuckles. He kissed her flesh instead of the air as was proper. He looked deeply into her eyes and murmured his pleasure in making her acquaintance. Her guess was that he was a rascal through and through.

"That will do, Peter. You need not make a cake of yourself." Sheldrake took Olivia's hand from Mr. Blessing's and tucked it into the curve of his arm.

She stiffened, but let her hand rest within Sheldrake's grasp. She noted that none of this escaped Mr. Blessing's notice, and she received a raised brow from the newcomer. She looked away.

"Come, you are in time for breakfast," Sheldrake announced to the new arrival.

"I do hope I have not come at an inconvenient time." Mr. Blessing cast a pointed look at her middle.

"Not at all," Sheldrake said. "I expected you to make an appearance."

She felt the heat rise to her cheeks. Mr. Blessing made no attempt to conceal his ogling of her condition no matter how uncomfortable she must seem to him. Sheldrake kept a hold upon her arm.

In the light of day it appeared that Sheldrake was not going to hold a grudge against her for asking him about the rumors. But she knew as he must, that the question remained between them. The warmth of his hand resting upon her own caused her enough distraction that she had to concentrate on walking with even steps. The breakfast room seemed an eternity away.

When they entered, Lady Evelyn immediately rose to greet Mr. Blessing with a kiss upon his cheek. Olivia regained her composure while the introductions were made to Susannah and Aunt Agatha. Soon everyone settled down after filling their plates at the sideboard.

"So, Peter, where is your new bride? You did not bring her? And what news do you have from London?" Lady Evelyn asked.

Mr. Blessing chuckled at the barrage of questions. "London is ever the same, Lady Evelyn. No doubt quiet now with summer. But I came from Scotland, and Winifred needed to attend to some family affairs."

"And do you live in London year round, Mr. Blessing?" Aunt Agatha asked.

"I did. 'Cept for when I come here to play the rustic with Shelly." Mr. Blessing grinned. "But now that I have married, I'll be making my home at my humble estate in Kent. I may yet become a country gentleman like yourself, Shel."

"Please do not say that you cut short your honeymoon to visit us," Lady Evelyn said.

"Ah, so you have heard?"

"Richard read it in the *Morning Post* the other day. Your bride I hope is not ill?" Lady Evelyn patted Mr. Blessings' hand.

"No, no, nothing like that. There was only so much we could do at my brother's hunting lodge. We both thought it best to get back. Winifred has been itching to get her hands on Trenton Manor, so I expect she is already there giving the place a good cleaning," Mr. Blessing said with a somewhat forced smile.

Olivia sipped her tea and observed the look that passed between Sheldrake and Mr. Blessing. She also noticed that despite Mr. Blessing's marital status, he was a flirt. He charmed every female in the room. Susannah positively beamed under his attention. Olivia tended to think there would be no playing with her sister's affections, but she could not be certain. She would definitely keep her eye on Mr. Blessing.

"Well, I hope the lady is worthy of you," Lady Evelyn said.

"She is most worthy in the *sum* of her attributes," Mr. Blessing said with a charming Gallic shrug.

Sheldrake burst out laughing.

Olivia found herself smiling in spite of herself. He obviously married for money and appeared very pleased with himself for succeeding. Perhaps she would find a way to obtain the same goal in time.

After breakfast, Sheldrake led his friend to a comfortable chair in his study.

"Well?" Peter asked.

"Well what?"

"Are you going to tell me about the beauty with the bulging belly? And is her expectancy any of your doing?" Peter wore an ear-to-ear grin upon his face.

"Not mine. She's Beresford's widow," Sheldrake said. At Peter's look of confusion, he added, "Remember Robbie Lawton? We were all up at Eton together. He was a bit younger than our set, but a good enough chap."

"I say, Beresford was Robbie Lawton? I never paid much attention to the connection. Beresford was up to London constantly. I heard he kept mistresses by the twos and threes. How'd he turn up his toes?"

Sheldrake suffered a sudden and strong dislike for the man. "Died in a hunting accident on the field a few months back." He wondered if Olivia knew of her late husband's dallying. If it were up to him, she would never know. The man must have had maggots in his head to stray from such beauty for Haymarket ware. Sheldrake dragged his thoughts back to his friend.

"You don't say. I didn't know you knew her. Invited her here to drown her grief in your arms, did you?" Peter smiled fully at him.

"No, nothing like that. She and her sister toppled their carriage at the bottom of the hill. Lady Beresford cannot travel until after her child is born, and her aunt is here to play protector."

"Ah, yes, the violently evil Lord Sheldrake. I bet the aunt will raise a breeze with you sniffing around her niece," Peter said. "You seem quite taken with this *enceinte* enchantress."

"We met only two days ago."

"Ah, but even Rome was not built in a day." Peter winked.

"You know I am in no position to play Romeo. She is simply a nice lady. And her aunt keeps watch nonetheless. By the by, do have a care when flirting with Miss Susannah, the lady's sister. She is only sixteen, and I will not have you distress Lady Beresford."

"We cannot have that," Peter agreed.

"I am serious," Sheldrake said. "The chit practically worshipped you in there. She hung on your every word."

"Don't worry, I'll be good. I am a married man now. Besides, it was only the tales of London that interested her, not me." Peter spread his hands in defense, then turned serious in a blink. "How are you, old boy?"

"Fine, I suppose."

"You look worn to a shade."

"Finished putting in the second planting, you know." Sheldrake did not mention he was up half the night thinking about his conversation with Olivia. He almost spilled it all to her right then and there when she had asked him about those bloody rumors. He wanted to chase away the shadows of suspicion from behind her eyes. Foolish, most foolish of him—he needed to keep his mouth shut tight. He dare not entrust her with the truth of what happened to Abbott. That could very well spell disaster for them all.

"How is Lady Evelyn?" Peter asked with a jerk of his head toward the door.

"She still does not remember. Acts too happy to be really so, but there it is."

"What does Pedley say? Will she ever remember that night?"

"Only time will tell. But I would rather that my mother never remember . . . ever."

They sat quietly for a moment, each deep in his own thoughts. Peter stood and slapped Sheldrake on the shoulder. "How about some target practice?"

"Where did you get this?" Susannah asked.

Olivia turned from her wardrobe to glance at the book her sister referred to. "Lord Sheldrake gave it to me to read."

"Goodness, since when have you wanted to read about farming?"

"He thought it might help me to fall asleep and it did. It is a bit dull." She closed the door to the armoire and sat down upon the settee in front of a hearth that had been swept spotlessly clean.

"You like him." Susannah sat upon the bed, the agriculture book still in her hands.

"He has been most kind to us."

Her sister smiled broadly. "But you like him, do you not?"

"Susannah."

Her sister raised her hand to keep Olivia from saying anything more. "It does not matter. I just wanted you to know that I would be glad if you liked him and he you."

"What about the rumors?" she asked.

"I don't believe them."

"Just like that?" Olivia could not believe her ears. In two

days her sister had changed her opinion completely. What did she know that Olivia did not? "What has changed your mind?" She watched Susannah twirl her hair on her finger as she sat quietly in thought.

"I do not know. Perhaps it is because he does not act like a murderer."

"And how would you even know how a murderer should act?"

"All I do know is that Lord Sheldrake has given me freedom to roam about the grounds, wherever I please. Would a murderer be so generous? And he did not scold me when he caught me going through some papers in one of the rooms the night we first came here."

"Susannah, you did no such thing!"

"Please don't be angry," Susannah said quietly. "I know it is shameful, but I was simply curious, and there was nothing to find. I merely think that if he had something so terrible to hide, he would act more sinister."

"Susannah, not every villain acts like a villain." Olivia sighed, her sister was too trusting by half.

"Well, I believe that you had the right of it all along. If the authorities called it an accident, then that is good enough for me."

"What about paying off the law as you said? He is a viscount after all, is that not what you told me?" She did not understand why she felt the need to push her sister's reasoning.

"He would never do that! Can you imagine Lord Sheldrake doing something so underhanded? I think not."

She was right of course. Olivia could not imagine Lord Sheldrake stooping to bribery. It was not his style at all. The man loved farming, but he also loved his mother and his land. If either of those were threatened somehow, would he kill in order to protect them? To continually speculate was sheer madness. She simply had to know.

"What are your plans this afternoon?" Olivia asked.

"Well, I had hoped to try out his lordship's stables, and

then of course there is the afternoon tea." Susannah was twirling her hair again.

"What tea?"

"I thought Aunt Agatha would have told you. Lady Evelyn has asked us to join her for tea at one of her neighbors' homes."

"I see." Olivia could not help but feel a bit disappointed in not being asked nor able to attend. In her condition, it would be highly improper, not to mention that she could not travel very far.

"And if I am to get that ride in, I had best change and be off." Susannah started for the door.

"Do be careful and heed Lord Sheldrake's requirement that you take a groom with you." Olivia watched her sister roll her eyes, but she nodded just before leaving.

Olivia sat back with another sigh. She was not about to spend the entire day indoors when the sun shined so brightly out of doors. Gathering her sewing basket and needlepoint, Olivia headed out of her chamber. She'd while away the afternoon in the garden.

Susannah reined in the sweet mare she rode and waited. She checked the small watch pinned to her habit. She was early, but only by minutes. What if the captain decided not to ride here today?

She watched as Lord Sheldrake's groom trotted back to the stables. She had cleverly sent him on his way, since they were so close to the Hall. She told him that she would pick a few flowers; and there was no need for him to hang about for that. She had let out a held breath when he said that he did have chores yet to complete and gratefully headed home.

Susannah slid from her saddle with ease and let the mare have her way and munch the grass. She scanned the horizon, but still there was no captain. Absently, she picked wildflowers. Closing in on a blue cornflower, Susannah noticed a pair of black boots before her.

With a start, she raised her head and smiled. "Captain," she cried. "You came!"

"I did."

"But when? I did not hear you," Susannah looked about for his horse, then spotted Luna in the middle of the field.

"I just arrived. I rode pretty hard, so I walked for a bit, and then I saw you picking the flowers and I did not wish you to stop. So I kept quiet." He looked away.

"I am happy to see you again. How is your friend?"

"Fine—a bit depressed, but otherwise physically healing." He gestured toward the field and added, "Would you care to walk?"

"I should like that above all things." Susannah let the reins to her mount loosen, but held them firmly as she walked next to her new friend. The mare followed leisurely.

When the captain remained quiet, Susannah ventured to ask, "What is it that makes your friend sad?"

"He lost his leg and cannot think his life worth living without it."

She stopped to look directly at him. Staring deep into his clear blue eyes, she asked, "And what do you think?"

Shock registered in his expression, and then he turned thoughtful. "How old did you say you were?"

"I didn't." She grinned.

"Ah, a lady's prerogative to conceal her age. You must be close to having a season soon. Next year perhaps?"

"I should love it if that were so, but of course I have no dowry. I doubt there will be the ability for a season in town, but perhaps my aunt shall take me to Bath." Susannah had tried to sound matter-of-fact, but she wanted a season more than anything; and she could not keep the wanting of it out of her voice.

The captain bowed before her with a lighthearted smile. "Miss Susannah, you will not need a dowry to catch yourself a fine husband. Your beauty will knock the gentlemen on their ears whether you go to London or Bath."

"Do you really think so?" She fiddled with the reins in her hands, picking at the polished leather.

"I know so."

"Have you been to London?"

"I have. It is a sparkling place."

"So why have you not found a suitable lady to take to wife?" Susannah asked teasingly.

"That is very simple. I have not yet made my fortune." He smiled broadly; and she thought him the most handsome man she had ever laid her gaze upon. Which were very few indeed, but she did not care. Captain Jeffries had a pleasant face and a ready smile. His eyes crinkled when he smiled, and she would venture to say that they even twinkled beneath his long dark lashes.

"How do you plan to make your fortune, sir?"

"After the war is done, I think I shall join the East India Company and come back a brown-skinned nabob rich with treasures."

"That sounds grand indeed, but I do not think I should wish to leave England."

"Why not?"

"It is so pretty here and never too hot. I would melt in such a heated climate for sure."

He laughed at her and chucked her upon the chin. "Spoken like a true Englishwoman. But would you not like to travel abroad? See the sights, smell the smells, taste the different foods?" His excitement and rapt expression nearly persuaded her, but she continued to shake her head and argue the superiority of English food and sights until she realized the time.

Checking the watch pinned to her habit, she looked up. "Captain Jeffries, I must go. Lady Evelyn is taking my aunt and myself to tea, so I cannot be late."

"Of course, you must hurry along." Did she mistake the disappointment in his eyes? It made her heart tumble.

"Can we meet again tomorrow?" Susannah asked as she hurriedly gathered up a few extra flowers in her bouquet.

"That would be fine. I ride at this time every day," he said.

"Very well, until tomorrow." Susannah waved, then turned and ran toward the gardens of Sheldrake Hall, the mare trotting behind her.

She was out of Captain Jeffries' eyesight when he stooped to pick a cornflower. Inhaling the subtle scent, he whispered, "Until tomorrow."

Olivia sat upon the same wrought iron bench where she had sat with Sheldrake the previous evening. The warm breeze caused the leaves overhead to stir and rustle in the soft wind. Her needlepoint lay in a heap beside her as she leaned back to catch the warmth from the late afternoon sun. It had been a perfect day for outdoor activity. The storm had taken away every trace of the oppressive heat. Lord Sheldrake and Mr. Blessing had been gone since the morning meal. Every now and again, she heard a shot, but it had been quiet for some time. They must be returning.

Olivia gathered her things to leave. She had to wash and change for dinner. She stood slowly, rubbing her back to ease the dull ache, when she looked up to catch sight of two men coming in from the fields. The sunlight shone from behind them, casting them as dark silhouettes against the sky. Dogs trailed about their feet.

She noted how tall and proud Lord Sheldrake appeared walking next to the shorter Mr. Blessing. She watched them approach, shielding her eyes against the glare of the late sun. Did she imagine that Lord Sheldrake stared at her as he walked toward her? She could not be sure due to the distance between them, but she did not look away from him. A strange thrill raced along her spine as she watched him come nearer.

One of the dogs, the smallest, ran ahead. Its barking distracted her, and she turned in time to see the spaniel bolt past her into the courtyard. Within seconds, she heard a yelp and then the dog howled in pain.

Dropping her workbasket on the bench, Olivia pushed herself forward, lifting her skirts in an attempt to move faster. She came upon the little dog before the stables, where it lay with its foot caught in a small trap. Lord Sheldrake ran past her and knelt down by the dog. He opened the trap and released its foot, but the dog did not move. It lay there trembling on the ground while blood oozed from its paw. He examined the foot with a quick glance, then picked up the spaniel and turned to Mr. Blessing, who came up behind him.

"What happened?" Mr. Blessing asked.

Sheldrake's features were stone. "She got herself caught in a trap. One of the men must have dropped it on his way out to lay them."

"Here." Olivia pulled her handkerchief from her skirt pocket and advanced toward Sheldrake to wrap the dog's foot. Blood dripped from the dog's paw onto his coat sleeve. "It looks as though it needs to be stitched." She turned to walk back to the bench to retrieve her workbasket.

"Madam, we shall see to it," Sheldrake said, his voice gruff.

She turned around to face him. "What are you going to do?"

"Olivia, we shall see you at dinner." His voice was calm and soft but his eyes looked troubled.

"No! You need not put the animal down." She went toward him and grabbed his arm. "I can mend it! Robbie had a dog with a wound much worse than this; and I tell you we saved it."

"Even so," he said and shrugged off her hold. "I'll not see her suffer." He walked toward the stables with Mr. Blessing.

As quickly as she could, she retrieved her workbasket and followed them to the stables. It was not far, but she walked much slower than the men. Determined to save the dog, she set her shoulders and entered the stable.

The smell of hay assaulted her nose, mixed with the scent of horse. She looked around, wondering where they could have gone. A groomsman jerked his head toward the back of the stable and growled out a terse "They be in the tack room, straight a 'ead to yer left."

She nodded her thanks and hurried to catch up before they did something she would regret. As she passed through the line of stalls, she absently noticed the prime blood Sheldrake kept. It was no wonder that Susannah was anxious to ride. They were splendid, every last one.

She found the tack room and entered. Both men stood hunched over a table. She scanned the room quickly, and it, too, was swept clean and tidy as was the rest of the stable. The dog lay upon the table with Sheldrake's jacket bundled around it. The dog whined.

She did not hesitate. She hurried to them and leaned against the roughened tabletop. "You will need to hold her still." She pushed up her sleeves.

"Olivia, the cut is quite deep," Sheldrake began, his voice strained. "She is a weak little thing as it is, and I fear infection will set in. It is far better to put her out of her misery now."

She gazed into his eyes. "I can save her."

His expression was controlled, veiled. "Give over, the dog is done for." He stopped and looked away.

She touched his sleeve, her fingers grazing the skin of his arm where his shirt was rolled to his elbow. "Please, let me try."

Sheldrake glanced at Mr. Blessing, who shrugged, then he turned to look at her. She sucked in a breath as she stared into eyes filled with such grief. The man was truly affected at the thought of killing his spaniel to put it out of its misery. Surely, this was not the reaction of someone who had willfully killed his stepfather.

"Do what you can," Sheldrake said with a sigh.

She turned to Mr. Blessing. "I shall need some hot water and basilicum powder and gauze for bandages."

As Mr. Blessing turned to leave, Sheldrake cleared his throat. "Find my mother and tell her to hold dinner."

Mr. Blessing nodded and left.

Silence settled over them as they waited. She watched Sheldrake scratch the dog's ears and stroke its fur over and over. His gentleness struck a chord of sympathy deep within her. The fact that the dog suffered distressed him. He mumbled words of encouragement every time it whimpered.

"How long have you had her?" she asked. Her voice sounded loud to her ears.

"Five years. I took her from one of my tenant farmers. She was the runt, and he planned to destroy her. I brought her home in my coat pocket." He smiled weakly and scratched the little dog's ears again. "That is how she got her name, Pockets."

"Well, Pockets," she cooed. "This will hurt a bit, but you will be right as rain in no time." She smiled at Sheldrake, who smiled in return. "I must thank you for lending me the agricultural manual last night."

"Ah, so it did put you to sleep." He continued to pet the dog.

"Yes, it did eventually, but there were some interesting theories laid out. Do you practice all of them?" She was glad to have something to fill the time as they waited for the list of items she'd requested.

"Some," he said. "I started with two plantings a couple of years ago, and it has nearly doubled our yield. I plant an early and late wheat. The latter is heartier with more of a nuttiness to it, but it is good and sells well. I have come to prefer it in my bread, much to Cook's chagrin. She likes to work with the more refined varieties."

"I must confess to liking the whitest of breads, so I must agree with your cook," she said.

A servant entered with the supplies she had requested of Mr. Blessing. When asked if there was anything further needed, Sheldrake dismissed him. Olivia breathed in deeply. The tack room's walls suddenly seemed much closer as she felt the weight of the task before her. She had to save the dog.

She bathed the wound gently. Pockets howled when she felt up and down its foot. "It may be broken, but I am not certain." She looked up at Sheldrake, waiting for him to give her his approval to proceed further.

His gaze locked with hers. He raked a hand through his tousled hair. "I can splint it. Go ahead, do what you can."

A dark lock still hung across his forehead. Seeing him thus, she fought the urge to smooth it aside, shocked at the strength of her longing to do so. He continued to stare deeply into her eyes, and a warmth ignited within her. She looked away, cursing her weakness toward him as she pulled out a spool of fine silk from her workbasket. She fumbled with it when she tried to slide the strand into the needle. Her hands shook, and she failed to thread the eye. She licked her dry lips and tried again.

"Are you sure you are up to this?" Sheldrake asked.

She nearly jumped, so quiet was his voice. "I am. Are you?" She looked up quickly. If Pockets were to die, would he blame her for meddling where she had no business?

His hands covered hers, stilling them. "I accept whatever happens. Do what you can."

She nodded and threaded the needle. She bent her head down to concentrate on the dog's foot. The pad gaped open, completely cut. "Hold her still."

He held the dog down, but Pockets jerked and howled in pain. Sheldrake's head bumped into Olivia's when she pierced the pad with her needle. Blood trickled down onto her fingers. She worked as quickly as she could. Sheldrake's head rubbed against her own, but he held fast to the dog as she stitched the pad with tight little knots. Her fingers were stained with blood, so she absently wiped them on her skirt. The dog squirmed, but eventually lay still when she tied off the last knot and bit the thread to break it.

She stood up straight and kneaded her back with one hand to ease the tension of leaning over for so long. "That should do it." She wiped at her sweating brow with the back of her hand. "I can hold her while you fashion the splint."

"Are you all right?" He reached out to cup her elbow with a free hand.

She looked up to see his expression of concern for her. *Stop it,* she thought. She did not want these feelings, these yearnings. The warmth from his hand upon her sleeve seeped through the stiff bombazine of her dress and threatened to weave its way into her heart. She backed away, causing his arm to fall from hers. "I am fine. Thank you."

"I am the one who must thank you, madam. You have done a splendid thing."

"You can tell me that after we see how well Pockets fares in a few days." She was not sure how to respond to the look of admiration in his eyes.

She bent down and concentrated on holding the dog still as Sheldrake fashioned the splint out of wood stakes that were in the room. His fingers constantly brushed hers as he wound gauze around the dog's leg that she held. Their heads were once again close together, and she could inhale the spicy scent he wore.

Would he ever answer her question from last evening? Were the rumors about him true? They couldn't be, she told herself as she watched him tenderly tuck the last bit of bandage in place. He was so gentle. To her in the carriage and now to this little unwanted runt of a dog he had rescued and cared for.

As he took the animal from the table to lay it in a wood-bin filled with hay, she let her hands stray to her belly. He would no doubt treat a child with as much care and kindness.

She watched him tuck his fine coat around the dog as it quivered. She wondered if he would care for a child this completely or would he give the babe over to a nurse.

"Olivia." He stood in front of her. "Olivia, is something wrong?"

She had been standing there staring until she snapped back to reality upon hearing the concern in his voice.

"You were miles away. Here, come and sit down." He

reached out and grabbed her elbows to steer her to the chair. But she remained standing.

"I beg your pardon." She shivered as a breeze blew through the opened window.

"The deuce, I'm sorry," Sheldrake corrected himself. "You are cold, and I have no right to let you tire yourself this way."

"Truly, I am fine. I was just thinking is all, and got carried away, I guess."

She cast her eyes down at her hands, and he pulled them into his own. He stepped closer and chafed her skin roughly to warm them. She looked up at him. He let his hands move up her arms, forcing the heat from his palms to chase away her chill. He stepped even closer, and she could feel the draw of his body, the heat that emanated there. She wanted to lean into him, let him rub out her worry as easily as he buffed her arms into a heated tingle. A stable boy walked into the room, then turned to dart back out. The spell was broken. She stepped away from him.

"George," Sheldrake called after the boy.

He pulled his forelock of hair as he responded, "Yes, sir?"

"I need you to run and ask Cook for some of that foul salve to put on the dog's bandages to keep her from licking them. And have Cook give you some prime scraps. Tell her I sent for them."

"Yes, sir."

"And hurry back," he added.

"Right away, sir." The boy left at a run.

"Well done, Lady Beresford. I thank you." Sheldrake leaned against the table.

"You are welcome, sir." She had stepped back and bent over to pet Pockets. "I should like to check on her."

"I do not wish to tax you any further. George will look after her, and I can keep watch on her progress."

"Keep a close eye upon her tonight, in case her paw becomes inflamed. The next two or three days will be the most critical."

"I will consult with you if there is any change for the worse. Now, come, let me walk you back to the Hall. Your aunt is likely frantic with worry."

She looked down at the dog, who had drifted off to sleep. She could do no more but hope for its full recovery. Not willing to endure Sheldrake's touch, doubting she could withstand the pleasure of it, she said, "I can find my way easily enough. Stay here and help young George with the salve."

He nodded, and she slipped out of the tack room and headed back to the Hall.

Chapter Seven

Olivia looked in a wall mirror to check her appearance before entering the dining room. Her cheeks did not need pinching. No doubt her high color remained due to the conversation she had had with her aunt when she returned from the stables. She knew her aunt meant well, but Aunt Agatha had given her a thorough scold for being alone with Lord Sheldrake. Her aunt had behaved as if they had arranged a secret rendezvous instead of mending a little dog's foot. She gave no consideration that Olivia may have saved the spaniel's life.

She glanced at the clock standing in the corner. Eight o'-clock. It was the latest she had ever eaten dinner and she was ready for it. Everyone had already gone on ahead to the dining room when she had gone to fetch her shawl. Hoping her grumbling stomach could not be heard, she entered the dining room.

"Ah, Lady Beresford, again, well done." Mr. Blessing stood up from his seat and bowed.

Lady Evelyn motioned for her to sit down. "Yes, my dear. We are so very grateful to you for saving little Pockets. Richard quite adores the dog. The little scamp stays in the Hall all winter long as he fears she will catch cold in the stables."

"That will do, Mother. You needn't make me sound like some old woman." Sheldrake held out Olivia's chair. When she sat down, he leaned to her and added, "But I am grateful to you."

"Thank you, everyone. It was the least I could do to repay his lordship's kind hospitality," she said with a pointed look at her aunt.

"You are a marvel, dear niece." Her aunt smiled a bit too broadly.

"I should say so," Lady Evelyn added. "You are a brave girl. I do not know how you could have stood the sight of blood. I promise you that I would have swooned the moment I spied the wound."

Olivia turned to respond, but was interrupted by Sheldrake who stood suddenly and asked if anyone wished some wine. His voice seemed strained as he proceeded to explain how he purchased the French wine years ago and had forgotten he had it.

She watched him exchange a look with Peter Blessing, who then took over with a story about the wonderful cellar his club kept in London. She noticed that Sheldrake cast Mr. Blessing a grateful smile and relaxed slightly. But after he sat down, Sheldrake did not take his gaze off his mother, who seemed oblivious to this verbal dancing by the men. Lady Evelyn filled her plate with the delicacies offered by the footman.

Olivia wondered if anyone else had sensed the tension in the room just a moment ago, but as she scanned the table, no one seemed concerned. Susannah questioned Mr. Blessing for more information regarding London. Her aunt was also busy filling her plate. Olivia watched Sheldrake watch his mother. What had been said to cause him distress?

After dinner, the gentlemen lingered only a short while with their port before joining the ladies in the drawing room. Mr. Blessing took a seat next to her and smiled. She nodded, but watched Sheldrake round up his mother, Aunt Agatha, and Susannah for a game of whist.

"Lady Beresford, what causes you to frown so?" Mr. Blessing asked.

"Oh, I did not realize I was doing so. I was only thinking."

"About Shelley?"

She turned shocked eyes upon him.

Mr. Blessing grinned at her in return. "I apologize, ma'am, that was too bold of me."

"I should say." She twisted the ends of her shawl, positively itching to ask him what exchanged between him and Sheldrake at dinner. "May I also be bold, sir?"

"I should like that above all things, my lady." He leaned closer to her and cast her a melting look.

Surely he did not expect her insides to turn to butter as must the maids of the *ton* at his attentions. She sat up straighter and looked him directly in the eye. "Tell me, what manner of man is Lord Sheldrake?"

Mr. Blessing suddenly became serious and returned her direct approach with a steady gaze. "A very good one."

"And yet there are rumors."

He leaned back, his charming self once more in place like a mask. "Lady Beresford, one thing I live by is never believe everything you see or hear."

A swell of hope surged within her. "Are you saying that they are not true?"

She did not receive her answer as Doctor Pedley chose that moment to be announced. He had completed his rounds and wanted to check in at the Hall to see how she fared. After a brief private discussion with her and her assurances that she felt fit, the good doctor left her side to join Mr. Blessing and Lord Sheldrake, who offered to sample brandy in his study. The three men said their good nights and left. Olivia pondered Mr. Blessing's comments, wishing again that she had something concrete regarding Sheldrake's innocence or guilt in Mr. Abbott's death.

Clearly, she needed to take matters to the next level of inquiry.

The day looked to be an uneventful one. Olivia had checked on Pockets straight after breakfast and was happy with the dog's good progress. The bandages would come off in no time. She did not see Lord Sheldrake though. She missed him when she had gone down to breakfast. He and Mr. Blessing had left early, Lady Evelyn had said.

Her questions surrounding Lord Sheldrake had no promise of being answered any time soon, so she sought out information from the servants she came across as she wandered about the main floor of Sheldrake Hall. She had spent the good part of the morning questioning a footman and a chambermaid, and even a stable boy, where she could. She received little other than praise for Lord Sheldrake as a good master and curses for Mr. Abbott as a scoundrel dealt what he deserved. All references to Abbott were whispered quietly and with great looking about. This served only to add to her confusion.

She had to admit that she felt less suspicious of Lord Sheldrake the more time she spent in his company. But a mystery lay beneath the rumors, and she positively had to know the truth. The fact that her curiosity demanded its due was beside the point.

Luncheon was served in the breakfast parlor, and Olivia entered with Susannah. Lady Evelyn and their aunt were already seated at the table.

"Olivia, dear, how well you look today," Lady Evelyn said.

"Thank you." She smiled as she sat down. Her mourning clothes were simple since they had to accommodate her increasing form, but the dove gray morning gown she wore was comfortable. Made of the softest layers of muslin, it draped her swelling middle nicely. The wide rounded neckline stayed modest with a lace fichu discreetly tucked into the bodice.

"Lady Evelyn, I must thank you again for your invitation to tea yesterday. That was most gracious of you to take us with you," Aunt Agatha said.

"Yes, thank you," Susannah chimed in.

"Olivia, I am so sorry you were unable to attend. Many

of my neighbors send their regards to you." Lady Evelyn nodded to Mrs. Boothe to commence in serving the soup.

"I am glad that you had a lovely time. Susannah said she had never seen so many beautiful ladies in such finery," Olivia said.

Lady Evelyn explained, "Lady Belham's niece brought an unexpected group of visitors from London for an extended stay at her manor. The ladies from the house party joined us at Mrs. Hardcastle's."

"One of the women took quite an interest in you, dear," Aunt Agatha said.

"Me? Why ever for?"

"A Lady Framingham said she knew Robbie, and she sends you her deepest condolences. She said that she was sorry to have not been able to meet you in person, but understood your reason for staying behind," her aunt said.

Olivia noticed that Lady Evelyn became rather fidgety at the mention of the lady's name. "Mmm, I do not believe I ever remember Robbie mentioning her name." But then Robbie had spoken very little to her about his activities in London, and he had never taken her there.

"Her name is Belinda," Susannah said. "And she told me about all the parties she attended during her season in London."

Lady Evelyn dropped her knife with a clatter and everyone became silent.

"Lady Evelyn, is something amiss?" Olivia asked.

"Please," she started. "I hate to ask this of you, but I must. Please do not mention that Lady Belinda Framingham was present at the tea yesterday afternoon to my son." She wiped her mouth with her napkin and looked terribly guilty.

Olivia's eyes widened in surprise, but she held her tongue and waited for her hostess to continue, as did Aunt Agatha. Susannah started to speak, but Olivia kicked her under the table and gave her a look to keep quiet, which, gratefully, she did.

Lady Evelyn looked at each of them, then she swallowed

and continued. "It is a silly thing to ask, I know, but I must just the same."

Aunt Agatha was the first to ease the tension in the room. "Of course, Evelyn, we shall be completely discreet. It will be our secret, between us ladies."

Susannah nodded her agreement, as did Olivia when Lady Evelyn giggled nervously and patted Aunt Agatha's hand. But she could not help but wonder why on earth Lady Evelyn would ask such a thing. And what could this woman possibly mean to Lord Sheldrake?

They continued with their meal, discussing the latest London gossip they had heard, but Olivia's mind wandered to what had just happened and why. When they had finished, Lady Evelyn and Aunt Agatha decided a walk in the gardens was needed. Susannah chose an afternoon ride, so Olivia went to the library to choose a book to pass the time.

On her way down the hallway, she passed Sheldrake's study. The door was wide open, and she could not keep herself from stopping in the doorway to peer into the room.

Drawn like a moth to flame, she stepped in and glanced about the cherry-paneled walls and wondered just how many secrets swirled like invisible mist around Sheldrake Hall. Everywhere she went, every subject seemed laced with them. She could not venture forth without stumbling into the mist.

Walking about his chair, she could smell the faint scent he wore, and smiled. The hearth was swept clean, and a fresh stack of wood lay waiting to be used. His desk was neat and tidy like everything around him. His papers were stacked neatly in a pile with a large iron paperweight upon them. His ledgers were tied closed with thick ribbon. Above the fireplace hung a portrait of a handsome man so close in looks to Sheldrake that it took her a few moments to realize it was not him but an older man who could only be his father.

Stepping closer, she looked at the austere tilt of the man's chin, the gray slashes of hair near his temple, and smiled. He looked formidable and intimidating. She understood the truth in Lady Evelyn's words that her son tried to live up to his father. He obviously was a man of high expectations, but she knew by looking upon him that he had been a good man. His eyes were soft and warm with an expression of contentment in them. The artist had captured the man's soul with brush and paint, and she found she wished that she could have met him.

Shaking off her fanciful thoughts, she left the study to find the library. She promised herself that she would ask Sheldrake to tell her about his father. And she dearly hoped that she could refrain from asking about a lady named Belinda.

Sheldrake and Peter entered the stables, their horses still slightly damp with sweat from a bruising ride.

"Lord Sheldrake?" One of his grooms motioned for a moment to speak with him in private.

"Go on ahead, Shelly," Peter said. "I need a good soak in the tub before dinner. I'll catch up with you then."

Sheldrake nodded and approached his groom. "What is it, Sam?"

"The young lady, sir, I thought ye should know."

Alarm ripped through him, but he stayed calm. "Tell me, is she harmed?"

"Nay, not a bit, but she's been meetin' regular like with a cove from the army."

"What?" Sheldrake ran a hand through his hair. *She is just a child!* "When?"

"Today, yesterday I think, I don't know how many other times."

Sheldrake motioned for Sam to come out of the stable for more privacy as stable boys and the head groom took care of their horses. With a quiet voice, Sheldrake said, "Sam, you had best start from the beginning and tell me exactly what transpired."

Sam pulled his forelock and nodded. "Aye, well, yesterday Miss Susannah said fer me to go on a'ead when we was done with our ride. She said she wanted to pick some flowers and wouldn't need me standing there just to watch. We was just beyond the gardens there." He pointed. "And so I went, I had chores to do yet."

"This was yesterday," Sheldrake interrupted.

"Aye, sir. I saw the chit bring the mare back not more than three quarters of an hour later, so's she wasn't picking the flowers overly long. I didn't worry none." The groom looked at Sheldrake, seeking his approval. The man obviously felt he had made the wrong choice by leaving the girl.

He nodded at his groom. "It is all right, Sam. She was safe in the field and you kept a good eye out waiting for her return. Go on, tell me what happened today."

"We was riding, and I was keeping a proper distance behind 'er, and wouldn't ya know she suddenly waves at this cove on 'orseback who was waitin' there in the field, like he was waitin' fer her."

Sheldrake let out an oath. "And then what happened?"

"The cove approached, and well, seemed like a good sort and all. He introduced 'isself and then we's all went for a ride. I gave 'em some distance, likes I should and just got back. I thought you should know."

"I see." Sheldrake rubbed his chin. It appeared the man was a gentlemen then, or so he hoped. "Sam, this army fellow, what was his name?"

"Jeffries, sir, Captain Winston Jeffries."

"Did Captain Jeffries treat Miss Susannah in a forward way? Make any advances or try to touch her?"

"No, sir. And that's why I thought 'im a good sort. He was friendly like, but not in that way, sir."

Sheldrake let out his breath. "Thank you, Sam. You have done well in coming to me. In future as you accompany Miss Susannah, do not let her out of your sight. Is that clear?"

"Completely, sir." Sam bowed and returned to the stables.

Sheldrake continued to stand outside, deep in thought. He was not sure what to do. Susannah Lacey was a lovely young lady, and in a year or two she would have men clamoring for her attention. But this was now and she had no business meeting with army captains.

"Lord Sheldrake?"

The object of his thoughts stood before him, and he nearly choked on his surprise.

"Miss Susannah," he said. "I believe we need to have a chat."

"My thoughts exactly, my lord." Her blue eyes shone with an earnest determination he could not help but be softened by.

"Shall we sit in the gardens then?" he offered.

"Yes, that will be fine."

They walked in silence, side by side, and he realized that she did not fear him. She tripped over a stone, but regained her balance with a shy smile and a reddened face. He chuckled. She might not fear him, but she was certainly nervous. When they sat down upon a couple of wrought iron chairs facing each other, she finally looked up at him.

"I saw you speaking with your groom."

"Yes." He'd let her say what needed to be said.

"I am assuming that he is a trusted servant and has told you that I rode out today with a certain gentleman." She cast her gaze down to her lap, where her hands were clasped tightly.

"Yes, he said that you met with this man yesterday as well, is that true?"

Her gaze flew to his in surprise.

"When you sent him on his way since you were going to pick flowers?"

"But I did pick flowers, my lord. They are in a vase in my chamber. You can ask Mrs. Boothe."

"That is not necessary. Did you meet with Captain Jeffries yesterday?"

She bent her head down and mumbled, "Yes, I did and the day before."

"What was that?"

"And the day before." She looked directly at him this time. "Please do not tell Olivia; it will only upset her."

"Susannah," he said with a frustrated groan, "she has a right to know, even more so your aunt."

"Please no, not my aunt." She had reached out and grabbed his sleeve. "She will banish me to my rooms for the rest of our stay and will make me eat bread and water, I am sure!" Her voice held a trace of humor, but he knew she was serious about being confined to her room.

"Tell me about this captain then."

"He is a gentleman. He happened upon me in your field the other day, and I met him the same time yesterday and again today. He wanted to come to your door and introduce himself, but I made him promise not to for fear of my aunt's reaction. He gave me his calling card to give to you if you should wish to call on him. He is staying at the constable's home, visiting his wounded friend."

"Dickie Matthews," Sheldrake said. "I know the family well." He sighed, then stood up to pace the short courtyard. "Miss Susannah, you place me in an awkward situation. You are far too young to be meeting gentlemen. And no proper miss meets a man unescorted."

"But Captain Jeffries is my friend, and he is having a hard time of it. He cannot accept Dickie's condition, and he's afraid to go back to the battlefield. I cannot abandon him, not when he needs me." She had spoken with such passion in her voice that her eyes filled with tears.

"He needs you, eh?" Sheldrake did not like the sound of that at all. Men fearing they were heading for their deaths were opt to do things they would not ordinarily do, like play fast and loose with an innocent. He did not like it one bit.

"Yes. I listen to his dreams of travel, and I tell him silly stories. We spend only a brief time together, not more than an half hour. It is totally harmless, I assure you. Plus, he is leaving in a few days."

Sheldrake stood in thought, amazed at how mature she sounded as she delivered her case. She had come to him, too, which said much for her character. He knew the chit was telling the truth. He also knew that if he forbid her to see this Captain Jeffries, she was just foolish and stubborn enough to defy him and meet with the man in secret, which he did not want. If he told her aunt, the results would be worse if not the same; Susannah would find a way to meet the captain and things could turn decidedly improper.

Fingering his chin, he looked at Susannah sitting upon the edge of the chair, awaiting his wisdom. He felt completely inadequate in dealing with this matter. He had failed to keep his mother away from Abbott when he had forbid her from seeing him. No doubt he would fail if he tried to keep Miss Lacey away from Captain Jeffries. And so far, the gentleman had proved himself to be a gentleman.

"Miss Susannah," he said, "I need an oath sworn by you on your honor to uphold to meet this Captain Jeffries only in the presence of a chaperone. Do you understand?"

She flew from the chair and threw her arms about him and hugged the life out of him. "I knew you would understand, I knew I could trust you, sir, I just knew it!"

He had to admit, he was moved. His arms came around the girl for a quick squeeze before he put her aside from him. "Listen to me. Do you swear to me here and now, that you will meet this man only in the brightness of day, with my groom present?"

All serious, but with the remnants of an impish smile, she agreed. "I swear upon my honor, Lord Sheldrake."

"Very well. I will have a meeting with this Captain Jeffries of yours. And I will check with Sam daily, so if you try to give him the slip, I will go directly to your aunt, is that clear?"

"Perfectly. Thank you, Lord Sheldrake." She gave him a curtsey, if a bit clumsily.

He watched her turn and run into the Hall. He hoped and prayed he was doing the right thing. She was a sweet girl, one who deserved a happy future. Looking down upon the card of Captain Winston Jeffries, he turned on his heel and headed for the stables. He'd visit the gentleman now, before dinner, and make sure the man kept his intentions pure. And he decided he'd send two grooms out with Miss Susannah and her captain. He did not care how backed up the stable duties became. He'd make sure the girl was kept safe.

Dinner had been strained and quiet, Olivia thought as she sipped the last of her lemonade. The ladies would leave Lord Sheldrake and Mr. Blessing to their port in a moment, and she could hardly wait. Mr. Blessing had carried most of the conversation with Aunt Agatha and Susannah. Sheldrake appeared deep in thought and watchful of his mother and Susannah.

What on earth had Susannah said or done? she wondered, hoping her sister had not snooped about in any more rooms.

Then, as Mrs. Boothe brought in the bowl of nuts and the decanter of port, Mr. Blessing gave her a wink. Olivia had first thought Peter Blessing a shameless flirt, but she now knew it was his way with females, regardless of age or looks. Mrs. Boothe clearly doted on him.

"Ladies." Lady Evelyn rose from the table. "Let us leave the gentlemen to their port."

Olivia sighed with relief. Sheldrake must have heard her as his gaze connected with hers with questioning concern. She smiled, hoping to convey that all was well. She would speak with him when they joined them in the drawing room overlooking the gardens.

"What shall we do this evening?" Aunt Agatha asked Susannah and Olivia. "Cards?"

"Not for me," Olivia said. She was not much of a player. She picked up her needlepoint and sat in her favorite chair by the window. She was surprised to see the gentlemen enter. They had evidently passed on the port.

Sheldrake handed over a new deck of cards for the latest game Mr. Blessing introduced.

"A round of piquet, anyone?" Mr. Blessing asked.

She leaned against the cushions of her chair and basked in the mellow warmth of the drawing room. She nodded her head to decline.

"Olivia is right, I cannot play another game tonight. I would much rather listen to Susannah play the pianoforte. I wish we had someone to sing. We used to have . . ." Lady Evelyn stopped in mid-sentence and looked down at her hands.

Olivia sat straighter at the sudden silence in the room and noticed that the tops of Sheldrake's ears had turned red. *What had Lady Evelyn been about to say?*

"Olivia can sing," Susannah said. "We accompany each other all the time at Aunt Agatha's."

The tension eased.

Lady Evelyn clapped her hands. "Oh, Olivia, please do sing! It has been an age since we have had a musicale."

"I have quite an ordinary voice, so please do not expect much." She set aside her needlework and followed Susannah to the pianoforte.

"Keep it simple," she whispered when her sister leafed through the sheet music.

Susannah's slender fingers skimmed the keys, and strains of music filled the room. Olivia turned to find four sets of eyes upon her. She began to sing.

Love's bitter song changed me
My heart is heavy from its tune
Fore when my love left me to cry
I could not sing again, I could not sing again
My tears have dried upon my eyes
but my heart continues to weep
Where dreams are stored and kept dear

My heart waits upon its door, my heart waits upon its door
One day another love will come
And rescue me from my despair
My dreams will be unleashed
And my heart will sing again, my heart will sing again

Olivia sought Sheldrake's gaze and held it. Her insides threatened to melt as he looked at her, his expression wistful, almost sad. Encouraged to sing another, she picked a lively tune to sing with Susannah. She hoped to erase the look of sorrow from Sheldrake's eyes.

She succeeded, for it was not long after the first verse that the gentlemen chimed in. Lord Sheldrake's voice rang deep and smooth and not surprisingly, Mr. Blessing was an excellent tenor. Soon everyone joined in the chorus. And then another song was played and sung, and another.

Out of breath and laughing, Olivia walked back to her chair and sat down. Absently, she rubbed her belly while Susannah played on with their aunt turning the pages for her. She looked up to see Sheldrake approaching.

"A lovely evening," she said when he stood before her.

"Made lovelier by your angelic voice."

"Your compliment is a bit exaggerated, I fear. If heaven holds angels with voices as plain as mine, I pity the saints who must forever listen."

He laughed. "Truly, your voice is very good."

"Thank you." Overheated, she used her embroidery hoop to fan herself.

"Would you care to take a turn in the courtyard? The sun is about to set." He held out his hand.

"I should like that above all things."

Sheldrake held her hand gently cradled in the crook of his arm. As they walked past the double doors, the sweetness of the air from roses in full bloom hit him. It had remained warm, and the sun rested low in the western sky, setting the clouds ablaze with color. Slowly, they walked toward the bench that overlooked the lake, and neither had spoken.

The melody of Olivia's first song kept weaving through his mind. Her breathy voice echoed the lyrics that told of the cycle of love gone awry to redemptive new love. An interesting choice considering Belinda's jilting had soured him, and he had yet to find redemption from a new love.

As he had listened to her, he imagined her singing to her child, rocking the babe to sleep. The bare longing that image produced in him left him empty and wanting.

"Watch your step," Sheldrake warned as he felt the ground turn soft beneath his boots. Instinctively, he pulled her closer, pleased when she did not pull away.

He knew she wanted to know what had happened the night of Abbott's death. Her question from the other night lurked between them like a tangible thing waiting to be answered. She was doing her best to get those answers, too; Mrs. Boothe had told him that she was asking the staff questions. He would have to put a stop to that, but carefully. If he took her to task for it, he was pretty certain that it would only make her all the more determined.

He smiled as he thought of how he had reasoned the very same thing with respect to Susannah and her captain. He could certainly tell the two were sisters, both headstrong. But he dare not tell her the whole. He did not know her well enough to be sure of what she would do if she knew the truth.

"What are you thinking about?" Olivia asked as they sat down upon the bench.

"Your aunt did not looked pleased to see us leave."

"No."

"Does that not bother you? Upsetting your aunt."

"She will give me a good scold later. It will make her feel better." She waved her hand in dismissal.

"You must have been a hellion as a child." He stretched his legs out in front of him, reveling in the sight of the setting sun.

"I was a serious child, but determined to prove myself

whenever my aunt said I could not do this or that. If she said not to do something, the harder I would strive to do it."

"As I said, a hellion!" He felt more confident in his choice of action with Susannah. No doubt she could be as stubborn as Olivia.

"Come now, were you the pattern card of obedience?" He could hear the light sarcasm in her voice.

"Actually, yes. I adored my father." He stroked his chin. "He was larger than life to me, and I wanted to be exactly like him. I guess I did not quite follow through on that score!"

"Whatever can you mean? Your mother is very proud of you! She raves over all you have done with the farms. Truly, you do not give yourself enough credit." She had turned on her seat and was looking at him with a fierceness he appreciated. "I am certain that your father would be proud as well."

"Perhaps." He knew he had disappointed the memory of his father for allowing Abbott into their lives.

"What was he like—your father?" She had sat back and now gazed straight ahead at the lake. He noted the straightness of her nose, the beauty of her profile.

He was not sure where or how to begin. "He was a man many admired."

"I believe if you look about you, you will find the same admiration is given to you."

Sheldrake wanted to tell her how no one would have ever believed his father capable of the tales Sheldrake faced. No, the truth of the matter was that his father would never have left his mother so vulnerable to reprobates such as Abbott. In this, Sheldrake had failed bitterly. His father could never have been proud of him for that.

"What made him so admirable?"

"Everything, really. He was a man of his word, a fierce protector of his family, and a man who valued justice."

"He does not sound terribly different from you."

He smiled, thinking, how could she know that he would

never be half the man his father was. But he tried. "And what of your own father—you said he traveled?" He watched a fleeting expression of remorse and something very like hatred sweep across her features, only to be quickly controlled.

Her lovely lips formed a wry smile. "I believe the sun will set and rise again by the time I explain my father."

"If you are uncomfortable talking about him, do not. I understand." He did not wish to upset her.

"No, perhaps it is time I said aloud that my father was an evil man."

He kept quiet and tried not to show his shock at her words. He waited for her to continue.

Her bottom jaw worked, a tiny muscle flexing before she spoke. "My father, Mr. Charles Lacey, did not travel. He was forced to leave England for dueling."

Sheldrake swallowed the oath that was ready to spring from his tongue. "And you have not seen him since?"

"Not since I was seven years old and my mother died after Susannah was born."

Good Lord! He sat there like a dolt, not sure how to respond.

"And so, my father was a scoundrel. Not a man to be admired or a model of behavior."

She spoke with such a matter-of-fact voice that his heart twisted. "I am sorry."

"Do not be. You could not have guessed, and I needed to say it aloud. It has been an unspoken thing at my aunt's for Susannah's sake, and I never shared it with anyone, not even Robbie."

"Then you do me a great honor." He patted her hand still tucked into the crook of his arm, but he wanted to pull her into his arms and chase away her pain.

"Oh!" Olivia suddenly leaned forward.

He felt a stab of fear sear his insides. "What is it?"

"The babe, 'tis kicking is all, but that was quite a strong one."

"Kicking?" He relaxed and looked at her middle. He never really thought a baby moved much. He had seen foals roll about inside a mare's belly a number of times, but somehow he expected a human baby to stay where it was. There was little enough room for movement. "Does it hurt?"

"It is not comfortable!" She breathed deeply and leaned back almost against him.

He watched as the fabric of her dress moved to poke towards one side. He cursed under his breath in wonder. Then he laughed. "I saw it!" Sheldrake pointed. "Right there." He looked directly into her eyes. "That must feel terrible."

She laughed at him then.

"Does the babe kick all the time?"

"No, not all of the time. I think it sleeps during the day and wakes up after dinner. The babe is most active then."

He watched in awe, hoping to see another kick. He could not help feeling a little disappointed when nothing happened.

She must have sensed his disappointment. She felt about her belly, then took hold of his hand and placed it upon her abdomen.

"Here," she said and moved his hand about her middle.

He almost jerked it away. *The deuce!* Surely, he should not be doing this. Then he felt it. A tiny movement, like a ball being rolled under a coverlet. He stared in amazement, feeling his mouth crack into a smile. Then a strong kick met his palm. "There it is, a hearty lad for sure." He gazed up at her and stared deeply into her eyes. He was struck again by her beautiful face.

"The baby could be a girl, you know." She sounded hopeful.

"With a kick like that, not likely," he whispered with a smile. Then it dawned on him that this could mean the babe was getting ready to be born. "Does Pedley know about this?"

"I should hope so. He *is* a doctor."

"Seriously. The babe is pitching to and fro, is that, I

mean, does that mean you could . . ." He did not finish his question, knowing the answer. The babe would come soon, and then she would leave. His life could return to what it had been, lonely. He did not relish the thought, but knew it would be for the best.

"I imagine so," she whispered.

"You are frightened." He saw the fear in her eyes, the worry. "You needn't be. Pedley is the very best." He sat there, his hand under hers upon her belly. Heat radiated from her through his arm straight into his soul. He stared into the green depths of her eyes and started to drown. Suddenly panicked, he pulled his hand away. "Come, it is getting late and our sun has set."

Chapter Eight

They entered the drawing room, and Olivia immediately felt
her aunt's disapproving stare upon her. Susannah still played
the pianoforte, but Mr. Blessing now turned the pages. Lady
Evelyn sat with her eyes closed, seemingly lost in the music.
Aunt Agatha glared at Olivia. She sat down and picked up
her discarded needlework.

Really, she thought, *they were only gone a few moments.*
Her aunt need not work herself into a pet. She turned and
looked out the window and noticed that the bench where
they had sat was in full view of the drawing room's wall of
glass windows. Her aunt must have seen him touch her.
Small wonder that she received such a look! It was not the
thing to allow a man to touch her middle, to be sure. She
looked at Sheldrake, to see if he had noticed her aunt's
scorn, but his back was toward her and she could not see his
face.

Perhaps she should not have let him touch her, but he had
been genuinely fascinated, and then disappointed when he
did not spy another kick, so she had simply taken hold of his
hand on impulse. His reaction endeared him to her further.
Be careful, she warned herself, tender feelings lay just
around the corner, and if she did not watch where she
stepped, she would fall straight into them. She knew she already tripped much too close.

She glanced again in his direction. He stood next to Mr.
Blessing and Susannah, who was rummaging through sheet
music to choose which should be played next. She liked

him, as Susannah had said. She truly liked him. But could she trust him?

He might have killed Mr. Abbott, perhaps with good reason, yet she still was determined to know the truth. Lord Sheldrake represented the answer to her family's uncertain future. She would find out what had happened the night Abbott died, and once Sheldrake was proved innocent of murder, she would marry him. If he was willing, of course.

She looked up at her aunt and suddenly smiled with bravado. She knew what she was doing.

Olivia could not sleep. Try as she might to keep her eyes closed, no sooner had she counted to ten, did she open them and stare at the canopy above her head. She kept thinking of Sheldrake—the way he ran his hand through his hair when he was impatient or upset, the deepness of his singing voice, and how when he did laugh, it filled the room with joy.

Why did he not just tell her the truth and be done with it! Pushing the coverlet back, she heaved herself off the bed. Grabbing her wrapper, she headed for the door. Perhaps a cup of chamomile tea would help her sleep. There was no sense in waking Mrs. Boothe. She could find her way to the kitchens and fetch it herself.

Once downstairs, she passed Sheldrake's study. The door was ajar, and the room was dark inside. Slowly, she pushed the door open with her fingertips. It was empty.

A chill ran up her spine as an idea came to her. She could take a peek around and see if she found anything regarding Abbott's death. No, she could not—it would be base of her. But what if she could find something that proved Sheldrake innocent? She might never know the truth if she did not take this opportunity to search. She was looking after the interests of her family, after all. She had a right to know, did she not?

She argued with her conscience a moment longer before finally thrusting her doubts aside. She needed to know the truth before her child came and she had to leave; then it would be too late. With a deep breath, she entered the room and closed the door, leaning against it. She had to hurry, before she lost her nerve.

The candle she held in her hand shook. Her heart beat so fast she feared it might leap out of her chest at any moment. Was she insane to do such a thing? *Yes,* she thought—*insane with the need to prove Sheldrake worthy for marriage.* She had come to this, sneaking around a man's study in the middle of the night. Heaven forbid, her aunt would have her backside if she knew.

The fearful thrill she had often felt as a child when she willfully disobeyed her aunt rushed through her veins and urged her forward. She walked toward his desk and set down the candle. Its flame flickered, casting eerie shadows to dance upon the walls. She glanced up and stared into the eyes of Sheldrake's father. Under his gaze, she almost decided she would go back to her room.

"I must know," she whispered at the painting. "Can you understand that?"

She stood there staring at the portrait, hesitating. Then she turned and walked to the desk. His desk was big and took up most of the small room. There was no clutter. His papers and ledgers had all been put away. She expected that—Sheldrake was neat. She wondered if his father was as tidy, and guessed that he must have been.

Perhaps Sheldrake's tidiness was in some way a means to live up to his father's memory. Running her hand across the smooth desktop, she crept around to the other side. What if she found something incriminating? What would she do then? Looking back up at Sheldrake's father, she decided she would simply deal with whatever was to come when she faced it.

Pulling out the chair, she sat down. She bent to test the drawers. In the top right, she found stationery and his seal. The bottom drawer contained ledgers and books of balances and inventoried goods. Nothing there. Pushing back, she opened the top middle drawer. Inside lay a supply of pen quills, a sharpening knife, and a few geegaws, but a diamond stickpin caught her eye. She smiled. She had not seen him wear jewels. Apparently he thought little of leaving them about. Tossing the pin back inside the drawer, she closed it with a soft snap. She reached for the top left drawer and found it surprisingly empty. She sighed, then reached for the bottom left.

It was locked.

She let go as if she'd been burned. Her breathing came short and hard. Her stomach churned. What did he have that he needs must lock the drawer? If a diamond stickpin lay carelessly among pen quills, what was so important to be kept under lock and key?

She had to know.

Closing her eyes, her conviction wavered as doubt filled her mind. She should have listened to her good sense and passed the room by. She dare not look back at the portrait. She knew what expression she would see there, and it all but screamed that what she did was wrong.

"Too late, I am here now," she whispered to herself and the portrait. Reaching into the middle drawer, she pulled out the stickpin. Placing it in the keyhole, she jiggled it left then right until she felt the drawer give when she pulled.

It opened.

She sat for a moment, struggling with her conscience, which refused to leave her alone. If Sheldrake knew what she was doing, he would never forgive her. That thought gave her pause. Her pulse raced and pounded in her ears. She could stop now and go back upstairs, forget all about it, and he would never know she had been there.

But her curiosity and need to know more about him got the better of her, and she peered into the drawer. It was larger than the others and deeper. She reached in and felt a small bundle. Dozens of letters were bound with ribbon.

She looked up quickly, thinking she heard a sound. The door remained closed, the house quiet. Taking the small bundle of pink parchment in her hand, she knew the letters were from a woman. She sniffed the ribbon, catching the scent of rosewater. Did he keep a mistress? Jealousy stabbed through her with a fierceness that almost made her sick at such a thought. She fervently hoped he did not. And he seemed too proper to do such a thing, too proud and just.

The top letter slipped from the ribbon holding them together and fluttered to the ground. It lay open and the signature at the bottom caught her eye.

Belinda! Was this Lady Belinda Framingham whom Lady Evelyn had mentioned? It had to be.

Snatching up the parchment, she flicked it open and began to read. Her fingers stilled and a numb dread filled her. She read the letter again, but nothing had changed. Over and over she read it.

Dearest Richard,

I must beg you to leave off trying to see me or communicate with me further. The strain is too much to bear. I cannot attach myself to a man capable of the things you have done. I understand why you did it, but please know that when you chose to take Mr. Abbott's life, you chose to say farewell to the life you once knew, the life I was to share with you. I have taken the liberty of sending the notice of our cancelled engagement to the papers. I am sorry. I will always love you, my dearest.

Your Heartbroken,
Belinda

Olivia closed her eyes as tears burned down her cheeks. Was it true? Did he confess such a thing to Belinda? Is that why she wrote to break off their engagement?

"Woman! You will explain yourself."

She nearly fell from her seat as she looked up to see that Sheldrake stood in the doorway, wearing a heavy silk robe and little else. He showed an expression of such hurt and anger that she shrank back against the chair.

"I . . ." Her throat turned dry, and she choked on her tears.

He leaned over the front of the desk, his voice controlled. "Well?" At that moment he looked very capable of murder.

"Stop shouting at me!"

"I am not nearly shouting, madam, but I will be happy to oblige you. How prettily you repay my hospitality with your deceit."

She flushed to the roots of her hair. She was more than ashamed. He was right of course, but something inside her gave way, and she braced her hands on the desk as she stood slowly. "My deceit?"

"What would you call sneaking into my study in the middle of night?" Fury dripped from his low voice, his harsh whisper.

"I call it self-preservation!" she snapped, surprised at her tenacity.

"What!?"

"I cannot go on not knowing what happened to your stepfather. Not knowing if you are innocent," she blurted.

His expression changed to one of disappointment. "You have already condemned me by coming to my study to look for proof." He walked around the desk to stand in front of her, taking the letter from her hand.

"How dare you!" she hissed. "Can you not imagine my feelings? My sister is here, sir, as is my aunt. I bear my child in your home! Do you not think I have a right to know? I have asked you, and you refused to tell me, so what choice did I have?"

"Right! What of my rights? It is you who have broken into my desk."

She stood staring at him. His face was inches from hers, the letter crumpled in his fist. She breathed heavily, unsure what to say. She was wrong; she knew that. But if he only understood why she had done it, then maybe he would stop looking at her with such hurt and disappointment.

"What do you want from me?" he whispered, all the anger gone out of his voice.

"I want the truth."

"I cannot give it to you, not now, not ever."

His dark blue eyes bore into hers, but she did not flinch. "Why? Please tell me. I want to understand."

She did not waver in her gaze, and she saw a bleakness behind his eyes, a loneliness she recognized easily, since she often felt it, too. She reached out to him with her hand up toward his face.

"Lord what you do to me," he hissed as he captured her face between his hands and brought his lips down upon hers.

She stiffened and tried to pull free, but his hands held her head captive. His mouth moved hard against her own. She pushed at him, but he only pulled her as close as possible. His lips were demanding, desperate. Then they softened.

Olivia's mind stopped. Her hands fell from him, and she swore her arms felt as heavy as lead. She vaguely sensed his fingers threading through her hair, tangling, positioning her so he could take more of her lips.

She opened to him and knew she was lost. Her hands finally grasped his waist and rose of their own volition across his broad back. The rough silk of his robe could not hide the muscles she felt there. She could not get enough of him. Higher her hands journeyed, until her fingers splayed across the wide breadth of his shoulders. She hung on as if her life depended upon the attention he gave to her mouth.

His tongue laced around hers, and he deepened the kiss instantly. She heard a low moan and realized it had come from the depths of her. She became as one famished, and starved as she was she returned his kiss with a fervor she did not know she possessed.

Then he pulled away.

She heard his roughened breathing, saw his eyes. His pupils were huge, taking over most of the blue. He raked a shaking hand through his hair as he stepped back. "Olivia . . ." His voice was hoarse. He reached out to her, but she could not look at him. Nor could she face the realization that she had lost her heart the moment their lips met.

She pushed past him, choked back a sob, and did not look back as she fled the room. She had not gone far when she heard his curse and the sound of glass breaking as it crashed to the floor.

He sat down and looked at the mess he had made when he threw the lamp from his desk against the wall. What had he done? He had kissed her. He realized he had wanted to for a time now, but he wished it had been different. He did not expect to feel that much, to want that much. He did not like it—not one bit.

She had been so furious with him when she had been the one in the wrong. Her hair, a long rope hanging down the back of her nightdress, was something he wanted to see undone. Even her condition stirred him. Her hard belly pressed against him as he ravished her mouth ushered in visions of her carrying his child. The depth of his longing for such a thing took him aback and scared him.

He looked down at the crumpled letter from Belinda that lay at his feet. He picked it up, smoothed it out, and read the words that had frozen his heart two years before. Somehow it did not matter to him anymore. What Belinda had done to him, jilting him and putting about the rumors about him, seemed far off and small compared to what he felt now.

He was in no mood to analyze it, he only knew that he had to make it up to Olivia. God only knew what she must think of him now after reading Belinda's rubbish.

He reached down and picked up the remaining letters from off the floor. It was stupid of him to keep them as some kind of reminder of his failure.

Why did she have to find them? Grabbing the candle Olivia had left behind, Sheldrake stood and walked over to the fireplace. After lighting their corners, he tossed the letters onto the grate and watched them burn. He did not need them anymore.

"Olivia?" Susannah called out.

"I am in here." She sat by the window of her sitting room, nibbling on toast. The rest of her meal lay untouched on the tray beside her.

"We missed you at breakfast. Are you feeling poorly?" Susannah asked.

"Just a bit tired."

Aunt Agatha followed Susannah into the sitting room and took a seat next to Olivia. "You were not at breakfast and we were worried. His lordship appeared to be also. He asked after you, wanting to know how you fared this morning."

Olivia felt her face flush.

"What is it—what has happened between the two of you?" Her aunt's concerned gaze cut through her.

She looked down. She could not begin to explain what had transpired between them. How could she tell her aunt about her unforgivable behavior in breaking into his desk, Belinda's letter, and then that kiss.

"I fear you are forming a serious *tendre* for the man." Her aunt put a hand to her forehead, checking for fever as she had done since Olivia was a child.

"Aunt, I really do not wish to talk of it." She looked to her sister for help, but Susannah was not paying a bit of attention. She had disappeared into the bedchamber.

"His lordship looked as though he had not slept a wink last night, and here I find you moping in your room."

"I am not moping."

"What is it then?" Aunt Agatha took one of Olivia's discarded muffins and sank her teeth into it. "I cannot like what I see. I do not want you to get hurt," her aunt said, her mouth full.

"You need not worry," Olivia remarked.

"Needn't I?"

"I shall have nothing further to do with Lord Sheldrake."

Her heart ached as she said the words. "There, I have finally decided to heed your advice."

"Well, they do say there is a first time for everything," her aunt teased.

"You were right, I was wrong," Olivia added.

Her aunt put a hand to her forehead again. "Are you sure you are well? I thought I heard you say that I was right."

That comment forced a laugh out of her. "Well, perhaps I go too far."

Her aunt gave her a shrewd look. Susannah entered the sitting room with one of Olivia's hats in hand. Aunt Agatha addressed her. "Susannah, do stop dawdling and go change into your riding habit."

"I shall in a moment. Olivia, can I borrow this?" Susannah asked as she twirled a small black cap.

"Go, Susannah," Aunt Agatha responded. "We meet everyone in half an hour. I do not wish to keep them waiting."

"You are going riding?" Olivia nodded her permission for Susannah to take the hat.

"Yes. Mr. Blessing suggested we go out of doors. The day promises to be fine, and you know how these clear skies cannot last forever."

"And Lord Sheldrake is going with you?" She did not wish to see him.

"Yes, he is coming with us. Olivia, please, tell me what troubles you. What has Lord Sheldrake done?"

"It is nothing, Aunt." She tried for insouciance, but failed miserably. Her voice sounded shrill, and her smile was forced. She knew she did not fool her aunt for a moment.

But Aunt Agatha merely shook her head, then stood. "We shall return in time for luncheon." Then she bent down and kissed her forehead. "Do I need to have a talk with our host?"

"No." She answered too quickly. "No, you need not. He has been nothing but kindness to us, and I do not wish to cause him any further grief with our presence by having you scold him."

Her aunt eyed her too closely for comfort.

"Go, Aunt Agatha, I am simply having a case of the doldrums, which is very normal for a woman who is increasing." She forced a smile. "Go on, you do not want to keep everyone waiting."

Her aunt leaned over and kissed the top of her head, then giving it a pat as she used to when Olivia was a child, she left without a word.

She watched her aunt gently close the door. Her throat was so tight, she feared she would have broken down into a fit of sobbing at any moment. She loved her aunt. Despite their differences, Olivia knew her aunt loved her and Susannah as if they had been her own children. No doubt, had she asked, Aunt Agatha would have given Sheldrake an earful.

But she could not fault the man for being angry with her for breaking into his desk. Nor could she fault him for making her insides turn to jelly whenever he looked her way. The fault was entirely her own. She should have heeded her aunt's advice and kept her distance.

She ran her fingers across her lips, where he had kissed her. Despite the accusations in Belinda's letter, she wanted him. She wanted to feel his mouth on her again. Feeling this way was not at all what she needed, but she had to concede that her situation still remained grim. Her child needed a future, and Susannah deserved a season. But could she truly consider Sheldrake to provide both? And what of her? She feared that she loved him. Could she risk losing her heart only for it to be broken in the name of her security and her family's future? She simply did not know if she could withstand the pain this time.

If only he would explain himself and tell her what really happened. She took another bite of the cold toast, then tossed the rest of it onto her plate. She rose from the couch. She was not sure she could trust herself. She wanted to believe the best of him too much. How was she even to know if he told her the truth? At least she did not have to face him to deal with the situation this morning.

She paced her room for at least half an hour, then decided the riding party must have left. Slipping out of her chamber, Olivia gripped the staircase railing as she quietly descended the main stairs. When she entered the hallway, she heard Sheldrake's and Mr. Blessing's voices.

She panicked. She did not want to see him, not yet. She turned to open the door to her right, but it was locked. Hurriedly, she went to another door and it opened. She dodged into the library and waited with her eyes closed, hoping the men would not enter. She strained to listen and heard the voices fade, the footsteps quiet. They were gone!

She released her pent-up breath with a whoosh. After counting to ten, she peered out into the hallway. No one. She walked back the way she had come and passed the locked door. She stopped. It seemed curious that a main-floor room should be locked. Her fingers twitched, and she retraced her steps until she stood directly in front of the door.

She tried to turn the knob again, but it was securely fixed. She wondered what lay inside the room. She had never noticed it before, and she had gone past it when she entered the library on several occasions. Perhaps it was only a closet. But then it was the only door for a considerable amount of wallspace.

She scanned the hall and realized the room was situated on an outside wall. She considered that perhaps she could find her way to the room from outside of the house and look into the windows if there were any. It was worth a try if only to divert her thoughts for a time.

The vision of Sheldrake's face when he found her going through his desk rose before her mind's eye. She dismissed the image. This was completely different. She saw no harm in finding a room from outside. Anyone could do so if they wished. Such a thing was no great invasion of privacy merely to look.

She walked down the hallway into the drawing room and

out of doors into the courtyard garden. The sun shone brightly between puffy white clouds in a brilliant sky of blue. A perfect day for riding. She walked along the outside wall to the south end of the house. A room jutted out. Surely, this was the locked room.

She peeked in the windows and found it to be a conservatory. She followed the walls of glass until she came upon a door. She tried it and it gave way. *Odd.* Why keep the interior door locked and the outside entrance open?

She entered and looked around. It was beautiful, but bare. She imagined it filled with potted palms and roses and wondered at the current state of vacancy. Sunshine filtered through thick beveled glass windows that acted as prisms, casting rainbows upon the marble floor. She watched dust motes dance in shafts of light that streamed in through the open curtains.

She circled the room. It was not an overly large space, but with nothing in it, her steps still echoed. She checked the walls for any hidden nooks. Nothing. She stopped to ponder. She was doing it again, looking for proof, anything to clear Sheldrake of killing his stepfather. Her insides sank at the knowledge that after reading Belinda's letter, she was even more desperate to find him innocent. Tapping her foot with impatience for her weakness, she looked down.

In the brightness of the day, the marble floor looked discolored. She could not bend down to look closer, so she backed away hoping to see more clearly from a distance. There was a definite stain, a good-sized darkened spot. She wondered, what would stain marble? A chill raced up her spine.

Could it be blood?

Olivia entered the dining room with Susannah. Due to the fine weather, luncheon was being served alfresco on the terrace. Her feet felt as if she wore slippers of brick, so slow were her steps.

Susannah pulled her along. "Olivia, please hurry, everyone is seated."

She pulled her hand away from her sister's. A growing weakness took root in the pit of her stomach. She could not face him, she could not! She wiped her hands along the skirt of her dark gray cotton morning gown. She had not bothered to change.

When they emerged through the dining room doors to the terrace, Susannah walked around the table and sat down, but Olivia hesitated. She felt everyone's eyes upon her as she stood in the doorway, wrestling with her courage. Daring to look up at the small party gathered around the table, she felt frozen in time. She noticed the crisp linen and polished silver, the pretty crystal glasses that caught the sunlight and sparkled.

Her gaze strayed to Sheldrake. He was everything a country lord should be in his buckskin breeches and morning coat of bottle green. Dare she look at his face, his eyes? She feared what he would find in her own.

"Good afternoon, Lady Beresford," Mr. Blessing addressed her. "Come, sit next to me. You must meet our guest, who happened upon us this morning on our ride."

Olivia nodded and took the seat offered and pulled her gaze to the man seated next to Susannah. He was dressed in a cavalry uniform.

"Lady Beresford, this is Captain Winston Jeffries," Mr. Blessing began. "A neighbor of Shelly's, so he invited the fellow to lunch."

"How do you do, sir," she said.

"Very well, ma'am. And you, how do you feel these days?"

He had a very nice smile she noted, and then she noticed that Susannah was paying particular attention to his every word. *Oh dear,* she thought. Susannah was too young, but the captain was just the type of man to turn a young girl's head. "I am feeling fine, if a bit tired. And you, sir, are you home for good?"

A shadow crossed his face as he answered, "No, my lady, I leave in a couple of days."

Relief filled her at his answer, and she mentally checked him off her worry list. Regardless of Susannah's admiration, she could hardly form more than a schoolroom affection in two days. Besides, he must look upon Susannah as the schoolroom miss she was, her hair still down and all. "Then godspeed your return home safely," she said.

"Thank you, ma'am." The captain nodded.

"Here, here," Sheldrake said from the end of the table, and everyone added their agreement and wishes for a safe return.

Olivia shook out her napkin and put it upon her knee. Her insides in turmoil, she cursed herself for causing herself this distress. But she knew, given the chance to turn back the clock and do things differently, she probably would have done the same thing regardless.

"How are you feeling today?" Mr. Blessing asked.

"I am well." She took a drink of her lemonade.

"Our ride was most wonderful," Susannah said, then continued to chatter about the sights.

Olivia glanced at Sheldrake. He was quiet. She watched him as he cut his food. He gripped the knife so hard, his knuckles whitened. So he was tense as well. She wondered if perhaps he did not wish to face her. He looked at her. His eyes were a blue storm of mixed emotions she could not read. Still, they threatened to pull her in, so she looked away.

"Your sister and your aunt are accomplished riders," Mr. Blessing stated.

Lady Evelyn chuckled. "Goodness yes, they quite rode circles around me."

"Are you an adept rider as well?" Mr. Blessing asked, drawing Olivia into the conversation.

"I am adequate, sir. My aunt always kept a respectable stable. She encouraged us to ride hard even though we are ladies."

"Very intelligent of her." Mr. Blessing leaned forward to

cast a wink at Aunt Agatha, who sat on the other side of Olivia.

"I am glad the ladies were able to keep up with you and Captain Jeffries. Richard did not mind keeping a sedate pace with his mama," Lady Evelyn said as she patted her son's hand.

Aunt Agatha helped herself to the thinly sliced ham. "Nothing like fresh air and exercise to encourage the appetite."

Everyone agreed, but Olivia picked at her food, swirling it about her plate.

Prodded by Susannah, Mr. Blessing regaled them with tales of riding in Hyde Park at the fashionable hour, which Captain Jeffries added to with his experiences there. Susannah sat listening with a rapt expression, clearly enjoying the tale and tellers.

"And did you meet your bride at this spring's season?" Susannah asked.

Mr. Blessing took a moment to answer, appearing deep in thought. "Sorry, yes, I did meet her this spring. Come to think of it, I met her at a ball. We actually spied each other from across the room. I managed an introduction and the rest is history, as they say." Mr. Blessing grinned.

"She must be very beautiful," Susannah whispered.

"In her own way, she is. Not the reigning diamond, mind you. That title is reserved for you, Miss Susannah."

Captain Jeffries nodded and took a drink of his lemonade.

"I should so love to have a season in London. It sounds like a fairy-tale place." Susannah's voice sounded wishful, but resigned to go without.

Olivia's heart twisted. Her sister was a good girl who deserved a chance at her dreams. And her own child deserved a future, too. Sheldrake could easily give them those things.

She looked up at him. Her thoughts drifted to the conservatory and the stain she had seen there. There had to be an explanation. Everything she had witnessed of him thus far was completely at odds with the notion that he had killed his stepfather in a rage. There had to be a justifiable reason.

When he found her in his study, he had been angry, but he did not rant or rave. He was in complete control of his emotions until he had kissed her. That had shaken him; it had shaken them both. And then there was the crash of glass she had heard. He obviously broke something. Which meant he had a temper, but was it so violent that he could kill?

She supposed that would depend upon what the stepfather might have done to ignite Sheldrake's fury. Her own father had roused bitter anger in her at a very young age due to his ill-treatment of her mother. But she had been only a child and could do little about it. What would she have done had she been a grown woman?

He looked up at her then, and she stared into his eyes, wishing he could understand her turmoil.

"Olivia?" Aunt Agatha asked in concern and nudged her.

She dropped her fork; the clatter against the dish startled everyone into silence.

"Olivia?" Aunt Agatha whispered to her, "Dear, what is the matter with you?"

"Sorry, terribly clumsy of me," she mumbled, her cheeks hot.

Mr. Blessing hurriedly covered the awkward moment by telling of the time he dropped his plate at a supper dance. Olivia was grateful. She peeked up at Sheldrake to see his frown deepen.

Finally, the meal came to an end, yet no one hurried to leave the serene surroundings on the terrace. Except for her, she was ready to run. After what seemed liked centuries, Lady Evelyn rose to leave. "I will take my lemonade to the gardens. Would you ladies care to join me?"

Olivia agreed. She wanted nothing so much as to leave.

The gentlemen also stood.

"Thank you for your kind invitation, Lord Sheldrake," Captain Jeffries said. "But I must take my leave as well. I have promised to play checkers with Dickie."

"Give him my regards, would you?" Sheldrake said.

"Yes, do," Lady Evelyn added. "And Captain, perhaps you can escort us to the gardens on your way out."

"I would be honored." The captain bowed, then led the ladies down the steps and into the gardens.

Sheldrake sat in silence after the women had left. He watched Blessing help himself to more wine, then crack a nut with his fist.

"Do you want some?" Blessing offered him the bowl of nuts.

"No."

"What are you going to do?"

"Do?"

"You did say you kissed her last night when you found her in your study. By honor's standards, you have some repairing to do." Blessing picked out pieces of nutmeat from the broken shell.

"What are you getting at?" Sheldrake muttered, feeling as if he had been hit in the head repeatedly. He had drunk too much last night and slept too little.

"I'm just saying that the honorable thing to do is to offer for her."

"Since when did you get honorable where women are concerned," Sheldrake snapped.

"Since I got myself a wife. Now listen to me, you have got to do something. Talk to her. Did you not see how jumpy she was?"

Did Peter think him blind? It tore up his peace to see her in such a state. But what could he do? How could he possibly do right by her with an offer of marriage? She would never accept him without knowing the truth and once that was revealed, she would no doubt have nothing more to do with him. It would be better for everyone if he just left it alone.

He sighed heavily. "She found and read that cursed letter from Belinda."

Blessing swore, then added, "If not for Belinda, there would have been no rumors."

"If not for me stating repeatedly that I wished Abbott six feet under, Belinda would have had no grounds to accuse me," Sheldrake said.

"Belinda was a fool." Blessing took a drink of his wine. "You should just tell Lady Beresford what happened."

"I cannot risk my mother's memory. What if Olivia tells her aunt or sister or worse yet, decides something must be done and she goes to my mother!"

"Tell Lady Beresford not to say anything."

"Trust a woman not to tell a juicy bit of a torrid tale? No, I will not risk it." Sheldrake picked up a nut and juggled it from hand to hand.

"Lady Beresford does not appear the type to give over to gossip."

"Neither does she seem the type to break into a man's study, yet she did."

"So, what are you going to do?"

"The deuce if I know," he answered as he tossed the nut off the terrace to a waiting squirrel.

Chapter Nine

Tea was about to be served. Susannah and Aunt Agatha shared the settee, Lord Sheldrake sat near the fireplace, Mr. Blessing stood, and Olivia shared the divan with Lady Evelyn when Simms announced a group of ladies visiting from Lady Belham's.

Lady Evelyn's hand suddenly shook, causing the delicate silver spoon to rattle indecorously against the Spode china. Sheldrake lept to his feet; the tops of his ears were red, and he looked ready to bolt.

Olivia watched in fascination as the woman announced as Lady Belinda Framingham entered with a rustle of yellow silk and feathers. She was tall, slender, and auburn-haired with flashing blue eyes. Susannah had been correct—she was beautiful. And she had written that horrible letter found in Sheldrake's study. She was Belinda.

"My goodness, Sheldrake, how good to see you again." Belinda extended her hand. "I did not expect you to be home."

Stiff-backed and looking none too pleased, he bowed over her offered hand. "Where else would I be, Belinda?" he drawled, then amended, "but that would be Lady Framingham now, I believe."

"My goodness, yes, it has been a long time. I would have thought you to be hunting or planting or some such activity. Ah, Mr. Blessing." She turned her attention to him. "You are still visiting Sheldrake in the late summer I see. And you have married, too. Poor dear, she must be exhausted from all the travel, but where is your new bride?" Belinda looked about.

It was the first time that Olivia witnessed Mr. Blessing gazing upon a female with clear dislike. He did not even try to hide his disdain for her as he bent over her hand. "My wife is at my estate in Kent, getting the place ready for us to reside there permanently. I will join her there soon."

That seemed to satisfy her. She turned around and gazed at the ladies seated, much the way a bird of prey searches for her next catch. She focused on Sheldrake's mother. "Lady Evelyn, after seeing you at Mrs. Hardcastle's, I simply had to call."

Lady Evelyn came out of her stare, flashed an apologetic smile toward her son, then ordered Simms to bring more tea.

Olivia merely sat quietly as the introductions were made, and a loaded tea cart soon appeared. Belinda narrowed her eyes as she looked directly at her. "Lady Beresford, I was acquainted with your husband. Please accept my deepest sympathy." Her words were all that was polite, but her eyes remained as cold as sapphires made of ice.

"Thank you," Olivia answered.

"And how interesting that an accident should bring you to Sheldrake Hall."

"Is it?" Olivia asked.

"Why yes. How fortunate for you that you were able to come here instead of some other place." Belinda accepted a cup of tea from Lady Evelyn and sat down upon a vacant chair. The other ladies gathered near the windows to admire the gardens with Mr. Blessing.

Olivia cast a glance at Sheldrake, who had calmed himself considerably as he leaned against the stone fireplace. His gaze caught hers and held. She tried to decipher his thoughts, but could not, and finally she looked away.

Belinda had not missed the exchange between them, and now openly stared at her. Olivia felt even more uncomfortable. It was as if Belinda had come to call expressly to check her over.

"Lady Framingham," Lady Evelyn started, a slight quiver in her voice. "It is so nice of you to take time out of your busy schedule to call upon us."

"I simply had to give my condolences to Lady Beresford in person. And it was lovely meeting Miss Lacey and Miss Agatha Wilts at Mrs. Hardcastle's. How could I not call and wish them well before I return to my estate in Kensington." Belinda smiled in their direction, but there was a smugness Olivia could not like. "I wish to extend an open invitation to tea should you ever come to London."

The comment was laced with hidden meaning, as if she knew that they could never afford such a trip to London. Olivia felt the heat rise to her cheeks as she considered the possibility that Lady Belinda Framingham knew the state of Robbie's finances after he had died.

It was not surprising really, since some of Robbie's bosom bows were present at the reading of the will and at the auction held soon after to settle the bills. Feeling the tension mounting in the room, Olivia was at a loss to know what to say or do. The last thing she wished was to talk of inconsequential drivel with Sheldrake's former betrothed, who proved herself to be neither pleasant nor gracious.

Thankfully, Aunt Agatha perked up just in time to ask the other ladies how they were enjoying their stay.

"I do so love rusticating in the country," one of them said from near the windows.

Olivia's nerves were drawn to the breaking point. She had put off speaking with Sheldrake all afternoon, knowing she would have to face him at tea that afternoon. She had not been prepared to meet the author of the letter she had read condemning Sheldrake for ending Abbott's existence.

Lady Evelyn rose to join the other ladies, and Belinda quickly took her seat. Olivia's spirits sank, evidently she really was the target of Belinda's visit.

"Lady Beresford." Belinda's voice was low, almost a whisper. "I do hope you will have a care while you stay here."

Olivia turned shocked eyes upon her. "Why do you say such a thing?"

"Have you not heard what is said about Lord Sheldrake?" There was an evil glint in the lady's eye as she waited for her reaction.

But Olivia had had enough of the woman. "Surely, those rumors cannot possibly be true, or you would not be here." She smiled sweetly at Belinda, who suddenly looked at a loss for words.

Olivia then glanced at Sheldrake. He had overheard them. He had a satisfied smirk upon his lips. She was not about to let him get away from the situation. "More tea, Lord Sheldrake?" she asked. When he nodded and handed her his cup, she did the pouring since the tea cart was closest to her. "Do sit down, my lord, and we three can have a lovely chat." She patted the vacant spot next to her. Belinda sat on her other side.

A grin split Sheldrake's face as he gingerly sat down next to her, looking ready to laugh. "Lady Framingham, do tell us, how is your husband? Last I had heard he was having some trouble with gout," he said.

Olivia turned her attention to Belinda, who was not at all pleased with the turn of events. She and Sheldrake presented a united front in the face of the rumors Belinda was trying to use against them. She looked positively enraged.

"My goodness." Belinda suddenly looked at the small watch dangling from the chain she wore. "It has indeed grown late. I mustn't overtire you, Lady Beresford, considering your condition." Belinda cast a pointed look at her middle, then rose to collect the other ladies. In a few moments the whirlwind of ladies left as they had come, completely unexpected.

"Thank you for that." Sheldrake leaned toward Olivia as he put his cup upon the cart.

"You are welcome," she answered.

"Richard, I beg your pardon, dear. I had no idea she would come to call," Lady Evelyn said.

"Not a problem at all, Mother."

Lady Evelyn looked ready to say something else, but thought better of it. She turned and said something to Mr. Blessing, who laughed and put his arm about her.

Sheldrake remained next to her. He leaned closer. "We need to talk."

She turned to him and whispered back, "That is the Belinda from your letter, is it not?"

"The very same. Quite the charmer," he said sarcastically. "Come, take a walk in the gardens with me, we must talk."

She turned her head to see Mr. Blessing helping himself to a scone. Susannah offered to pour him a cup of the still warm tea, and he nodded his acceptance. Lady Evelyn and Aunt Agatha chatted on.

"I have nothing to say to you," she lied. She had so very much to say to him, only she was not prepared and his nearness threw her off balance. Purposefully, she set her attention back to her cup of tea.

He took the cup from her hands. "Please."

She looked up into his eyes with a sinking feeling. He melted her resolve when he looked at her that way. Breathing a sigh, she took his offered hand to help her stand.

Across the room, she caught her aunt's questioning gaze. "We are going for a short stroll in the garden. Perhaps you can join us when you have finished with your tea." She did not wish to be alone with him overly long.

They walked in silence, and Olivia could feel the apprehension in him. Once in the gardens and well out of earshot of the opened windows, she turned to him. "You wished to speak with me, my lord?"

"So it is 'my lord' again?" Sheldrake asked.

"Under the circumstances, I believe it is more appropriate." She held her hands firmly clasped and draped across her belly.

"Under the circumstances! Olivia, it was *you* who broke into *my* study."

"Yes, and shameful as it was, what else was I supposed to do? You refuse to explain what I found, what I know."

"But you know nothing," he stated.

"Then tell me." She stepped closer to him, looking up into his eyes. "Here, now!" She heard the sounds of the others coming outside to join them.

He did, too. He pulled her aside, close to a tree and out of direct sight of the others. "I want you to trust me."

He stood so close to her that her heart clamored in her chest. She wanted to trust him, her heart begged her to, but she just could not, not yet. She finally found her voice. "Trust you? Sheldrake, how can you expect such a thing after I read that letter."

"That letter is untrue," he said. "You met Belinda. Do you think her a pillar of truth and honesty?"

"No, but . . . are you telling me that you did not kill Abbott?"

The others were in the courtyard, coming toward them. He looked up in their direction and did not answer. Her insides were in turmoil, and then she remembered the stain on the floor of the conservatory. She grabbed hold of his arm. "What about the conservatory? Why do you keep the inside door locked?"

He looked startled, and her concern grew. Her breath caught in her throat at the look in his eyes. He looked worried, almost guilty.

"You were in the conservatory?" He took a strong hold of her shoulders.

"Yes, today. Why is the room empty? What is the stain on the floor?" She could not stop her questions or the fear tearing through her at the expression on his face. It was a haunted look, one filled with emotions so deep, it terrified her.

"Did you tell or ask my mother about it?"

"No, but—"

"Olivia, swear to me here and now that you will not mention that room again, ever."

"Why?"

The others were almost upon them.

"Promise me." He shook her gently.

"Yes, but . . ."

He let her go.

"Lovely afternoon, eh?" Mr. Blessing asked loudly before he led the ladies to them.

"Indeed." Sheldrake raked a hand through his hair.

Olivia nodded. Something *did* happen in the conservatory. She was convinced that was where Abbott had died. The way Sheldrake reacted, the look in his eyes confirmed it for her.

She realized that he must keep the room locked out of consideration for his mother. But his reaction was so strong. What happened that night? Her mind reeled. He admitted only that Belinda's letter was untrue. She recalled the contents of it—*when you chose to take Mr. Abbott's life . . .*

Did he or did he not kill Abbott? She knew that he did not murder the man, but he still may have killed him. Why and how did it happen? There could have been a row and then an accident that left his stepfather dead. She would do her best to understand, if only he would tell her and be done with it.

Her aunt's words that Abbott had died from a gunshot wound while he cleaned his gun ran through her thoughts. Would anyone clean their firearm in a conservatory? And how could anyone accidentally shoot a man?

Her thoughts in a whirl, she looked at Lady Evelyn. Perhaps it was she who kept the room closed and locked to keep away the unpleasant reminder of her husband's death. But why the letter from Belinda? Why would she accuse Sheldrake of murder? What could that woman possibly have to gain by such a letter written only to Sheldrake? Olivia's mind churned and ended straight back where it all began. *Belinda's letter!*

She looked at Sheldrake. He was conversing with Mr. Blessing. Dare she trust him?

The garden stroll became a great walk the length of the

lake and back, but she did not venture farther than the bench she had shared with Sheldrake on several occasions. She sat quietly and watched as he showed Susannah how to skip flat rocks across the lake's still water. Her sister clapped her hands when she finally accomplished three skips in a row. The gentlemen soon fell into a competition with her while Lady Evelyn and Aunt Agatha picked the pretty white wild-flowers that grew along the south end of the shore.

Olivia leaned her head back and closed her eyes. She desperately wanted to believe in Sheldrake, yet there were so many questions, so many secrets. She could no longer avoid the inevitable. He had been correct—they needed to talk in private. But not now, she was too tired. Slowly, she rose from the bench and waved to her aunt. She needed to rest before dinner.

Susannah dashed out of the gardens and into the field. Captain Jeffries was there standing beside his horse waiting, just as she had asked him before he left the Hall earlier. Her heart skipped a beat, and she waved.

She was so grateful to Lord Sheldrake for inviting him to ride with them this morning and then again to luncheon. It made it considerably easier for the captain to write to her, since he could also include her aunt and her sister for propriety's sake.

"Have you been waiting long?" She was out of breath by the time she reached him.

"No, and I will stay only a moment. We are not chaperoned."

"Oh, piffle," she said with a huff.

"My dear Susannah, there are rules that must be followed." He smiled, and she felt as if the sun had just dimmed in comparison.

"I know, but I just wanted to ask you, since I did not have a chance earlier, if you would be so kind as to . . ." She hesitated, then stuck a piece of paper into his coat pocket. "Please write to me. I have given you my aunt's address."

His smiled again and retrieved the paper to read it. Then he folded it carefully and tucked it into his waistcoat pocket. "I shall write to you, Miss Susannah Lacey."

"Good. Now, when do you leave? Tomorrow, is it not?" She tried to keep the waver out of her voice. She would miss him dearly. Her captain, her own dearest friend and love. She knew the moment she had spotted him in the field that she loved him. She would love him forever.

"Tomorrow evening I must head for Plymouth to rejoin my regiment. But I shall see you tomorrow at the Hall. Lord Sheldrake has invited me to call."

"He is a good man. I do hope he marries Olivia," Susannah said. Surprise registered upon her captain's face and Susannah giggled. "Can you not tell that he is mad for her? And I think she likes him very much, in turn."

"You could certainly have that season you wanted." His voice sounded bleak.

"Yes, I suppose I could." She looked up into his eyes, suddenly feeling shy. "And I could meet you there."

His eyes turned serious as he gazed at her. "Susannah, do not do anything so foolish as to wait for me."

She was not sure how to respond, but it hurt to have him scold her. She decided to smile brightly and flirt. "Perhaps it will be you who will have to wait for me."

That did it. His frown cleared to be replaced by a lop-sided grin. "Yes, I suppose I just might." He gently chucked her chin, which she hated, but tolerated it considering they had so little time together. "You must return, Susannah. Dinner will no doubt be served soon, and I do not wish to make you late, nor cause Lord Sheldrake to seek you out."

She nodded. "Tomorrow then?"

"Tomorrow."

She turned and ran back into the gardens, praying the whole time that Captain Jeffries would indeed wait for her.

*　　　*　　　*

Olivia entered the stables to check on Pockets. Dinner was not for half an hour yet, but she could rest no longer. She looked around until her gaze landed upon the stable boy.

"Good day, George," she said.

"Ma'am." The boy pulled his forelock in greeting. He was careful to look directly at her face. Her bulging middle clearly made him uncomfortable as he often reddened when he looked at that part of her.

"How is our little patient?"

"She be doin' jus' fine, ma'am." He hurried to escort her to the tack room.

In the corner a box filled with fresh hay housed the sleeping spaniel. She sat down in a chair and asked George to bring the little dog to her. He carefuly lifted Pockets, and the dog yawned herself awake.

"Well now, Miss Pockets, let us see how your foot fares, shall we? George, hold her still please." She reached out toward the dog's bandaged foot.

"Here let me." Sheldrake had entered the tack room.

She tried to quell the sudden shiver of sensation she experienced at the sound of his voice. She said nothing as he pulled another chair close to hers and took Pockets from the stable boy. She sat watching him as he stroked the dog's head and murmured his greetings.

"If you will give me her paw, I will check the wound," she finally managed to say.

"George, run along to the kitchens and ask Cook for some scraps."

"Yes, sir!" With a hasty bow, the young boy hurried to do Sheldrake's bidding.

"I did not have a chance to apologize," he said when they were alone.

"Apologize?" She carefully unwound the gauze from the spaniel's paw.

"For my behavior last night. It was unthinkable."

She felt his gaze upon her, but she continued to unravel

the bandage. "You were provoked, and I had no right to go through your things."

She tried to concentrate on her task, but he reached out and stilled her hands.

"I was referring to my kiss. I should never have taken advantage of you that way."

She stopped breathing.

"Olivia, please look at me." He reached out and touched his finger beneath her chin, gently forcing her to look at him.

She gazed into his eyes of deepest blue. "Can we not simply forget it?"

"Yes, I suppose we can." Sheldrake sighed. "But I have some repairing to do."

Her heart raced. Was he going to offer for her? This was exactly what she wanted, and yet she could not accept until she knew the truth about him. She had so many questions to ask, but she merely sat like a stunned ninny, unable to articulate what she needed to say. His nearness always set her at odds with her good sense.

"Sheldrake," she began, trying to keep him from asking the question she was too tempted to answer with acceptance regardless of his secrets. "I still do not know what happened"—she paused knowing she must tread lightly—"to Mr. Abbott."

"Can we not leave that alone for now, just for now?"

"Then I can have no interest in your *repairs,*" she said abruptly and stood, turning her back on him.

"I suppose I deserve that," he said. "After you came here, I took the liberty to send a note to my solicitors in London to check into the matter of your late husband's will."

Olivia turned back around and stared at him. "Why?"

"To see if it is solid and legal. To see if something could be done."

"And?"

"Tight as a drum. Edmund is the lawful heir unless you give birth to a son. There is no provision otherwise." He continued to sit with Pockets in his lap, absently stroking her fur.

It was painfully obvious to Olivia that Robbie thought little of females and his own wife in particular. Had he ever truly cared he would not have left her in such a state. "But what does this have to do—"

"Please, let me finish," he interrupted. He set Pockets back into the box, her foot temporarily forgotten as he stood and walked toward her. "As I have no right to deal with this Edmund as I would wish to, I would like to at least make a provision for you as recompense for my behavior."

"Your behavior?" She backed up and leaned against the tack room table.

"Last night."

She remained silent. What was he saying? He wanted to give her some sort of pension as payment for a stolen kiss? He had no intention of offering for her! A deep disappointment settled with icy coldness in the realm of her chest. Of course, he would not marry her. How stupid of her to ever think he would want her in such a condition.

"I do not know what to say," she sputtered. It hurt. It hurt so deeply that she felt her knees would give out if not for the table she leaned upon.

"Say nothing; only accept it knowing that I would be more than grateful if you would do so."

"To absolve you of your many sins, or to keep me from asking about them?" She knew she had answered more sharply than she had meant to when she saw him flinch. She knew not the amount of his provision, but no doubt it would be adequate enough to give her security. Until he decided he no longer needed absolution.

Sheldrake said nothing about her harsh remark, but his eyes were soft and sorry. "Please, just think about it."

What could she say—what could she possibly do but accept? She needed the funds. She felt more than defeated. "I shall think about it."

He nodded and looked away.

She walked past him and picked up the dog, then resumed the task of checking the dog's foot, while Sheldrake looked on. An awkward silence had settled over them, so she hurried in order to get the thing done so she could leave.

"It looks good," he said when the paw was revealed with a stitched wound that was healing nicely.

"Another day or two and I think the bandages can stay off."

"Thank you," he whispered.

She nodded, overcome with feeling, with hurt and the need to cry. But she would not do so in front of him. She could not allow him to see the heartbreak that she felt. She finished changing the bandages in silence. She could feel his gaze on her, but she dared not look up for fear of what he would see lurking in her heart, the love that lay there. Heartache tended to uncover it and lay it open for anyone to see.

When George returned with the scraps, she saw her opportunity to escape. She lay the dog down and stood. "Well, George, Pockets looks very good indeed." She coughed to clear her throat and swallow the unshed tears. "I shall leave you to discuss her progress with his lordship."

Sheldrake watched her go. He'd made her angry and he'd insulted her, he thought as he sat there staring at her back as it disappeared around the corner of the tack room.

"Here you are." Peter suddenly entered the room.

"Here I am," Sheldrake sighed.

"Didn't go well, did it?" Peter nodded in the direction of where Olivia had retreated.

Sheldrake stood and gave George instructions to put more salve on the dog's bandages and to let him know if anything changed. He walked out with Peter into the early evening air. "Why do you say that?"

"Because I ran into Lady Beresford exiting the stable with tears in her eyes, and there you were sitting like a bump on a log."

Tears! Sheldrake ran a hand through his hair. He had made a mull of things—again.

"What did you do?" Peter asked.

"What do you mean?"

"Did you tell her what happened to Abbott?"

"No."

"Did you offer for her?"

"No."

"Blast it, Shelly, what *did* you do?"

"I offered her a pension," he said flatly.

"You what!" Peter stopped dead in his tracks and turned to look at him. "Why didn't you offer for her? You know you want to!"

"Because I can't, Peter. I can't do that to her, to my mother . . . to me."

"Shelly, you have got to come back to the living. What happened to Abbott and Lady Evelyn was not your fault. You have to stop blaming yourself and stop with this noble cock-a-brained notion that you don't deserve to be happy, that you failed."

"Peter, that's enough." Sheldrake clenched his fists at his side. He had hit too close than was comfortable.

"Oh, no, it is not nearly enough. Somebody needs to knock some sense into you."

"What do you know about it?" Sheldrake was facing Peter now, almost shouting.

"I know all about failure, and I know you are far from it," Peter countered.

"But I could have prevented all of it." Sheldrake's anger then deflated to be replaced with despair.

"You are throwing away a chance to be happy for a big *what if.* What if your mother remembers the night Abbott died, what if she cannot recover from it, what if—"

"But those are pretty big *what ifs.* The deuce, Peter, do you not think I would offer for her if I thought it possible? How can I risk my mother's state of mind? How can I bring a bride into a home filled with such secrets and insanity?"

"She's already here, Shell. She's already here. Give her a chance to make up her own mind. Don't bloody well make it up for her."

Olivia sat in the drawing room, looking out the window at the gardens beyond. Dinner would be any moment, but she felt no appetite for it. She cursed herself as a fool. She had such grand plans of catching Lord Sheldrake for a husband, thinking she could keep her heart safe and her family's future secure. She had failed on both counts. Her heart was sorely abused, and her security was based on the whim of a man who wanted to make a provision for her out of guilt. And when he decided to marry, her pension could quite possibly be cut off, and she would be back in the same predicament.

And what made matters even worse, she still knew no more about Abbott's death than when she first set foot in Sheldrake Hall. He had said that Belinda's letter was untrue. Perhaps she should just believe him, accept his provision and be done with the whole thing. Her child would come soon, and then she could leave this place.

Her heart suffered at the thought of leaving, at not being a part of Sheldrake's life, at not seeing him put more of those farming techniques he studied into action, at not crossing strains of roses with him, at not being held by him or kissed.

She looked up in time to see Sheldrake enter the room. Her body reacted to seeing him with the usual shiver up her spine and flutter in the pit of her stomach. But this time she also felt hurt.

"The others have gathered in the dining room for dinner." His gaze was steady, but he looked unsure of himself, almost awkward. "Susannah said I could find you here. I thought perhaps I could escort you," he said softly.

"Thank you," she replied rather woodenly as she stood and took his proffered arm.

He wrapped her hand around the crook of his elbow and

patted it with reassurance. She looked up at him and he gazed back. But he said nothing, so she looked away. They walked in silence to the dining room. There was a new tension between them, and Olivia tried her best to act normally, as if nothing bothered her.

Once in the dining room, Sheldrake pulled out the special chair he had found for her after she had trouble getting out of the other dining chairs. Her heart twisted painfully. It was such a small thing really, but she thought it so kind of him, to spare her further embarrassment.

Was she wrong to give up on him so easily? Perhaps she should fight for his affection, not just let him go. She shook her napkin out onto her lap with a vengeance. She was tired of enduring the heartaches in her life. She was tired of sitting back and letting them happen. It was high time that she sought out what she wanted in life. And that included Sheldrake. She would make him see somehow that he must have her as his wife.

Chapter Ten

"A picnic?" Olivia asked. She let her needlework fall to her lap. She had come to her sister's chamber to while away the rest of the morning.

"Yes, Lord Sheldrake has arranged for us all to go on a picnic. We are to leave in an hour. Of course, he and his mother were still discussing it at breakfast, but now it is settled. Is it not grand?" Susannah asked. "And we will not go far, due to your condition. The weather is so fine, it shall be splendid."

"Splendid," Olivia murmured. *A picnic?* She wondered what made Sheldrake think of it. She could not quite reconcile him as a man lazing about on chaise or upon a blanket. Then again, he had surprised her last night at dinner; he had been most congenial. The awkwardness between them was still there, but he had done everything he could to put her at ease.

He had even gone out of his way to speak to her aunt, and Olivia knew he had scored considerable favor with Aunt Agatha as he had made her laugh quite often.

And now a picnic. The fine weather continued to hold, and she reveled in it. She had made her rounds of the courtyard garden that morning and was not in the least against spending the afternoon out of doors as well.

"What should I wear?" Susannah asked. She held a dress in each hand.

"Does it matter?" Olivia padded over to where her sister stood before an armoire, holding a meager selection.

"Of course it does, silly."

"How about the peach gown," Olivia said.

"But he has already seen me in it."

"Susannah, Mr. Blessing is married. You have no business trying to impress him."

Her sister flushed with embarrassment. "It is not him. Lord Sheldrake has invited Captain Jeffries to the picnic."

"Has he?" She'd have to speak to him about playing matchmaker with Susannah. She was far too young for Captain Jeffries. "When does this captain return to his regiment?" She saw the light dim in her sister's eyes.

"Tomorrow. He leaves for Plymouth later today."

At her downcast eyes, Olivia's heart twisted for her. She walked over and put her arms about her sister. The dresses fell in a heap as Susannah returned the embrace. "I am sorry."

Susannah looked up at her with wide eyes. "He is a very nice gentleman, Olivia. You'd like him."

"I am sure that I would." She stayed that way, silently offering Susannah comfort. They did not mention the chance of the captain falling in battle. She knew that was her sister's fear, but there was nothing she could do to take it away. She kissed her on the forehead and said, "What about the primrose yellow? That one looks very fine on you."

"Yes, the primrose, I think." Susannah pulled out of her embrace and picked up the fallen dress. Once into it, she turned for Olivia to fasten the tapes in the back.

It had been an old dress of Olivia's that Susannah had refurbished with a deeper flounce and a lace ruffle secured to the rounded neckline. It looked very nice indeed for something handed down. But then, Susannah made anything she wore look that much nicer.

"What about me?" Olivia asked. "Do you have a pretty bonnet that perhaps I could wear?"

Olivia looked into the enormous oval mirror on the wall in Susannah's bedchamber. A pale woman stared back. The dark gray morning dress she wore did little for her complexion. She had told Aunt Agatha to forgo making up a mourning wardrobe for Susannah, and save the money. It had been nearly six months since Robbie's death when Susannah came to Adberesmere. Susannah had come only for a short visit. But when Edmund asked Olivia to leave, at least Susannah was present to give her company on the long journey to their aunt's, where she could spend her confinement.

Trying on a plain straw bonnet lined in deep rose, she turned to Susannah. "May I borrow this?"

Susannah broke into a wide grin. "You see, I am not the only one trying to impress a gentleman."

Olivia felt her cheeks redden, but it was true. She wanted to present herself to advantage with Sheldrake.

"Yes, it looks very nice on you." Susannah took away the bunches of cherries on the side, to replace it with a single white feather dipped with crimson. "There, that looks much better."

Olivia scrutinized the effect in the mirror. The rose lining of the bonnet enhanced her coloring, bringing a glow to her cheeks. Susannah also produced a crimson ribbon, which she fastened around the straw brim, then drew it under her chin. The ribbon's color brought out the green of her eyes. Satisfied, she nodded to Susannah, who smiled in return.

"You shall enslave him with your beauty!" her sister teased.

"Susannah, really. I am certainly not trying to *enslave* anyone." But that was a fib. She did hope to bring him to his knees, with but one question to ask.

"But you do wish to attach Lord Sheldrake's affection, do you not? You already have his attention."

Olivia said nothing, which made Susannah all the more determined. "Are you trying to secure Lord Sheldrake's affection?"

"Perhaps." Olivia smiled in spite of herself. She would win his hand, and if she was fortunate, she would win his heart as well. She retied the crimson ribbon to set the bow on the left side of her jaw, just under her ear.

"Are you ready?" Susannah stood before her, dressed in the jaunty primrose yellow gown.

"Yes, I suppose so." Olivia took a moment to examine herself in the large mirror. The dark gray cotton morning gown was overused. She wore it almost daily, but it was cool and comfortable. Her belly stuck out and looked lower than it did just a few days before. She adjusted the bonnet slightly and patted its bow before following her sister to the door.

The picnic was set for an apple grove just beyond the lake, Lady Evelyn had informed her. Olivia reclined against the soft leather seat of Sheldrake's well-sprung open gig as Lady Evelyn drove. She marveled at being driven in such comfort. The gig was obviously new.

The dirt road leading to the orchard lay very flat and straight, and since they moved slowly, Olivia was not jostled a bit. She lifted her head to the sunshine as it peeped out from behind a cloud. Agatha and Susannah had gone ahead with the gentlemen.

"A very fine day for a picnic," she said to Lady Evelyn.

"Yes, very. I applaud Richard for suggesting it. It has been an age since we have done anything like this."

"It was his idea then?" Olivia asked.

"Yes. He wanted to enjoy the outdoors to the fullest, before the weather turned cold. See, dark clouds are already forming."

Olivia did in fact notice the clouds on the horizon. She hoped the rain held off until after their picnic.

"You are good for him, my dear," Lady Evelyn suddenly said.

Olivia was not sure how to respond to such a statement so she simply nodded. But it warmed her considerably to know that Lady Evelyn approved of her for her son.

They drove along the edge of the orchard until they came to a slight clearing upon a small hill. Olivia's breath caught at the sight before her. A white tentlike canopy billowed in the center of the opening. The orchard surrounded the clearing on three sides. The fourth and open side overlooked the lake with a gradual slope leading to it. The apples, not yet fully ripe, lent the air a sweet freshness that nearly made her mouth water.

A couple of small tables were set upon a huge tapestry that was laid upon the ground with oversized cushions for lounging. There was even an overstuffed chair for her to sit in comfortably. Servants scurried about making ready for a feast.

Lady Evelyn stopped the gig, handed over the reins to a waiting groom, and jumped down. The groom extended his hand for Olivia to hold as she carefully stepped down from the gig. Lady Evelyn stood ready to escort her the rest of the way, and they linked arms. She spied the gentlemen engaged in a game of battledore and shuttlecock. Olivia and Lady Evelyn walked toward them.

They stood watching as Mr. Blessing and Sheldrake furiously hit the shuttlecock from one to the other. Both gentlemen had removed their jackets and waistcoats. Their fine lawn shirts pressed against their chests in the warm steady breeze. Olivia tried not to stare at Sheldrake and looked away. Aunt Agatha and Susannah, along with her captain, were not far off. They waved cheerfully and returned to the checking of apples for signs of ripeness.

"I think I shall join them," Lady Evelyn said, and she walked toward Aunt Agatha. Olivia nodded, but stood transfixed, her attention caught by the game being played before her.

Sheldrake's tall form moved with effortless grace to return each of Mr. Blessing's volleys. His bare forearms flexed as he gripped the racquet. There was such strength there.

She closed her eyes as the memory of the kiss they had shared in Sheldrake's study scorched her memory. The strength of it still had a potent affect on her. Absently, she ran her fingers across her lips.

Olivia opened her eyes in time to see Mr. Blessing taunt

Sheldrake, who laughingly returned the shuttlecock with lightning speed. Mr. Blessing was fast in his return, but he hit the shuttlecock too far, which spelled victory for Sheldrake. The two men jostled each other as they departed from the area of play.

Sheldrake noticed her and smiled. "How long have you been here?" he asked as he came up alongside her, shrugging hurriedly into his waistcoat.

"Not long." He wore no cravat, and his neck was a smooth tanned column. She wanted to reach out and touch his heated skin, feel the texture of it. Instead, she turned to Mr. Blessing, who approached them. "Good afternoon, Mr. Blessing."

"Lady Beresford." He bowed. "I do hope I was spared your witness to my defeat."

"Unfortunately, sir, I did see your losing shot."

"Aha, you see, Peter, it's obvious you were trounced!" Sheldrake slapped him on the back.

"I do have to let you win on occasion." Mr. Blessing mopped his brow with his own cravat. "I am in need of refreshment. Lady Beresford, do forgive me for running along."

"Of course." She nodded.

"How are you today?" Sheldrake asked softly once Mr. Blessing had gone.

His dark hair lay tousled by the wind and exertion. He looked more handsome than she thought possible. "I am very fine, indeed. And you?"

"I have been anxiously awaiting your arrival." His gaze was direct and melting.

Olivia felt the familiar flutter in her stomach that his nearness always produced. "Thank you for the transportation. That was most thoughtful, as is bringing such a large chair for me to sit in," she said as she pointed to the white canopy.

"You are most welcome. Peter thought it too nice a day to stay indoors. I hope you agree."

"Most heartily," she responded.

"Come, walk with me a bit." He held out his arm.

She wrapped her arm about his. He did not wear his jacket, so her fingers rested upon his skin just below the roll of his shirtsleeves. Warmth flooded through her fingertips and raced up her arm to her heart, causing it to pound terribly.

They walked into the apple orchard and out of sight of the others. She breathed deeply in order to calm her racing pulse. "The air is sweet with the smell of apples. It is lovely."

"And your cheeks are as rosy as any apple here." He stopped to reach up and pluck an early apple that was nearly red.

She stopped as well, and he moved away from her. She watched as he leaned against the tree's trunk and slowly polished the apple against his waistcoat. He brought the shiny fruit to his lips, took a bite, and swallowed.

"Very sweet," he murmured, then handed it to her. "Here."

Was he actually flirting with her! Now was her chance to reciprocate with full force. She stepped forward, took the offered apple, and raised it to her mouth. A tremor ran through her as her lips touched where he had bitten. It was sweet indeed. Looking up, she caught Sheldrake's gaze and sank her teeth in deeply with a crackle. She saw his eyes darken.

Chewing slowly, she offered it back to Sheldrake. His heated gaze never left hers as he took another bite. She could not breathe. Her fingers and toes were numb, and her insides churned with desire. She dared not break the spell as he handed back to her the apple they shared.

She savored every moment. She ignored the secrets of Sheldrake Hall and all the questions that lay there. She simply indulged in the moment. They might never share more than this, but she knew she wanted more. She wanted more of him than just the sensations he created by sharing an apple. And if she succeeded, he would want those things, too.

The fruit was gone too soon. He took the last bite and threw the core away. Then he reached out and stroked her cheek with his fingers, and she trembled.

"I have been such a fool," he whispered.

But she barely heard him; all she wanted was for him to kiss her. She wanted to feel his mouth on hers again. She leaned forward slightly, even closed her eyes when she heard Susannah's call.

"Olivia? Where are you?"

She jerked away from Sheldrake as her sister came upon them.

"Here you are. Oh, Lord Sheldrake. Hm, luncheon is served." Her sister's face flamed.

"Thank you, Susannah, and not a minute too soon. We were ready to eat the orchard!" Sheldrake wiped his mouth with his hand.

Olivia forced a smile, knowing her disappointment must show. Looking down to watch her steps, she did not take Sheldrake's arm. She did not dare touch him, not just now. But she felt that they had made some progress of sorts. He wanted her, and that pleased her beyond words.

Sheldrake followed a safe distance behind Olivia. *Eat the orchard!* He would have devoured Olivia had his lips touched hers. She practically drove him to distraction eating that apple. Did she know how desirable she was, gazing up at him as she took a hearty bite? He ran a hand distractedly through his hair.

As they came out of the orchard, everyone had taken a seat around the table. Once they were ready to be served, he looked across to the chair, where Olivia sat shaking out her napkin. She looked quite calm, while he burned with the memory of sharing that apple. If he chanced to be alone with her again, he would no doubt kiss those rosy lips, and be sorry for it.

He was not sure why he had taken her aside in the first

place. And he had teased her with that apple as she stood there staring at him. What had he been thinking? Obviously he had let the fine day and her beauty sway him into pretending he could have her. And he wanted her, he truly did. But had he kissed her a second time, there would be no escaping the honorable thing of offering for her.

Would that be so very bad? he thought. Perhaps Peter was right; his mother might never remember. Should he let Olivia slip away, only to regret it later? But he realized he should know her better, learn to trust her before he told her what had happened to Abbott. He certainly had to ensure his mother's safety and peace of mind. He needed to trust that Olivia would not upset that.

"Captain Jeffries, when must you leave?" his mother asked.

Sheldrake noticed that the captain was decidedly quiet during the meal. He seemed tense, reserved, almost fearful. And little Susannah was not her usual chatterbox self.

"Today, my lady. Straight after this picnic, actually." The captain took a drink of lemonade.

"Well, it has been delightful to have you with us." Lady Evelyn bit into her buttered bread.

"I thank you for welcoming me." Captain Jeffries sent a pointed look in his direction, and Sheldrake nodded.

"Perhaps you will write to us when you have a chance," Olivia added in a hopeful voice.

Good for her, Sheldrake thought. He was glad that he had brought the young captain into their fold. It gave Susannah the chance to share her feelings rather than keep them hidden. And should the young man fall, Susannah would need her aunt and sister's support.

"I will do my best." Captain Jeffries nodded to Olivia, but his gaze slid to meet Susannah's. And Sheldrake saw it. The affection, the caring, and Lord help him, it looked a bit like love shining from the captain's eyes.

Suddenly, he did not feel so confident in his actions. He wondered if he had done the right thing, allowing them to continue meeting. But what else, short of locking her in her room, could he have done to protect her? Susannah was headstrong and foolish; she would have found a way regardless.

But now they both faced heartache, and he was sorry for that. And Susannah was young, too young to be thinking so fondly of Captain Jeffries. He knew that the captain knew that as well. He'd said as much to him. He only hoped the young man returned home safely.

They had finished the meal and were chatting of the forthcoming turn in the weather, when Captain Jeffries stood.

"I thank you again for your kind invitation to luncheon," Jeffries said. "But I must take my leave."

Susannah also stood. "Captain, I shall escort you back to Sheldrake Hall." It was then that everyone seemed to understand the way things were and where her heart rested.

Before Sheldrake could intervene and require a chaperone to accompany them, Jeffries hurriedly added, "Perhaps just to the lake. Would that be permissible?" Jeffries waited patiently for Agatha Wilts's response.

Sheldrake turned to Olivia's aunt. But Olivia was the first to answer, much to her aunt's disapproval. "By all means, yes, Captain Jeffries. And you shall be in our prayers for a safe and speedy return, sir."

"Thank you, ma'am." He bowed to all of them as each person raised a goblet for a silent toast, then offered Susannah his arm, which she shyly took.

Once the two had left, her aunt whispered, "Olivia, what are you doing? Susannah is far too young."

"Now perhaps, but in a couple of years, she will be just the right age. How could you possibly forbid them goodbye? Susannah has formed a *tendre* for the man. Besides, they are in our direct view, so it cannot be improper." She looked at Sheldrake for reassurance.

"I assure you, Miss Wilts," he said, coming to Olivia's aid, "Captain Jeffries is a gentleman. He has only the most honorable intentions toward your niece. In fact, he has said as much to me. He considers Susannah too young to trifle with her affections. He will tread lightly and be gone. By the time he returns, Susannah will no doubt have formed an attachment elsewhere."

"But they have only just met," the aunt continued to whisper. "How can Susannah be so serious in her affection."

"Love knows no time," Peter added softly.

"Why Peter, what a lovely sentiment," Lady Evelyn said as she patted the aunt's hand. "It is quite all right, Agatha. Do you not remember having a schoolgirl infatuation at that age?"

She giggled in response and waved her hand in dismissal. And the discussion was dropped.

Olivia looked at him as if there were more to the story than Sheldrake had shared. Another situation they would have to discuss, he thought. He knew he had to tell Olivia about Susannah meeting her captain days ago. Now that the captain was leaving, he must tell her. "Would you care to walk to the lake as well? That way, we can keep an eye on them."

"I should like that above all things." She extended her hand.

He bent down to help her rise. His face was close to hers, and her skin looked so smooth and cool, he longed to touch her. He straightened quickly and offered his arm. They walked in silence, her hand tucked around the crook of his elbow. His other hand covered hers, making circles with his fingers along her knuckles.

"Are you enjoying yourself?" he asked, not sure where to start.

"Very much. Thank you. This was a wonderful idea."

They came close to the lake's shore, and Sheldrake nodded to Captain Jeffries as he stood talking to Susannah, who was trying to be brave in her good-bye. They continued along, away from them.

"Tell me, my lord, how long have you known Captain Jeffries?" Olivia asked.

"Not long." *Here it comes,* he thought.

"And how is it that you have deemed him acceptable to try and matchmake him to my sister?" Her eyebrow had cocked upward, but she did not look angry.

"I must be truthful," he started. "Your sister and the young captain met quite by accident some days ago."

She turned to him. "And why did you not tell me this sooner?"

"I promised Susannah that I would not. She feared it would only cause you upset. And I agreed. You have had so much on your mind, I did not wish to add another worry to your already full plate. I made sure she was properly chaperoned when she rode with him."

"She's been riding with him? Sheldrake, it was not your place to decide such a thing." The breeze was playing havoc with the white feather of her bonnet. It dipped across her cheek and tangled in strands of her hair that had come loose.

He sighed. "I know, and I humbly beg your forgiveness if I overstepped my bounds. But I feared that if I did not treat Susannah as more of an adult young lady, she would become stubborn and hell-bent on meeting the captain in secret, which would have ruined her reputation."

She listened intently to his reasoning and nodded. "Yes, I quite see what you mean."

"Your sister said that should your aunt find out, she would have been confined to her room."

"Yes," Olivia agreed. "That was the way of it with Robbie and me. I did find a way to meet him, though. No doubt Susannah would have done the same. Forbidden fruit has a way of looking much more appealing than it truly is."

"Exactly so." He patted her hand. "With the good captain leaving in but a few days, I saw no harm in letting them continue with their friendship under a chaperone. Friendship was all it appeared to be, until today. I do believe Jeffries is smitten."

"Oh no, truly?" Olivia stopped walking and cast worried eyes upon him. "Susannah is quite taken with him as well, and I do not believe it is simply a schoolgirl affection."

He nodded. He had thought as much.

Olivia seemed lost in thought as she slowly rubbed her swollen middle.

"Does the child kick?" he asked, feeling the need to change the subject.

"Actually, he has been quiet today—not much movement at all really."

"Oh." They continued walking, slowly.

"Sheldrake?"

"Yes?"

"Did you love Belinda?"

The question hit him like a splash of cold water. When he did not answer right away, she turned to him, her big green eyes searching his. "I beg your pardon," she said. "But I could not help but think about the letter and how horrible it must have been to receive it. I want to say . . . I need to say, that I am truly very sorry for having read it. And for having gone into your study to find it."

Her eyes were huge as they implored him for forgiveness. How could he not. "Your apology is accepted."

When she remained quiet, he thought he may as well explain Belinda's part, at least, in the rumors she had heard.

"Yes, I loved her, but I was blind. Fooled by what I thought she was." They resumed their walk.

"What was she then?"

"She cared more for my title than she did for me. Framingham is an earl, an older gent. I believe she saw a larger and richer fish in the pond, and so she needed a reason to break off her engagement with me. Abbott's death was as convenient a time as any. There would have been no rumors if not for her."

Olivia stopped walking and turned to face him again. "Do you mean to say that Belinda spread the rumors about your killing your stepfather in a rage?"

"Yes. To be fair, I think she thought them true, from her perspective at least."

"I do not understand. You said they were not true, that her letter was not true."

He reached out and adjusted the white feather of her bonnet. So very much depended upon his answer. He decided that he had to tell her something, ease her suspicions about him. "I admitted my loathing for Abbott to Belinda. I had even gone so far. as to say I wished him dead. Once she heard about Abbott's death, that was enough for her to wonder, to accuse, and then to talk."

"She should have stood by you," she stated, "found out the truth."

"As you are trying to?" Sheldrake asked. When she nodded, he continued. "Look, it was a terrible accident, Olivia, one that I cannot tell you about just now, for my mother's sake. I will not lie to you and say that I wish the man alive, but I did not kill the man in cold blood. It was an accident."

Both her hands rested upon his arms. He gathered them and brought them to his lips, kissing the back of each hand. "Please, trust me. Someday I will tell you everything there is to tell, but now is not the time. Besides, this is too pleasant a day to soil with such a tale." At the doubt he saw flit across her features, he turned her right hand over and kissed her palm. "Just know that I am not a killer, Olivia. Trust me."

"I know that you are not, my lord," she whispered. "And I want to trust you, with all my heart, I do."

He tucked a stray dark curl that fought against the ridiculous white feather back under Olivia's bonnet. He took his time and let his touch linger along the side of her jaw. Their gazes locked and held until he noticed that the sky had completely clouded over with what looked like rain. It was time to leave.

He knew he had to offer for her and he wanted to. But until he told her the whole story of what had happened to Abbott, he knew she would not accept him. And why should she? He asked her to trust him, yet it was he who needed to trust her. He needed to trust her with the truth.

Still, it felt good telling her about Belinda's betrayal. He felt that that part of his past with all its hurts was finally closed and sealed. He need not experience the pain at the memory of being jilted; it was over.

They walked back to the canopy, where the servants had packed the remains of their picnic into the wagon. The wind had picked up considerably by the time Sheldrake helped Olivia into the gig.

"My mother will be with you soon," he said, and he gave her hand a squeeze. When she did not let go, he bent toward her.

"Thank you for telling me," she whispered. "And thank you for taking care of Susannah. I am truly grateful to you."

Her eyes were shining, and he had the urge to blurt a proposal of marriage right there. He kissed her fingertips instead. "I shall see you at dinner this evening."

She nodded, and Sheldrake walked away from her feeling more lighthearted than he had in a long time.

Susannah followed Captain Jeffries to the lake shore. Her arm rested in his, and she was nervous. She feared she would cry and knew that would only make matters worse. She had to be brave, for his sake. They strolled along in silence until finally Captain Jeffries stopped and turned to her.

"Susannah." He looked into her eyes with a seriousness she had seen only briefly before. "I want you to know that I will carry the memory of our friendship and these past few days together into battle with me. It will keep me safe."

She felt a lump form in her throat, and she swallowed twice before she could trust herself to speak. "My prayers and those of my family go with you, Winston." It was the first time she had called him by his Christian name. "That will keep you safe and bring you back to me."

"Thank you, but, Susannah, you mustn't think like that. You mustn't wait for me. Promise me that you will have your season, either in Bath or London." He took her hand. "Promise me that you will enjoy yourself and flirt shamelessly with all your suitors and find a rich and worthy man to take care of you for the rest of your life." His voice was soft and full of emotion, like that of a man who expected to die.

"Do not worry about me," she said. Her eyes welled up with tears, and one tripped over her lid to run down her cheek. She did not care how long it took, she would wait for him.

"Promise me," he insisted.

She sniffed and said, "I promise I shall have my season."

He nodded and seemed satisfied with her answer. He reached into his waistcoat pocket and pulled out a stickpin, one a gentleman would wear in his cravat. It was a small butterfly encrusted with tiny diamonds and rubies. He offered it to her. "I want you to have this. It was given to me by my brother, who tries to make a proper gentleman out of me, but I cannot wear such a feminine thing. I want you to have it, and think kindly of me when you wear it."

She cradled it in her hands, then affixed the pin to her dress, just under the shoulder. "It is beautiful, thank you."

He shrugged his shoulders. "A trifle really."

She thought a moment, wondering what she could give him in return, when an idea struck her. "I want you to have something of mine as well."

"Susannah, you do not have to give me anything."

"But I do." She reached back and snatched a hat pin from her bonnet. It was made entirely of paste jewels, but it sparkled in prisms of blue and gold. "You may feel funny carrying around a lady's hat pin, but maybe you can use it as a weapon." Handing it to him, she giggled despite her tears.

"A wonderful idea." He smiled broadly and took the hat pin and settled it into the lapel of his uniform.

"And think of me when you wear it," she whispered.

"I will," he said. He looked up at the darkening sky. "Susannah, I must go."

"I know."

"Do take care." He took her hand and brought it to his lips.

"And you do the same."

He reached up and caressed her cheek, then walked away. Susannah watched his long strides take him away from her, and then she remembered to remind him. "Do be sure and write to us," she called after him.

He turned and smiled and waved. She forced herself to smile and wave in return, but her heart had never felt so heavy. She stood alone for what seemed like an eternity, when finally her aunt came to stand next to her.

"Are you all right, dear?" Aunt Agatha asked softly.

"Oh, I am so afraid for him." She sobbed and threw herself into her aunt's embrace.

Chapter Eleven

Due to the large meal served at the picnic, dinner was held late. Olivia entered the dining room with her aunt and sister and immediately looked for Sheldrake. He stood casually by Mr. Blessing in conversation. She took her seat as did the rest of the ladies. Slowly, she shook out her napkin and placed it upon her lap. Every fiber of her being hummed with the awareness of Sheldrake standing across the table from her.

She looked up to see if she could catch his attention, but he was still deep in discussion. With a sigh, she peered out the windows, shielding her eyes from the late-day sun's glare with her hand. The afternoon rain and clouds had cleared to reveal a brilliant sun about to set.

"Richard, pull the curtains, dear. The sunlight is getting in Olivia's eyes," Lady Evelyn said from the head of the table.

He turned to go to the windows, but Olivia held out her hand to stop him. "No need. The sun will soon set, and I do not wish to deprive anyone of the view. I shall simply move my chair." She started to push herself out of the chair.

"Richard, do help her," Lady Evelyn said as she rose from her seat.

In a moment he was behind her. She could feel the warmth of his body as he bent to help her rise.

"Good evening," he whispered, letting his lips caress her ear.

A tremor of pleasure raced down her spine, and she

looked about quickly to see if anyone noticed his intimate gesture. No one appeared to have seen a thing. Even Aunt Agatha did not pay a bit of attention to them.

He gently cupped his hands under her elbows to give her leverage as she rose. Lady Evelyn had walked over and now stood next to her. She asked her a question, but Olivia was too preoccupied with her son's nearness to hear her.

When Olivia finally turned to face her, she was taken aback by the odd expression on the lady's face. "Lady Evelyn, you were saying?"

Lady Evelyn stood staring at her a moment, then she shook her head. "It is nothing." She returned to her chair at the head of the table.

Olivia noticed that Lady Evelyn's hand shook when she unrolled her napkin. Sheldrake had moved Olivia's chair closer to his mother, to get out of the sun's glare. Once seated, she placed her hand over Lady Evelyn's. "Are you all right?" she asked.

"Yes, yes, please do not mind me." Lady Evelyn would not look at her.

She wondered what she had done to offend her hostess. She pondered it further, but could not be sure what had upset her. Everyone was seated, and soon the tureen of soup was served. She offered to fill Lady Evelyn's bowl.

"Thank you," Lady Evelyn responded, yet again without looking at her.

She reached out and placed her hand upon the older woman's hand, which trembled. "Please, let me know if I can be of any further assistance."

She earnestly searched the face of her hostess. When Lady Evelyn did look up into her eyes, Olivia thought the woman looked as though she beheld a ghost. Lady Evelyn stared at her with a haunted expression.

Olivia felt an icy chill grip her heart, constricting it, forcing it to beat harder. *What was wrong?* "Lady Evelyn?" she whispered.

Lady Evelyn's eyes widened, and then she stood abruptly. Her gaze never left Olivia's.

"Mother?" Sheldrake called. "What is it?"

He rose from his chair and came toward her, his expression grim. Lady Evelyn's head whipped around to her son. She finally blinked, but backed away from the table, knocking over her chair.

It crashed upon the floor.

Everyone, including the servants, went still. An eerie silence filled the room. Olivia watched as every movement made by Lady Evelyn progressed with a trancelike slowness. She was frozen in shocked silence, unable to do anything but stare as Lady Evelyn continued to act as if a terrible dream unfolded in visions that no one else could see.

Lady Evelyn, wild-eyed, backed up against the wall. She stared at nothing in particular, and she gripped her hair as though ready to pull it out.

"Mother!" Sheldrake reached out to her.

Then she screamed.

Olivia had never heard such a sound. Once started, Lady Evelyn did not stop. She screamed again and again, as if from the depths of her soul.

Olivia noticed that Susannah, tears running down her face, was nearly sitting in her aunt's lap. Aunt Agatha held her sister, but stared mutely at Lady Evelyn.

Sheldrake grabbed hold of his mother's arms, trying to calm her, but she fought against him. Mr. Blessing jumped up and raced toward them with a glass of wine.

"Richard. Oh, my dear son!" Lady Evelyn finally spoke in a hoarse, emotionally ragged whisper.

"No, Mother, do not talk now, here have a sip of this."

"No." She pushed the glass away, and it shattered when it hit the floor.

The wine seeped forward, leaving a dark pool of liquid on the gleaming wood.

Olivia watched Lady Evelyn stare at the stain. "So much

blood," Lady Evelyn murmured. "Why did you do it, Richard, why? You lost Belinda because of it."

A gasp was heard, and Olivia realized it had come from her. Lady Evelyn fell to the floor in a faint as Susannah let out a choked scream that sent everyone into motion at once.

Aunt Agatha bundled Susannah into her arms and took her out of the room. Sheldrake lifted his mother and shouted for someone to send for Doctor Pedley. Mr. Blessing quickly did his bidding. The two footmen also scattered at Sheldrake's orders to bring a blanket to his study along with burnt feathers.

Olivia sat as if she had been slapped.

But he needed her.

With a force of will that amazed her, she pushed all the horrible thoughts that were tearing through her aside. She stood and asked, "What can I do?"

"Come with me. I may need you," Sheldrake said, then he remembered her condition. "Can you?"

"Lead the way." She followed him out.

Walking behind him, she tried to swallow the lump of dread that seemed lodged in her throat. Nothing seemed real, and yet it was all too real. Lady Evelyn's nightmare had just enveloped them all.

Sheldrake took his mother to his study, where he laid her down upon the sofa. Stripping off his jacket, he quickly tucked it around his mother's bare arms. Olivia placed her shawl, bundled up as a pillow, beneath Lady Evelyn's head.

He sat quietly, holding his mother's limp hand.

Olivia walked to the shelf behind Sheldrake's desk. She opened the decanter and poured a healthy portion of what looked like brandy into a heavily cut crystal glass and handed it to him.

"Thank you." He took a deep pull as Mr. Blessing entered the room.

"How is she?" he asked Sheldrake.

"She is so cold."

Olivia stepped back as Mr. Blessing knelt by the sofa.

"Why did she react so, do you think?" Mr. Blessing asked.

"I do not know." Sheldrake turned to her and asked, "What did you say to her?"

"Nothing! She asked me a question, and I turned toward her to ask her what she had said. She looked at me in an odd fashion, then began to tremble and stood up and began to scream." She looked from Sheldrake to Mr. Blessing. "You must believe me."

"Of course," Sheldrake said, and she knew that he did.

She sat quietly in the chair behind Sheldrake's desk as the two men tried to rouse Lady Evelyn with burnt feathers and a vinaigrette the footman delivered, but to no avail. Over and over Olivia heard his mother's voice echo in her thoughts, *So much blood, Richard, why did you do it?*

The lump lodged in her throat gave way to a pain deep within her chest. *He lied. He had lied!*

She felt herself beginning to crumble inside, but she held herself together, she knew she had to. Now was not the time to come apart. She stared at Sheldrake until he caught her gaze over Mr. Blessing's head and stared back. He looked at her with such a desperate plea of sorrow and remorse that she looked away. She was transparent to him, and she knew he could tell what she was thinking.

She kept her eyes closed to block him out, and to rally as much strength as she could. Hot tears seared her lids, and she pressed her eyes shut even tighter until the tears subsided. She did not know how long she stayed that way, but when she finally opened her eyes, Sheldrake stood at the door with Doctor Pedley.

She gratefully rose from her chair and left the study when Doctor Pedley asked it of her. She was glad to leave. Her eyes burned. She made her way to her chamber, completely spent, and both Aunt Agatha and Susannah rushed to her side.

"Olivia, thank goodness. What happened? Has Lady Evelyn recovered?" Susannah asked.

"No, Doctor Pedley is with her now."

"But it cannot be true, it just cannot be." Susannah started to sniffle. "Lord Sheldrake is all that is kindness. He could not have murdered anyone."

"Susannah, please dear, why do you not go to your room, and I shall meet you there directly," Aunt Agatha said. When her sister hesitated, Aunt Agatha grew impatient. "Susannah, go, I do not want you to upset your sister."

"But I did not mean—" Susannah wailed.

"Not another word," their aunt scolded.

Susannah grabbed hold of Olivia's hand and placed a kiss upon it with a sob.

That was her undoing. The tears began to fall, and the lump in her throat only grew and threatened to choke her. Aunt Agatha guided her to the settee by the empty fireplace and motioned for Susannah to leave, which she finally did. Her aunt helped Olivia to sit. She took a pillow and crushed it to her chest, rocking slightly.

He lied to her.

"Stay right there. I shall fetch us some tea from Mrs. Boothe. That is what you need." Aunt Agatha darted out the door.

Lady Evelyn's words echoed again in her mind. *So much blood, Richard, why did you do it?*

Why did he do it, why did he kill Abbott?

Belinda's letter, the locked door to the conservatory, the fear in his eyes when she told him what she had discovered there—they all pointed to Sheldrake having killed the man. But what had triggered Lady Evelyn to react in such a way as if the demons of hell were coming to take her? Was she seeing what had happened to Abbott being played over in her mind?

After a time of quiet consideration, Olivia threw her pillow to the floor. She rubbed the tears from her eyes in anger. Sheldrake had said he did not murder Abbott. He had said that it was an accident! Should she believe him? she wondered. Was she jumping to conclusions again?

But the look in Lady Evelyn's eyes as she stared in horror at the wine soaking the floor was something Olivia would not easily forget. The woman was obviously seeing something else. Olivia's thoughts conjured up the stain on the conservatory floor. Perhaps the spilled wine looked like the blood Lady Evelyn had seen the night Abbott was shot. But why would Lady Evelyn ask him why had he done it unless he had been the one who killed Abbott?

Enough was enough, she decided. It was time that she found out what had happened that night. Sheldrake killed Abbott. His own mother accused him. But the reason why, and the circumstances were still a mystery.

How she wished that he had told her what happened so she did not have to wonder, so she could have been prepared, so she did not have to feel as though someone had just pulled the carpet from underneath her. Why didn't he tell her!

Because the last time he trusted a woman, she started the rumors about him, she heard her inner voice say. Did he fear that she would spread gossip as Belinda once did? Surely he knew her better than that.

Olivia was relieved when Aunt Agatha returned with a steaming pot. She could no longer think.

"Aunt, here, let me help you," she offered, starting to rise.

"No, stay. Heavens, you will have a shock or spasm of your own." Her aunt poured the tea. "His own mother accuses him, Olivia." Aunt Agatha did not look at her as she handed her a cup of sweetened tea.

"We do not know what really happened." Olivia said this for her own benefit as much as for her aunt's. "It was two years ago. We do not even know for certain what Lady Evelyn referred to." She sipped the hot tea. She knew it was a feeble statement.

"Oh, come now. We both know exactly of what she spoke."

"There is an explanation. There must be," she countered.

"Why must you defend him? He may be guilty, and the rumor may be true. If that is so, perhaps we should send for someone."

"No, Aunt. He did not murder his stepfather," she said.

"And how do you know this?"

"Because he said that he did not."

"And what of the rumors?"

"They were put about by his ex-betrothed, our own Lady Framingham."

"He told you that also?"

"Yes."

"And you believe him?" Aunt Agatha asked.

That was the real question, did she believe him? When she did not answer, her aunt shook her head.

"Tsk, tsk. Olivia, dear, you often see only what you wish to see. Be careful in whom you choose to trust. I do not want to see you hurt again." Her aunt wrapped her arms around her.

She let her head fall onto her aunt's shoulder and took comfort in the embrace. She had trusted Robbie and he neglected her. She had trusted her father and he had left her mother to die. Dare she trust Sheldrake?

And if she did, what would be the cost to her this time?

She felt the tears come again, and she turned her face into her aunt's bosom. Gently her aunt rocked her, soothing her in her own awkward way that was both endearing and comforting. Olivia let herself cry until she was spent.

"It will be all right," her aunt whispered. "I promise."

She sniffed, but continued to hold fast to her aunt, praying that she was right.

Sheldrake walked to the window. The moon was full like a huge yellow ball taking up so very much of the sky. It bathed the grounds with soft light, casting shadows from the trees. He let the curtains drop and looked back at the bed where his mother now lay still and unmoving, but breathing steadily. She was so pale.

He feared for his mother's sanity once she woke, if she woke at all. Looking up at the portrait of Abbott, he cursed the man depicted. The artist failed to capture the cruelty that lay beyond Abbott's sardonic smile.

He went back to the window, and anger burned in him anew at the dead man responsible for so much unhappiness. It appeared as though Abbott would truly destroy Sheldrake's mother as she remembered how her husband had died at her own hands. And he wished again, for the hundredth time, that it was in fact he who had killed the man— not his gentle, frivolous mother. And she had finally remembered what had happened. She remembered it all.

His mother had acted much the same at dinner as the night when Sheldrake had found her, clutching her hair, staring at the blood, Abbott's blood, spreading across the marble floor of the conservatory. A still-smoking pistol lay discarded at her feet. A chill ran through him, and he tried to clear the image from his head.

Resting his forehead against the cool glass, Sheldrake thought instead of Olivia. What could he possibly say to her? Even if he told her the truth, would she hear it from him? She had heard his mother's words as did the rest of them. He wondered if she would believe him. He wondered if he should even bother trying to tell her.

He knew what his mother had meant when she uttered those fatal words. Peter probably knew as well. She wondered why he had kept her from remembering, why he had taken the blame on himself at the cost of losing Belinda, and why he had not let anyone know it was his own mother who killed Abbott. He had done the right thing in protecting his mother, and he'd do it again. But would he have to protect his mother from Olivia?

Sheldrake recalled the look on Olivia's face after his mother's ranting had registered with her—sheer shock. She sat there completely stunned. Then as she stared through him in the study, Sheldrake thought his heart would break at the disappointment he saw in her eyes—the hurt.

He had to make it up to her somehow. His happiness seemed to depend upon her now. Sheldrake scuffed his boot against the wall, his heart full with the knowledge that Olivia brought back something precious to the Hall. She had brought back life. The kind of life his mother would need to heal, if it was possible.

He now understood what Blessing had tried to tell him. Without Olivia, his life would be meaningless. He had to tell her the whole sorry mess and hope to God that she would accept his love. He smiled despite the heaviness in his soul. He had come full circle as Olivia's song promised. He had found love again. He only hoped it was not too late.

He went to sit at his mother's bedside. Could he trust Olivia with the truth? At this point, he felt that he had to try. And perhaps if he could put things to right with her, he could tell her that he loved her and wanted above all things for her to be his wife. The rest was up to her.

Chapter Twelve

Olivia hesitated before entering the breakfast room. She had spent a fitful night tossing and had decided that she must speak to Sheldrake directly. But faced with the prospect of actually doing so, she experienced considerable doubt. She did not wish to appear insensitive, considering his concern for his mother. Perhaps now was not a good time to approach him. She stood there, outside the breakfast room door, looking for an excuse to turn tail and run.

But the subject of Lady Evelyn's outburst needed to be dealt with as soon as possible, and she believed that putting off an encounter with Lord Sheldrake might make matters only worse. She chewed her bottom lip for a moment before she entered the room.

The sideboard was laid with steaming dishes, and the coffee smelled fresh. Her gaze rested upon Mr. Blessing, the only person at the table.

"Ah, good morning, Lady Beresford. You are up at an early hour."

"I was thinking the same of you." She poured herself a cup of steaming coffee, then poured a considerable amount of milk and sugar into it and stirred.

"I am quite used to early mornings."

"But I thought the London crowd rose much later." She did not mean for her comment to sound sarcastic, but she wished Sheldrake was the one present instead of Mr. Blessing.

"But I am not in London now, Lady Beresford, and so I

rise with the sun. I've even enjoyed a brisk ride." He leaned back lazily in his chair.

"How very good for you." She did not even try to keep the disappointment from her voice.

He rose from the table. "Here, let me fill a plate for you."

"Thank you." She sat down with her coffee, keeping her hands around the tall cup to savor its warmth.

In silence, Mr. Blessing chose buttered eggs, a muffin, and a slab of ham, and soon the plate was put before her. Olivia remained silent as she took only two bites of ham and egg, then proceeded to move the rest of the food around on her plate.

"Have you lost your appetite?" Mr. Blessing asked.

"Yes, it appears I have." She set down her fork. "Tell me, is there any news of Lady Evelyn?"

Mr. Blessing took a sip of his coffee. "She remains unconscious."

"And Sheldrake? How is he?"

"As well as can be, under the circumstances, no thanks to you."

She jerked her head up at his harsh words. "What do you mean, sir?"

"Simply that you looked at him as though you saw him do the old man in yourself."

"And did he?" She flushed with anger. How dare he question her reaction!

"I am not at liberty to answer that."

"And yet you fault me for my suspicions after what happened last night, after what Lady Evelyn said."

"Yes, I do. You know what kind of man Shelly is. You know he is not capable of killing the likes of Abbott, no matter how much he wished he had."

"Then you are saying that Sheldrake did not kill Abbott at all?" Olivia narrowed her eyes.

"I am saying nothing."

"No, you are certainly saying something. Why not simply tell me and be done with it!"

"I am by honor bound not to. I gave Shelly my word I'd not breathe of it to anyone." He slumped back in his chair and dusted off a speck of crumb from his sleeve. His voice turned gentle. "I know this must be difficult, but you are a strong woman, Lady Beresford. Do not judge Sheldrake harshly until you have heard him out. He deserves that much." Then he rose, his coffee left half full. "If you will excuse me, I have some packing to do."

Alarmed, Olivia blurted, "You are leaving? How can you leave him like this?"

"I must. I have a bride to get back to. I leave at first light tomorrow."

"But . . ."

"Be supportive of him, Olivia. You are the one he needs."

As he walked past, she grabbed hold of his sleeve, embarrassed as she did so. "Mr. Blessing, please, can you not see—"

He cut her off. "He is a good man. The best I have ever known. Follow your heart, my dear, and let it guide you. The heart often knows far more than the mind."

He gave her an encouraging caress to her cheek, then left the room. She sat staring at the door, pondering his words. She felt utterly defeated in her plan to demand an explanation from Sheldrake. It would be cruel of her to do so. He must be ill with worry right now, she realized. No, it simply would not do to demand anything from Sheldrake just now. But should she simply sit tight and keep an open mind until Sheldrake sought her out? Or should she seek him and offer, what, her support?

She picked up her fork and bit into another piece of ham. It was delicious, but might as well have been sawdust for all she cared. She did not feel like eating. Dropping her fork with a clatter, she rested her head in her hands.

After sitting alone for half an hour, she could think of nothing better to do than wait and see what happened next. With a heavy sigh, she decided she had best eat something, and so was finishing half the contents of her plate when Susannah entered. "How are you this morning, dear?" she asked.

"Well enough." Susannah went to the sideboard to fill her plate. A servant entered to check the chafing dishes, making sure they were still hot. Susannah sat next to her and pushed the small portion of food she had chosen around on her plate. Olivia's heart twisted.

Once the footman had left, Olivia leaned forward. "I know this is hard for you."

"Lady Evelyn's illness or Captain Jeffries returning to war?" Susannah asked.

"Both I suppose."

Susannah only shrugged her shoulders, but then she turned to look into Olivia's eyes. "What are you going to do?"

She reached out and grabbed hold of Susannah's hand. "All I can do right now is wait."

"Do you think he did it?"

"I am not entirely sure what to think, Susannah. But I do care for Sheldrake, and I owe him the benefit of hearing what he has to say on the matter."

Susannah shook her head in agreement.

It was painful for all of them, even Aunt Agatha. Lady Evelyn and Sheldrake and even Mr. Blessing had become close friends and dear to their hearts. It was difficult to stand by knowing that there was little one could do.

By midafternoon Olivia had had enough of waiting. She had argued with herself over and over. Her heart told her to trust the man and let him explain in his own time what had happened. Her head told her to withhold her trust until she was sure of him, until she heard the truth and measured it accordingly. And her soul cautioned her not to act rashly and throw away a chance of happiness and her family's security based on suspicions and unknowns. She tossed her embroidery down upon the open sewing basket at her feet.

"What is it, dear?" Aunt Agatha asked.

"Nothing. I cannot keep my stitches in line and am dreadful sick of poking in and out without making any headway with the pattern." She rubbed her eyes.

With eyes of sadness Susannah looked up from a book where she had barely turned a page. Her heart was breaking over Captain Jeffries, and there was nothing Olivia could do to make anything better. Frustration seared through her. She felt utterly helpless at the moment.

A fire crackled cheerily in the grate, chasing away the afternoon chill that a late morning downpour had brought. She turned to look out of the window. The sky had darkened considerably and the rain had turned to a lifeless drizzle. There had been no change in Lady Evelyn's condition, and the house remained as quiet as a tomb. She worried about Sheldrake.

Dare she seek him out? Olivia had thought long and hard regarding her discussion with Mr. Blessing. She could not deny that she found some truth in what he had said. He obviously thought she was being oversensitive in her misgivings. He did not understand how much was at risk to her if she believed in Sheldrake, if she trusted him, and he proved to be false. She shifted with an uncomfortable groan.

"Olivia, are you well, dear?" Her aunt studied her.

"Yes, just a bit restless," she said. She continued to look out the window, watching the raindrops as they made slashes of water that trickled along the glass. Was she too lonely and scared to know a worthy man when he stood before her? For pity's sake, she thought, Mr. Blessing had nothing to gain by lying to her.

She rubbed her middle and felt the child roll slightly within her. She would deliver soon, she could feel it. She swallowed the panic that always threatened when she thought of what lay ahead. She needed a diversion, something to keep her thoughts away from Sheldrake and her baby.

"I am going to the library to look for another book," she said. "Aunt Agatha, should I bring one back for you, too?"

"No, dear, I wish to finish this for the baby." Her aunt held up the long clothes she was working on.

"The baby will not be able to wear that for a while. Would you not rather read?" Olivia asked.

"No, I want to complete this, but you go on ahead."

She did just that. She pushed herself up out of the chair and padded out of the door, down the main stairs and hallway to the library. Silently, she pushed open the door and came to a halt.

Sheldrake!

Standing in the doorway, she watched as he shelved a stack of books. They were heavy volumes she would never dream of reading let alone lift. He turned to her as if sensing her presence.

"I beg your pardon." Her heart beat faster as he looked at her. "I did not mean to intrude." She backed away, flustered, unprepared, and ready to retreat.

"Come in." He walked toward her, book in hand.

"I came for a book to read." She looked down at the thick text he held. "Did you read that?"

"Some of it."

"How is your mother?" She still had not entered the room.

"The same. I had hoped this might give me some insight as to how long she would remain unconscious." He held up the medical book.

"And does it?"

He only shook his head that it did not.

"I am so sorry." She knew it was an inadequate apology for what he had been through. He looked tired. The dark circles beneath his eyes spoke of a fitful night of little sleep.

"Come in." He motioned for her to enter. "Perhaps I can help you choose something to read." He held out his hand.

She walked toward him, but did not take his hand. All the bravery she had felt in the morning when she thought she should confront him and demand the truth had escaped her. She felt uncomfortable, awkward, and guilty for mistrusting him. And she was a little scared that she would decide that it did not matter what happened. She was more than tempted to care only about easing the tension from his face.

"Now then, what are you in the mood for?" he asked, his voice dull.

"I do not know. Susannah likes Mrs. Radcliffe. Do you have any of her novels?" She moved closer.

"I may." He turned and walked to the far end of a shelf, examining the bindings as he went. "Actually, I have quite a few. My mother must be fond of them. Which one would you like?"

She came up to stand behind him, scanning the various titles, trying to remember the ones Susannah had read to her. Her fingers tapped the tops of each book. "Perhaps this one."

He reached for the book and covered her hand with his own as he pulled the book from its space on the shelf. Her skin tingled where his fingers had touched her. She looked up into his eyes.

"What else might you like?" His voice was low and filled with unspoken emotion.

"To trust you," she whispered as tears filled her eyes.

"Olivia, do not."

Suddenly, she was in his arms, pushing to get closer to him.

His arms came around her. "What you heard, what my mother said, it is not what you are thinking." He squeezed her tight.

"I know." She threaded her fingers through his hair. Her heart beat wildly, and she felt as if a heavy load had been lifted from her. It was right to be in his embrace; this was where she belonged.

They stood there wrapped around each other for what seemed like a blessed eternity when Sheldrake finally pulled back.

"I must tell you the whole story, only I fear—"

"When you are ready," she interrupted him and traced his

eyebrow with her fingertip. She decided there and then that she would follow her heart one more time. She had to. If she did not, she could very well make the mistake of a lifetime. She was not sure if she knew this based on what Mr. Blessing had said or if her heart had finally won over her mind and soul. "I am not going anywhere."

This earned her a smile from him.

"I am glad of that." He cupped his hands around her face, and his thumbs made circles along her jaw. "I hope that you will stay here for a long while yet, forever really, as my wife."

She looked up at him. Warmth spread through her, and she thought perhaps for the first time that she could finally have it all. She opened her mouth to respond, but Sheldrake placed a finger across her lips.

"Do not answer me yet. I must explain what happened the night Abbott died. You may think differently once you have heard it, but I owe you the truth. This is probably not the right time, but I doubt a better one will present itself."

He guided her to a leather divan and made sure she was comfortable. He remained standing, looking unsure. "You said that you wanted to trust me. Well, I understand exactly how you are feeling. You see, I want to trust you. In fact, I am choosing to, right now, just by telling you this. Your reaction, what you do with what I tell you affects my mother more so than it does me." He ran a hand through his hair. He looked thoughtful as if trying to find where to start with his tale. "My mother was very lonely when she met Abbott." He hesitated.

"Yes," she encouraged.

"He stayed in the village at an inn, and they came across each other at the summer fair. I discouraged her from furthering the acquaintance," he said. "But I was called away to Scotland to see to some investments I had made that looked as if they would sour. In the time I was gone, Abbott had courted my mother feverishly. I returned to find her wed."

Olivia sat quietly as he stared into the flames, seemingly lost in thought.

"I checked into his background, of course, but could find nothing confirming Abbott was what he boasted himself to be—a wealthy nabob back from India. To the contrary, the man had enough debts amassed for a dozen men. Needless to say, I urged my mother to have the marriage annulled. She would not. She was not the same woman I had left but six weeks before. She was withdrawn and quiet." Sheldrake stopped, his jaw working.

She reached out to him, but he was deep in a memory, one that caused him pain.

"She had a bruise one day, Olivia, right here." He gestured toward his temple. "I asked her what had happened. She had her hair fixed to cover it but I saw it." His expression took her breath away. He looked terribly remorseful, as if he had failed somehow, and her heart broke for him.

"She said she had stumbled." His voice was lower and thick with emotion. "Abbott had hit her, the filthy cur. I took him to task and bloody near pulled his cork for it, but my mother intervened. She begged me to stop, to let her handle it. She said that it was simply a married couple's spat." He gained more control, and his voice changed to solid steel as he continued. "I swore I'd kill him if he ever raised a hand to her again."

"And did he?" she asked, understanding completely the rage he felt toward the man.

"Not that I could tell. In fact, the two acted like happy newlyweds for a time. Things had settled down, but then—"

Mrs. Boothe knocked rapidly, then opened the door. "Your lordship?"

"Yes?"

"Lady Evelyn is awake, my lord, and calling for you."

Sheldrake dashed to the door. Looking back, he quickly said, "Olivia, I am sorry, but I must go."

"I know. Go and see your mother." She recalled Mr.

Blessing's advice. She would heed his words and indeed give Sheldrake her support.

Whatever had happened, it appeared to be justified. She remembered the bruises her own mother sported after her father's drunken bouts. She had been only a child, but the anger she had felt was real. She imagined that it must have been very difficult indeed for Sheldrake to have held himself in check.

She understood why he was loath to tell her about his mother and Abbott. She knew the shame one felt at having a loved one, your own mother, treated so poorly, abused. She had been afraid to tell him about her own father, and she had not even shared the half of it with him. And of course, his experience with Belinda spreading rumors all over the countryside made him even more cautious in telling her the tale.

She wondered if Belinda knew about Lady Evelyn's treatment at the hands of Abbott or if Sheldrake had ever told her. Something told her that he had not. Belinda did not seem to be the kind of lady that one could ever tell such a story.

She tried to remember what Sheldrake had said about Belinda—that she needed a reason to break off her engagement with him, and Abbott's death presented the opportunity. Perhaps Belinda spread the rumors about him in order to gain the sympathy she thought she needed to leave Sheldrake without besmirching her reputation. That made her all the more horrible.

Olivia felt a twinge of guilt; had she not planned to catch a wealthy man to marry with no desire for love? She relaxed against the back of the divan. But she knew better now. She loved Sheldrake, and the signs were there that perhaps he would tell her he loved her in return. She decided that she believed in Sheldrake, and she knew it was the right thing to do. She also knew that Abbott's death was justified. Sheldrake would not have let it be otherwise.

As for his mother's outburst, she was not entirely sure

what to think other than perhaps Lady Evelyn came upon
her husband and her son in the middle of a coil. She may
have blamed Sheldrake before she knew what had happened. Or perhaps there was an accident after her son had
been provoked. Whatever the situation, she would support
Sheldrake and do what she could to help his mother to heal.

   She stood and decided to return to her chamber. She had
to leave the mystery alone for now. He would tell her, and
she would then finally know what had happened. No matter
what, she decided that she would trust him.

   Sheldrake entered his mother's apartment. The curtains
were drawn, steeping the room in darkness. He thrust them
open. The dull gray light of the sodden afternoon seeped
through the windows, giving the room more light. The tick
of the wall clock broke the silence. He feared for his
mother's sanity and wondered in what state he would find
her.

   He hesitated outside of her bedchamber door, hoping and
praying that she remained sane. After a deep breath, he
slowly entered the room.

   She lay still, propped up with pillows, her eyes closed.
She looked peaceful in her sleep. He glanced up at the portrait of Abbott. It would have to come down. She could not
stop him from removing it this time.

   The man in the portrait was well favored, even though
Abbott was well beyond his middle years at the time of the
painting. Abbott's lids rested arrogantly low over his eyes as
he stared out of the canvas in boredom. Those eyes seemed
to watch Sheldrake's every move, making the hairs on the
back of his neck itch.

   "It will be to the attics with you soon—or the fire," Sheldrake mumbled.

   "Is that you, Richard?"

   "Mama." He rushed to kneel at her bedside. "I did not
mean to wake you."

   "I was merely resting." Her voice sounded hoarse.

"How are you feeling? We have been very worried about you. You gave us a quite a scare."

"I know."

"Would you like some water?" He grabbed the pitcher and poured her glass.

"No, I have had my fill already." Tears welled up in his mother's eyes.

"Mama, don't." He reached out to his mother, but she sat up and flung her arms about his neck with a strong hold that surprised him considering her weakened state.

"Richard, I am so very sorry."

"There, there." He patted her back as she cried on his shoulder.

"B-but I ruined everything." His mother gulped air, then dissolved into broken sobs that tore at his heart.

"No, Mama, you ruined nothing. Truly, it will be all right now."

"B-but I killed him, I shot him, Richard, and killed him."

"I know."

"I deserve to be hanged, taken to Newgate."

"No!" Sheldrake thrust her back so he could see her face. "Mama, do not be ridiculous. You had the right."

Her face crumpled as she began to cry again in earnest. He rocked her gently as she used to do for him when he was a small child. They sat that way for what seemed like hours when a knock at the door brought Pedley peeking his head in as he opened the door.

He walked in and draped his coat across a chair. "How is she?"

"I am not sure. She has been weeping this age."

"Probably will do her some good."

"I can hear you," Lady Evelyn answered with a muffled voice. Her face rested against Sheldrake's lapel.

Sheldrake looked up at Pedley, who smiled encouragingly. "I'm sure you can, Lady Evelyn. Richard, I shall be here awhile, then I want to look in on Lady Beresford before I meet you in your study."

Sheldrake felt his mother stiffen, then she sat up with a wild look in her eye.

"No," she whispered.

"Mama, what is it?" He watched his mother look at the portrait, her eyes narrowing. "What is it?" He looked, too, trying to figure out what his mother was staring at. He exchanged a glance with Pedley. "I will have the portrait removed at once."

"No."

"Mother, it cannot be good for you to have to look at it."

"Yes, of course," his mother said in a distracted way.

"Here, I will leave you with Doctor Pedley, but I will come back and remove that bloody painting myself."

"Yes. That will be fine," she answered as if she had not truly heard him.

His mother continued to stare at the portrait. Sheldrake worried that she had lost her wits, and he looked at Pedley for guidance.

"I'll be down to speak to you directly, my boy." The doctor nodded toward to door.

So he left. He walked down the hall to Peter's chamber and knocked. Peter let him in and asked, "Well? How is she?"

"I do not know. She kept staring at Abbott's portrait."

"He had it coming, you know."

"I know that. I need to make sure that she knows it." Sheldrake flung himself in the chair at the end of the bed. "When do you leave?"

"Tomorrow at dawn. Do you wish me to stay?"

"No, no, we will be fine. Thank you for coming." He tried his best attempt at a smile.

"Have you spoken to Lady Beresford?" Peter continued to fold his cravats and place them in his bag.

"Yes. And I have asked her to marry me." He fingered his chin.

"Good show." A wide grin split his friend's face. "And did she say yes?"

"I would not let her answer, not until I have told her the truth. She may feel differently when she knows my mother shot her husband." He shifted uncomfortably.

"Lady Beresford's a good woman, Shelly. She will do right by you. And I don't think it'll make a bit of difference to her."

"I hope so."

"Count on it, my friend."

They talked more of Peter and the trials he had had with his new wife, when finally Sheldrake rose from the chair. "I will let you finish your packing. I must meet with Pedley in my study, but if you wish to join me there, we can share a brandy or have tea before dinner."

"Delighted. You look like you need it."

Sheldrake slapped his friend on the back and left the chamber to go to his study. He ran into Pedley in the hallway.

"How is she?" he asked.

"Distraught, filled with remorse and guilt, but otherwise in good shape for a woman who has suffered such a shock," Pedley replied.

"What about her mind? Does she have her wits about her?"

"I think that she does." The doctor put his arm around Sheldrake's shoulders. "You see, the mind is a delicate thing. At the time, I think your mother simply could not face what she had done. And then your betrothal was broken, something your mother thinks happened because of her. She continued to bury this incident deep within herself so she would not have to face it or come to grips with it. She is weak, tired, and will no doubt go through her grieving period, but otherwise I think she is fit and completely sane."

Relief flooded through him. "What can I do?"

"Encourage her and give her time to adjust to the knowledge of what she has done."

"He had it coming," Sheldrake said.

"Yes, he did," Pedley agreed. "She needs you to assure

her, as I have done, that what she did she did in self-defense. And get that maid, Sally, back here. She can help your mother get through this, too, I think."

Sheldrake nodded. He would ask Peter if the maid still worked at his brother's estate in Surrey and send for her. His thoughts immediately turned to Olivia, and he asked Pedley, "Lady Beresford—have you seen her?"

"Yes, and she is doing very well. Close to her time, so she needs to be kept calm. How is she reacting to all of this?" The doctor adjusted his coat that was draped over his arm. He had not bothered to leave it with Simms, the butler.

Sheldrake walked with the doctor down the hallway. "She does not know exactly what happened, as I have yet to tell her. But she has an idea and is taking it very well."

"A good woman."

"The finest," Sheldrake agreed.

The doctor slapped him on the back. "Good for you, son. And about time, too." He winked at him, and he realized that the doctor knew where his intentions lay.

At the door, Sheldrake shook Pedley's hand vigorously and thanked him for everything he had done for them. As he headed for his study to meet Peter, he felt as though his life was on the brink of taking a new and happy turn. Things would be far better than just normal from now on. And he knew destroying that blasted painting was the last step that would finally put the past to rest for good.

Chapter Thirteen

"Olivia, will you stop that pacing?" her aunt cried.

"Yes, yes of course." She sat back down in her chair by the fire. They had moved to the drawing room to await more news after hearing that Lady Evelyn had recovered somewhat. But they heard little else since Doctor Pedley had left. She picked up her embroidery and stared at the stitches, her fingers working the frayed edges of the muslin.

She glanced at Susannah, who lay stretched upon the chaise, her book in her hands. She was making some progress. Susannah had actually turned a few pages, but she stared out the windows into the dreary afternoon with a faraway look in her eyes. She worried for her Captain Jeffries, and nothing Olivia or Aunt Agatha said had helped matters. They all knew the danger he faced.

With a gasp of pent-up frustration, Olivia stood again. Her back ached, and she could sit no longer.

"For pity's sake, go find the man and have done with it," her aunt admonished her.

"Thank you, Aunt. I simply must know how his mother fares. Sheldrake may . . ."

"Need you?" her aunt finished for her.

"Yes, is that a crime, to want to be needed?" She felt ridiculously close to tears.

"Heavens, child, no! It is not a crime at all. Now, tell me what is truly troubling you." Her aunt looked up at her with concern-filled eyes.

She was not sure where to start. She did not know if it was

the unfinished explanation of Abbott's death, or the unknown condition of Lady Evelyn that caused her fidgets. "Sheldrake has asked me to marry him," she said in a tumble of words.

Susannah dropped her book. She sat at full attention. "What did you say?"

"I have not given him an answer. He would not let me, not yet. Not until he has explained to me what happened to Abbott." She looked at her aunt, waiting for her response. When none came, she continued, "It makes perfect sense to say yes. My child would be assured of a future, and Susannah could have a season." She felt the need to point out the positives of the match to her aunt.

"Do not marry on my account," Susannah said with her hand raised. "I would feel terrible if you did not suit."

Olivia turned to face her aunt, sitting on the settee, and waited.

Finally her aunt said, "She is right. You must not marry to benefit others, my dear. You must marry because it is what you truly want and what you know is the right thing to do. You married Beresford impulsively and look where that left you."

"This is different. I am older now."

"I tell you there is but one reason to marry."

Olivia wrung her hands. "Love, Aunt Agatha?"

"Yes, dear. Love and trust." Her aunt continued to gaze at her, until Olivia felt almost nervous at such scrutiny.

"I do love him." She said it simply and aloud for the first time, even though she had felt it for some time.

She had loved her father and even Robbie, yet both had left her, hurt her, and made her unwilling to experience that kind of pain again. Although she had decided to follow her heart and chose to trust Sheldrake, she could not help but feel some uncertainty, some lingering sense of doubt.

You may think differently once you hear the truth, he had said.

Would she? Would the truth shatter what she felt for him? Trust was beginning to bloom within her soul, and she did not want anything to shake it loose. Abbott's death had to be justified.

"Have you not noticed that I stopped warning you to stay away from Lord Sheldrake?" her aunt asked.

It was true, she had not scolded her lately. "I had not noticed. Tell me what changed your mind."

"Many things, really. I cannot say that his kindness toward us has not impressed me. I like him, Olivia, I genuinely like him very much indeed. But more so, I like what I see when he is with you. He respects you and looks upon you with real affection. He is true, my dear, and if you can accept what happened to this Mr. Abbott, well then, so will I. I will trust your judgment."

Olivia's heart swelled with warmth, and she bent to hug her aunt. It was as if she and her aunt had forged a new and stronger relationship. Her aunt's approval and trust in her meant so very much. She no longer had to prove anything; she could rest assured in her decision.

Perhaps that had been part of her problem when she had married Robbie. She thought she knew herself so well. She had never stopped to consider that her aunt's notions were correct, that Robbie was not the man for her. And it had been true, he had not been.

Olivia glanced up at the clock. It was nearly three hours since Doctor Pedley had left her. He had given her no details other than Lady Evelyn was as well as could be expected. Since then, she had looked in on Pockets, who now lazed about in the stables recovering nicely, and she had worked on her embroidery. But Sheldrake had not sought her out.

Her thoughts straining for a solution to her restlessness, she wandered across the floor to stand before the windows. She stared out over the gardens to the wrought iron bench where she had sat with Sheldrake on several occasions. She could not imagine a life without him. In the short time she had been at Sheldrake Hall, had come to know its lord, he had become a part of her.

And he might need her. She knew she should go to Lady

Evelyn's chamber and offer her help, even if it meant sitting by her side and reading to her. It was nearly time for tea—as good a time as any. She turned and headed for the door, determined to do something.

"I shall return shortly," she said as she grabbed her shawl from the back the chair.

"Be certain, my dear. Be sure of him and of you." Her aunt nodded.

"I will, Aunt."

She glanced back at her sister, who gave her an encouraging smile, then she let the drawing room door close with a quiet click. She headed down the hall and entered the library. Skimming the shelves, she pulled down a book of John Donne's poetry and headed for Lady Evelyn's chambers.

The Hall was still quiet, but not nearly so tomblike as earlier in the day. Servants bustled about their daily duties. They must have heard that Lady Evelyn had awaken; the tense, furrowed brows she had seen earlier in the morning had eased. Once upstairs, she came upon the housekeeper carrying a tray laden for tea, struggling for balance.

"Can I help you with that, Mrs. Boothe?" she asked.

The housekeeper tried to keep a biscuit from rolling off the tray. "Oh, my lady, your condition." Mrs. Boothe hesitated, but looked very much in need of a second pair of hands.

"Here, I shall take this plate of biscuits that is giving you so much trouble. There, see, it is no strain at all."

"Thank you, my lady."

"Is this for Lady Evelyn?" she asked.

"Yes, and I am so grateful that she is well. She will recover fully in no time."

Olivia nodded with overwhelming relief and not a little bit of annoyance that Sheldrake had not informed her. But then she knew that there were any number of things that demanded his attention. She simply lacked patience.

She followed Mrs. Boothe through the hallway until finally they stopped before a set of paneled doors. Clutching the book of poetry closer, she hoped she was not too forward in coming. She could only assume that Sheldrake had not come to find her because he was sitting with his mother. Perhaps she could take some of the strain off him by reading to Lady Evelyn if his mother was up to having the company.

Mrs. Boothe spread wide the double doors to the apartments that were more than spacious. They entered a large sitting room decorated in shades of peach. A huge fireplace took up a good portion of the wall with two sofas facing each other next to the hearth. A fine rosewood desk and chair stood near the window.

The drizzly day out of doors could not dampen the coziness of the room. The fire blazed in the grate, and the set of doors leading to the bedchamber also stood opened wide. Olivia hesitated slightly as Mrs. Boothe stepped toward the bedchamber. Perhaps she should not go farther. She had not been invited and hoped that she was not intruding.

She inched forward. She would stay but a moment if Lady Evelyn was not feeling well enough for a visitor. The least she could do was offer her best wishes. Pushing aside her doubts, she followed Mrs. Boothe into the bedchamber. Her heart skipped a beat when she spied Sheldrake standing by the window.

He turned to acknowledge Mrs. Boothe as she set down the tray. Then he noticed her, and Olivia smiled at him. He looked surprised, but not at all displeased with her for coming into his mother's apartment. An answering smile curved his lips, and her insides grew warm. She could not tear her gaze away from him.

But he broke eye contact with her, and then she remembered where she was and why she had come. She looked at Lady Evelyn, who stared back at her with a strange look. It was different than the expression the night of her spell, but still Lady Evelyn looked puzzled, almost troubled. Olivia realized she should not have entered without an invitation.

She bowed. "Forgive me, I meant no intrusion."

"Not at all. My mother is much more the thing this afternoon." Sheldrake held out his hand to her. "Stay just for tea; she could use your company."

"If that is agreeable to you, Lady Evelyn?" She stepped forward. "I do not wish to tire you."

Lady Evelyn met her gaze and shook her head as if to clear it, then smiled. "Please do stay and take tea with us."

She continued to hold the plate of biscuits as Mrs. Boothe pulled the small tea cart near Lady Evelyn's bedside around and into the center of the room.

"Olivia, here, let me take that from you so you can sit down." His fingers touched hers as he took the plate.

Her entire arm felt his touch, and warmth flooded her heart. It was going to be all right. Lady Evelyn was well, and Sheldrake wanted to marry her. She glanced about to find a straight-backed chair and noticed one at the end of Lady Evelyn's bed. She turned to get the chair, then glanced at the fireplace and saw it.

She felt the pit of her stomach coil in horror and the edges of her mind turn suddenly fuzzy. Her heart raced, and she reached behind her for something to lean against, but there was nothing for her to grab for support. A portrait of a man with eyes the color of green so like her own faced her. It leaned precariously against the fireplace, an enormous painting of a man she thought she would never come face-to-face with again.

Dear heaven, a portrait of her father!

Olivia continued to back up. She felt as if she had been hit with something hard, and she held tight to her middle. Her breath had been knocked out of her as she gulped but could not get enough air.

"Olivia?" Sheldrake whispered as he came toward her.

She felt as if she were moving in a dream, a bad one. Her body was dull and leaden. "Where . . ." she choked out, "where did you get that?" She grasped her belly with one hand while her other hand continued to search for something solid behind her. She connected with one of the bedposts.

She backed toward it, feeling the pole wedge between her shoulder blades, and she leaned against it.

"What is it? What is wrong?" Sheldrake asked. He was next to her in an instant, his hand cupping her elbow for support.

"That man in the portrait . . . that man is my father." She heard the words come out of her mouth as if from a great distance. The humming in her ears threatened to drown out all sound.

In a panic, she glanced toward the bed. Lady Evelyn, poor Lady Evelyn, struggled to get up and walk toward her, her eyes sad and filling with tears. Olivia wished she had never come into this room!

She looked back at Sheldrake, and his expression was stone, his face ashen. He tried to guide her from the room, but her feet would not move and she held onto the post as if it could save her, keep her from falling into the darkness that threatened to overtake her.

The portrait was of her father! But why was it in Lady Evelyn's bedchamber? Then suddenly the answer came to her with painful reality. "Sheldrake," she whispered as he lifted her, "your Mr. Abbott is my father."

The thunderous hum in her ears blacked out the light from her eyes, but she heard his muttered oath before all went quiet.

Sheldrake scooped her up in his arms. Striding to one of the sofas in the sitting room, he laid her down gently.

"The poor dear. I thought maybe, but I was not sure. They really do not look alike, 'tis only the color of her eyes, her expression. Oh, what have I done! The dear girl," his mother babbled, tears streaming down her cheeks.

His insides were at war, and the cannons were aimed directly at his heart. And it burned where the shots hit him. *Abbott was her father!* Of all the . . . how? His head screamed in agony at the implications, at the knowledge of why she had seemed familiar to him. She did not look like Abbott, she did not! But his mother was right, there was something in the

color of her eyes and Abbott's that were similar. Why did he
never see it before?

"Mrs. Boothe, get Pedley back here now," Sheldrake
barked. He turned to his mother and added with a quiet voice,
just above a whisper, "When did you know this?"

"I think that evening at dinner when I had my spell. Something in the way the light played off her face, the expression
she had. It reminded me so much of Abbott that it all came
crashing in. My memory had returned."

He stayed quiet as he watched his mother smooth a stray
curl from Olivia's face, then finally he said, "You should not
be up, Mama."

She ignored him. "Poor dear. This is quite a shock."

He shook his head, defeated. Why had he not removed the
bloody portrait as soon as he had entered her chamber as he
said he would! Why had he lingered in his study with Peter
when he should have been destroying Abbott's portrait?

He knew there was no sense in telling Olivia what had
happened to Abbott. She would never accept him. Even if he
kept up with the farce that it had been an accident, or wove a
tale to protect his mother, no matter what he told her, the fact
remained that Abbott was her father and he had died at Sheldrake Hall.

But he knew that he owed Olivia the truth, and that was
the worst part. Was it better to let her think he had done Abbott in himself, or tell her the truth that it was his mother who
had killed her father. *Her father!* The look on her face when
she recognized the man in the painting was stamped into his
mind. He would never forget her widened eyes, her paleness.
Her words just before she fainted were lodged in his gut.
These words tore at him, made him sick.

"Richard?"

He jumped when his mother touched his shoulder.
"What."

"We have to tell her, dear. We owe her the truth," she said
softly.

"She need not know about your part in it."

"I will not have you protect me any longer. Not at the expense of your own happiness again."

He looked at Olivia's still form. He caressed her cheek with bitter dread. He touched her neck and found a strong pulse there. Then he rose from the floor where he knelt and went to the window to look out across the rain-soaked gardens. It did not matter what he told her; it was over for them. "Will she be all right?"

"She has fainted, dear. I am certain she will be just fine."

Mrs. Boothe entered the chamber with feathers to burn and a pot of sal volatile. He turned to his mother. "I will tell her aunt, and then I will be in my study."

Olivia gasped and pushed the offending smell away from her nose. She tried to focus and saw two pairs of concerned eyes staring intently at her. Lady Evelyn and Aunt Agatha hovered over her. She frowned. Something terrible had happened. She tried to remember. Suddenly, the memory of seeing that portrait rushed in on her with actual physical pain. She felt it deep within her, an ache that took her breath away.

Sheldrake had killed her father. But it had been an accident, or self-defense. And her father had beat his mother. She looked at Lady Evelyn, and their gazes locked. What did she think of her? Olivia thought desperately. Her father, Charles Lacey, had been posing as Abbott, the man who had made Lady Evelyn miserable. Olivia looked away from her, utterly bereft and unsure what to do.

Sheldrake!

Another pain grabbed hold of her, and it was hard to breathe. She tried to sit up when she felt an odd sensation. A trickle of wetness escaped from her. *Oh, no!*

Terrified, she knew this must be what Doctor Pedley had explained as losing her fluid before her baby was born. *Not now. Surely not this instant!* She closed her eyes tightly, trying to think of what she should do.

"Olivia dear, can you hear me?" Lady Evelyn asked with concern.

She opened her eyes. Sheer panic choked her; her throat felt as if it were closing.

Lady Evelyn's gaze narrowed slightly, then she looked down at the wetness that had formed a dark stain on Olivia's dress. "Oh, I see," she whispered.

She watched in silence as Lady Evelyn whispered to Aunt Agatha. Her aunt went pale.

"Aunt Agatha," Olivia croaked. Tears spilled from her eyes. She was so afraid, so very afraid of what was to come.

"There, there, Doctor Pedley has been sent for." Her aunt nervously patted her hand.

Her mind raced from her upcoming delivery to the revelation of her father's last identity. Did Aunt Agatha know Abbott was her father? She fervently prayed that Lady Evelyn had not told her. It was something best left alone for now. Seeming to understand her distress, Lady Evelyn shook her head no, then nodded toward the bedchamber. The doors were closed.

"Try to relax. Try to rest," Lady Evelyn said as she stroked her forehead.

"You are the one who should be resting," Olivia said, and she lay back, relieved that her aunt had no knowledge of the portrait.

"Gracious, yes," Aunt Agatha admonished. "Lady Evelyn, please do return to your bed. I can wait with Olivia until Doctor Pedley arrives."

"Nonsense, I am fine," Lady Evelyn said.

Olivia knew the woman fibbed. She looked wan and stretched to the breaking point as well. Even so, she reached out to her and grabbed hold of her hand. Lady Evelyn squeezed tightly in return.

She hoped that Lady Evelyn could forgive her for having Abbott as her father. *Strange,* she thought of him quite easily as Abbott instead of his real name. It was easier that way, as if he were not truly any relation to her. She hoped they could all get through this.

"Where is Sheldrake?" Olivia asked.

"In his study, dear," Lady Evelyn said.

"Is he all right?"

"He will be. Do not worry." She stroked her head again, then got up to pull a couple of chairs closer to the sofa.

Aunt Agatha continued to pat her hand, and she did not let go, even after she sat down. She looked terribly nervous, like a frightened rabbit ready to bolt at any moment. Had Olivia felt more lighthearted, she would have smiled at her aunt's expression. But she was not light of heart, she was afraid. She was not certain that she would live to see her baby's face.

Minutes passed, and she watched the clock on the wall. The ticking sound soothed her somewhat as she waited for the doctor's return. Her pains came every quarter hour. She rubbed her belly, hoping to quell the discomfort, but to no avail. The next quarter hour the aches returned on schedule.

She wondered about Sheldrake. He was in his study, no doubt reeling from the news, from the realization that he had killed her father. She hoped that Mr. Blessing was with him. For all the man's charm, Peter Blessing could be a surprisingly level-headed fellow.

A fierce longing for Sheldrake took hold of her. She wanted him, needed him, to be with her. She wished it were he that held her hand and gave her words of encouragement. He had promised her everything would be all right, that she would not die as her mother did. She concentrated on those promises he had told her. She recited them over and over in her head in an attempt to believe them.

A knock at the door caught her attention. Hoping it was Sheldrake, she could not keep from being disappointed when only the doctor entered.

"So, your time has come, has it?" he asked.

"It appears that way." She tried to smile, but even that was too much.

Doctor Pedley leaned over her and felt her abdomen. "How quickly are your pains coming?"

"Every quarter hour."

His brow cleared as he said, "You have time yet, Lady

Beresford, do not worry." Then he turned toward Lady Evelyn. "And you should be resting, my lady. You looked completely pulled."

"Yes, but . . ." Lady Evelyn glanced at her.

"Do, rest, Lady Evelyn." Olivia did not wish to see the lady suffer a relapse. "I shall be fine." But she knew she lied. Olivia wished that she could stay with her. She had borne Sheldrake, surely she had not forgotten. But she could not demand such a thing, not at the risk of Lady Evelyn's own health.

Finally, Lady Evelyn nodded in agreement.

"We can move you to your own chamber, Lady Beresford," Doctor Pedley said. "It will do you good to get comfortable, perhaps have a cup of tea and relax. We have plenty of time yet."

She nodded.

Lady Evelyn bent over her and kissed her forehead. "Do not worry, my dear. Everything will be fine, you shall see."

Olivia felt the tears starting again, and she cleared her throat with a cough. "Thank you," she whispered.

Aunt Agatha was on one side of her and the doctor on the other as they helped her to stand. She could walk, but they argued that they would both support her as they slowly exited Lady Evelyn's apartment.

They entered Olivia's sitting room to find Susannah curled up by the fire, reading. At the interruption, she looked up and her eyes widened. She rushed to her side. "Oh, thank goodness! I was worried when Aunt was summoned. Is it the baby?"

"Yes," Olivia answered with gritted teeth and in the middle of a pain.

"Come draw back the coverlet," Aunt Agatha told her sister.

Susannah rushed to fling back the covers. "Will the baby come now? Please let me stay with you."

"No!" Olivia answered too sharply. When she saw the hurt on her sister's face, she turned to her aunt. "Do not let her come in, I do not want her to see me if I . . ." She could not finish the statement, but her aunt understood.

"Hush, now." Aunt Agatha patted her shoulder. "You will be fine, dear, everything will be just fine."

"But I can help," Susannah protested, only to be silenced with a look from Aunt Agatha.

"It will be a good while before the baby is born," Doctor Pedley explained. "The best thing is to make Lady Beresford as comfortable as possible. Help her change into a nightdress, and I shall return."

"Where are you going?" Olivia asked wildly as he headed for the door.

"His lordship will want to know, my dear. And of course, I want to make sure Lady Evelyn is resting. I won't be long," he replied evenly.

Again she wished that she could speak with Sheldrake, that she could send him a message through the doctor. But she could not seem to form the words as the doctor left the room.

Olivia sat in anxious silence as her aunt and sister fussed over her until she felt ready to scream at them both. Her aunt, always frightened of any show of blood or injury, looked pale as a sheet. Her forced cheerfulness began to grate on her nerves as did Susannah's pleading to stay and watch the birth. She continued to refuse her. She did not want her sister to see her die.

The truth of the matter was that she did not wish for either of them to stay with her during the birth. She feared that if she had trouble as her mother had, then their last image of her would be her horrible death. They both had to leave when the time came.

Once tucked into a warm bed, and relatively comfortable except for the pains that racked her body, she wondered what Sheldrake was thinking and feeling. If only she could speak with him and make him understand that she knew what her father was like. She remembered clearly the cruelty he had been capable of inflicting. His death had to be justified.

"Would you like some tea, dear?" her aunt asked.

Shaken from her thoughts, Olivia agreed, then turned to Susannah. "Perhaps you could read to me?"

Her sister smiled and chose Byron's latest work that lay on the nightstand next to Olivia's bed. It was the first book Sheldrake had given her in what seemed like ages ago when their carriage had overturned. It seemed so long ago that she had felt afraid of him as he had watched her during the ride in his carriage to the Hall. So much had changed since then.

A servant arrived with the tea her aunt had ordered. Olivia sipped the sweetened brew and tried to concentrate on Byron. But her thoughts kept slipping. She wondered when her father had returned to England or if he had ever left. That he had not once tried to communicate with her or Susannah made her insides burn with anger. He had never cared for either of them.

A heaviness settled upon her heart. She grieved not so much for hearing that her father was dead. She expected that he had died years ago. In truth, had not she wished him dead many times in the years since he had left them? No, she grieved more because she had never had a loving father—a man a daughter could look up to as Sheldrake did his father.

Sheldrake!

He must think she could not bear to look upon him. A pain racked her body, and she tensed, breathing heavily and gripping the sheets.

Susannah paused in her reading. "Does it hurt terribly?"

"Yes." Her voice was hoarse, and she let her breath out in a whoosh when the pain subsided.

Aunt Agatha set her dish of tea down with a clink, then got up and walked to the windows to look out over the drive. Even more pale, her aunt's brow furrowed, and Olivia knew that her aunt would fare better in her own room, or in the drawing room where she could work on her needlepoint or pace. It was difficult for her aunt to remain motionless when she was nervous or upset. Olivia had picked up the same trait, so she easily recognized her aunt's anxious state of mind.

"Aunt Agatha, you need not stay. Susannah will read to me until Doctor Pedley returns."

But her aunt shook her head and sat back down at her bedside.

As the minutes passed into an hour, Olivia tried to lay as quietly as she could considering her pains were coming faster and her fear of the coming event increased. Doctor Pedley had not returned. Aunt Agatha seemed to grow whiter with every pain Olivia experienced.

Another pain took hold, and she braced herself for it, but could not keep from gasping and doubling up from it.

"That seals it! I am going to fetch the doctor!" Aunt Agatha announced and rushed from the room.

Olivia threw her head back against the pillows as the sharp ache crested, then finally began to recede. Waves of pain were washing over her, climbing and gaining in force, only to ebb and recede, leaving her hot and tired from the effort to fight them.

"Can I get you something?" Susannah asked, a worried frown marring her delicate skin.

"No, please read on. But once the doctor comes, then you will have to go."

"But if there is something I could do for you, hold your hand, I do not want you to be alone."

Olivia reached out, took hold of her sister's hand, and looked deeply into her eyes. "Susannah, if something should happen to me, if I should die as Mama did, I do not want that to be your last image of me."

Tears trickled down her sister's cheeks. She sniffed and wiped them away. "But—"

"Please understand," Olivia urged.

Finally, Susannah conceded and nodded her head. "What happened to Mama will not happen to you. She had been sick and was weak—you said so yourself."

"Yes," she whispered. It was true, her mother had not

been well. "And I will not be alone. Doctor Pedley will be with me and Mrs. Boothe. Do not worry. Go ahead and finish reading this page."

Olivia thought about her sister's words. In all her fears and panic, she had never stopped to consider that their mother had been in poor health before Susannah had been born. Their mother had been sickly for as long as she could remember. This gave her some relief, and she felt an odd mix of both excitement and dread. She looked forward to holding her newborn babe in her arms and rocking the tiny mite to sleep.

If she lived.

Images of her mother, deathly pale and exhausted, rose before her mind's eye as she called out for her father. *No!* Do not think of that, she told herself. Focusing on the canopy overhead, she lay still, forcing herself to focus on anything but thoughts of death.

Her sister read on as another pain took hold of Olivia. She turned her face into her pillows. She tried to breathe evenly, but ended up panting. A sick feeling settled in the pit of her stomach. Sweat trickled down her forehead to mix with the tears that flowed from her eyes.

Why did Abbott have to be her father? she thought wildly. Why did such a terrible man sire her? Why did he leave their mother to die, and why did she have to see it and now remember it all so vividly?

"Olivia?" Susannah asked as she gently touched her shoulder.

"Please see what is taking the doctor so long. Will you go find him?" Olivia sobbed.

"But Aunt has just left and I do not want to leave you," Susannah said.

"Please just find them."

Susannah kissed Olivia's cheek and promised her she would rush the doctor along.

It seemed as though an eternity had passed since she had been in Lady Evelyn's apartment. She lay on the bed, trying to reassure herself that she would be all right. She clung to Sheldrake's promise and Susannah's words that what had happened to her mother would not happen to her.

When Doctor Pedley entered her chamber with Mrs. Boothe in tow, pain after pain took Olivia and held her in its grip. Mrs. Boothe swathed her face with a cool cloth, and Olivia merely prayed silently that it would be over soon.

"Ah, now we are getting somewhere," the doctor said with a laugh. "I believe we can begin now."

Olivia groaned.

Doctor Pedley reassured her how wonderfully she was doing and that in no time she would have her baby in her arms as reward for her labors. He ordered the housekeeper to send for hot water and clean linens.

It was time.

Her mind racing, Olivia suddenly wondered what would be the fate of her child should she not live. Her aunt would surely take the babe in, but what of cousin Edmund, Robbie's heir? If she bore a son, he would be heir to Adberesmere and all alone. Edmund might require the child to live with him. Was taking the child away within his legal right? This new fear gripped hold of her, and she could not shake it loose. Not yet.

She needed to ask Sheldrake to look into the matter. She pulled herself up against the pillows. He would help her. He would see to it that the child was protected.

"My lady, please lie back. You will strain yourself." Mrs. Boothe hurried to her side.

"No. I must see Sheldrake," she said.

"Later, Lady Beresford, we have pressing business to attend to." Doctor Pedley rolled up his sleeves.

"It may be too late! I must see him. I demand that I see him. This is important, a matter of life and death!"

He nodded to the housekeeper to oblige her request, and Mrs. Boothe rang for a footman.

Chapter Fourteen

Sheldrake poured himself a second brandy. He had been sitting in his study, staring blindly at the flames from the fireplace ever since he had left his mother's apartment. After emptying the contents of the glass, he held his head in his hands. *Her father! Abbott was her father!*

Obviously, Abbott was not the man's real name; it was something Lacey. Olivia had mentioned his Christian name, he thought. No wonder he had such trouble finding information on the man's background. A scratch at the door brought his head up. "Enter."

Peter Blessing stepped into the room. Once he saw the decanter of brandy, he frowned. "I wanted to look in on your mother, see if she is up to a visit this evening, since I am leaving so early in the morning. How is she?"

Sheldrake cleared his throat, not sure he wanted his friend's company just then. "She is well and resting."

"So, why the brandy?"

He did not feel much like answering, and that was his mistake; Peter knew something was wrong. Peter sat in the chair opposite him, leaned forward, and asked, "Do you wish to talk about it?"

He looked his friend in the eye. "No, I do not."

"It is Lady Beresford, then."

"You do not give up, do you." He stood and walked the short distance to stand directly in front of the fireplace. The warmth of the flames did nothing to chase away the chill that had taken hold of his heart, his soul.

"I am nothing if not persistent." Peter lounged back in his chair and waited.

"Abbott is Olivia's father," Sheldrake said in a dull voice.

"How the devil is that so? What happened?" Peter asked in astonishment.

"She saw the portrait, the one I told you I was going to destroy. It appears her father had been exiled from England, but instead of leaving, he simply assumed another name. Who knows how many other names he used before settling on Abbott and making my life a living hell."

"What did she do?"

"Do?" He ran a hand through his hair. "She fainted."

"And is she all right—what happened when she came to?"

Sheldrake shifted uncomfortably. He had turned tail and run like the coward he was, before she had come back to her senses. He could not bear to see her pain-filled eyes. He knew he could not have watched her expression turn to contempt, scorn, or disgust for him at what he had done, or what she thought he had done to her own father. "I do not know. I left her with my mother and Mrs. Boothe, then fetched her aunt."

"I see."

Sheldrake turned to face him and shrugged.

"And what will you tell your lady when she asks for you?" Peter asked, his frown deeper.

"The deuce if I know."

A knock at the study door interrupted Sheldrake's gloomy thoughts. Could he not simply be left alone? "Enter," he barked.

Pedley stuck his head in before entering. He noticed the brandy and shook his head. "That'll not solve your troubles, dear boy," he said as he entered.

"How is she?" Sheldrake asked.

"She is set to give birth."

"Now?" Sheldrake's heart raced.

"Not for a time yet, but soon enough. I have sent one of

your servants for a wet nurse," Pedley said. "It may have been the shock at seeing that portrait of her father that got everything moving."

"My mother told you then."

"Yes. And she is resting now, as is your Lady Beresford."

Sheldrake refilled his glass, not bothering to offer some to the doctor or to Peter. "Of all the bloody luck!" he muttered.

"She is a smart gel. Tell her the truth of the matter." Pedley took the bottle and put the stopper firmly in place.

"He's right, you know," Peter added.

"It was her father. What difference does it make what I tell her? Abbott was Olivia's father." He looked at the two men as if they had both lost their wits thinking she could overlook what had happened. "Nothing I say or explain will ever change that!"

Sheldrake drained his glass and reached for the bottle again. He shot a look of disgust at the doctor and removed the cork. *Of all the people in the world,* Sheldrake thought miserably, *why did Olivia have to be Abbott's daughter? Why did he have to love Abbott's daughter? Why did any of it have to happen at all!*

He sat there quietly swirling the brandy in his glass as both Peter and Pedley looked on. He knew he had to pull himself together. Olivia needed him to be strong. And he needed to remain sober enough to make sense of this situation. He rose from his chair and put both the decanter and his glass firmly on the shelf. Then he turned and asked, "How on earth do I tell her what happened?"

Susannah paced the carpeted floor of her bedchamber. She had come upon Mrs. Boothe and Doctor Pedley in the hallway moments after leaving Olivia in search of them. She knew that her sister was in good hands, but it still hurt that she had made her leave. Olivia was being completely irrational in forbidding her to stay with her until the baby was born. The worst part was that there was nothing Susannah could do or say to take the fear of death away from her sister. She felt so helpless knowing there was nothing she could do but wait and pray.

She wondered what it must have been like for Olivia, a scared little girl of seven, facing their mother's death. Olivia had never blamed her for their mother's death, and Susannah was grateful to her sister for that. Olivia had told her time and again that their mother had been weak and sickly before Susannah had ever been thought into being. Her sister had always lovingly told her that their mother made sure she lived in order to bring Susannah into the world. Olivia often called her their mother's last and greatest gift.

A tear trickled down her cheek, and she sniffed. She could do nothing but wait—just as she had to wait for Captain Jeffries. And for him it could take years. Her life would be nothing but waiting!

"Enter," Sheldrake muttered to the knock at the door. It would be Peter, no doubt to convince him to come to dinner. Blessing was playing host in his absence to Susannah and her aunt. At the second knock, he knew then that it was someone else. "Enter," he said more loudly.

"My lord." A footman bowed from the doorway. "Lady Beresford is calling for you."

He was up in a trice. "Is she all right?"

"Mrs. Boothe says it's a matter of life and death."

He bounded from his study. Racing up the stairs, he prayed over and over that she was well. *Dear God, if anything happened to her.* His blood ran cold at the thought.

He stopped just outside the door to her chamber. He could hear her groan. Opening the door slowly, fearful of what he would find, he saw her. She looked tired, as if she had been working very hard indeed. Tendrils of her hair stuck to her forehead. When she saw him, she reached out her hand for him to come closer.

He quickly knelt at her bedside. "How are you?" he whispered. It was agony not to hold her, to smooth the lines of worry from her beautiful brow.

"I am frightened," she answered in a low voice.

For a moment he merely looked at her, willing her to stay strong. Then he turned to Pedley, "How is she?"

"Fine, Richard." The doctor wiped his hands on a towel. He looked a bit harassed. "She demanded that you be sent for, wouldn't lie back otherwise."

Taking her hand in his, he said, "It is all right, love, I am here."

"I need to ask you . . ." She hesitated between deep breaths.

"Sshh, not now. Later." He smoothed back her hair. He knew she would demand the truth about Abbott, but never expected her to do so now.

"No, you misunderstand me. Should I die . . ."

He laid a finger across her lips. "Never! You will not. Do not even think it."

"Sheldrake, please, if I do, will you see to the baby? Watch over him or her. Even if from afar. I beg you. Do not let Edmund raise and ruin the child."

Sheldrake felt a tightness in his throat at her request, that she would entrust him with such a task. Raising her hand to his lips, he said, "I would be honored."

He watched as her eyelids closed in relief, and she squeezed his hand. He held on tight. He started when she suddenly gasped and tensed, clenching his hand so hard that he marveled momentarily at her strength. She grit her teeth and held her breath.

"Easy, easy now." He soothed her much as he would a mare at birth time.

Mrs. Boothe gave him a cool, dampened cloth. "For her head, my lord."

He nodded his thanks.

"This is when the fun begins." Pedley smiled, then said to Olivia, "Now breathe deeply, my dear, here we go."

Sheldrake tried to pull his hand away, but she held fast. "Olivia, I must go now."

She turned wide, terrified eyes upon him. "No, you cannot leave me."

"Mrs. Boothe is here and Pedley—they will see you through."

"No." She tried to sit up.

"You will be fine, I promise." He tried to sound cheerful when he explained, "I should not be here at all you know. This is a very compromising situation."

She only cast those huge green pools of eyes at him, pleading for him to stay.

"Olivia."

"Please, do not leave me. I need you. I am afraid." The last was said in a faint whisper that stabbed his heart.

Had he not caused her enough grief without adding to it by leaving? he thought. "This will no doubt be talked about across the county." He would stay. Right now he would do anything to chase the fear from her eyes.

In a surprisingly calm voice, she said to him, "You have asked me and I shall give you my answer in front of these two witnesses; I shall marry you, Lord Sheldrake. And that should satisfy propriety, I think." She breathed deeply as she leaned back against her pillows.

His heart leapt, but she could not be serious. However, in the name of propriety he would accept her answer and release her from it later. "Very well, now what should I do?"

"Keep hold of my hand. Ohh!" she gasped and began to rock.

"Pedley!" He looked at the doctor in panic. "What do I do?"

"Here is some cold water for that cloth. Bathe her face with it and hold her hand as she said." Pedley handed him a basin of water. "Oh, and congratulations, Richard!"

Olivia's scream rent the air. He laid the cloth on her head with shaking fingers. He knelt close to her, holding her hand and feeling completely useless. He was nervous and more than a little numb. He could not imagine what she must be feeling. Keeping the hair from falling in her eyes, he sent a silent petition to heaven to keep her safe.

Olivia collapsed between pains. She thought she could not go on. She could not! Sheldrake never left her side. All she knew was that she had to get this done whether it killed her or not. The pains came so close together, she felt as if she existed in another world full only of pushing and agony.

She shuddered. Sheldrake smoothed her brow with the cold cloth and murmured words of encouragement. She tried to rally her strength, what little of it remained. She could feel the swell of pain and knew what she had to do. Looking deep into Sheldrake's eyes and taking a deep breath, she pushed when the doctor ordered her to push. Again, she pushed.

She did not take her gaze away from Sheldrake, and his eyes spoke volumes of pride and encouragement to her without saying a word. He squeezed her hand every time she pushed.

"Just a little more, my lady, almost there, I can see the baby now," Doctor Pedley shouted.

She did not hear the rest. She felt the need to push and did so with such vigor that she groaned. She gripped Sheldrake's hand hard and squeezed her eyes shut.

Suddenly, her baby's cry filled the air.

"A girl! And she's a beautiful little mite!" the doctor announced.

Olivia fell back against her pillows, exhausted. It was over and she was alive! *Alive!* She looked up at Sheldrake, whose eyes were unusually bright.

"You did it," he whispered as he brought her hand to his lips.

"Yes, I did." She had nothing more to fear. Although she was more tired than she thought she had ever been, she knew she was fine.

Sheldrake stood quickly when Doctor Pedley brought her

baby to her bundled in white linens. She had a shock of dark hair, a whole head full.

"I will name her Jane, after my mother," she said with tears streaming down her face. With little Jane nestled in her arms, she checked each tiny finger, each toe. She was perfection.

Looking up at Sheldrake, who stood there smiling, she whispered, "Thank you for staying with me."

"You are most welcome," he said quietly, then he cleared his throat. "But I must go now and tell your aunt and sister. They are no doubt waiting on pins and needles." He bent down and kissed her forehead.

She watched him leave, knowing that she trusted him with her very life. She cradled Jane, but the infant searched out her breast through her nightdress. She laughed and awkwardly managed to grant the child what she wanted.

Mrs. Boothe looked shocked. "My lady, we have sent for a wet nurse."

"No," Olivia said with pride. "I have no need of one. I will provide for my child all that she needs." She was completely spent, but content and incredibly proud. Everything would be all right as Sheldrake had promised. In fact, she was better than that. She had agreed to be his wife and everything was right in her world for the first time in many years.

With Jane nestled, now sleeping in her arms, a quick tap at the door brought Aunt Agatha and Susannah bounding into the room. Her aunt hesitated at the bedside, but Susannah reached out eagerly and Olivia let her scoop the bundled babe into her arms. "I named her after Mother," she whispered.

"She is so pink." Susannah laughed. "Oh, my precious Baby Jane, we shall have such fun together."

Olivia could not stop smiling. The fear of death that had haunted her thoughts these past months was finally gone. She had won. Perhaps one day she might even have another child, a playmate for Jane, if of course Sheldrake agreed.

Warmth spread through her at the thought of giving him an heir, a son. They would be a family, and she promised herself that despite her father's life and death, they would be a happy one.

"You have done well," Aunt Agatha said. She stroked Olivia's forehead lovingly. "I am so very proud of you, dear."

"Thank you." She reached out to take hold of her aunt's hand and gave it an affectionate squeeze.

Doctor Pedley soon asked everyone to leave, except for Aunt Agatha, who decided she would stay and watch over her and the baby. With Jane tucked safely beside her and pillows all around for protection, Olivia finally dozed off to sleep.

Later that evening, she woke to the sound of Sheldrake's low voice talking to her aunt by the door. He carried something in his hands.

"Sheldrake?" she said as she raised herself up and leaned on her elbows.

"I did not mean to wake you," he said, standing in the threshold of the door.

"What do you have there?" She adjusted Jane, who slept peacefully beside her. "You may come in."

"Yes, Lord Sheldrake, do come in and see the baby," Aunt Agatha said.

"Just for a moment," he said.

Olivia noticed that he looked tired as he walked toward her. Pride in him swelled in her chest. He had stayed with her and helped her bring Jane into the world. She loved him so very much that the magnitude of what she felt for him almost overwhelmed her.

"I brought this." He lifted a cradle and placed it next to the bed.

She stared into his eyes, again moved by his thoughtfulness. "Thank you, it is lovely." she whispered. "Where did you find it?"

"It was mine when I was a babe. I pulled it out of the attics." He remained standing, looking uncertainly at her and then at Jane.

"Would you like to hold her?" she asked, then burst into laughter at the panic that flitted across his face. "I may just dump her in your lap sometime, so you had best prepare for it."

That earned her a smile. "But not now. She is too small," he said.

"How is your mother?" she asked.

"Fine. She is sleeping, which is what you should be doing. It is late."

She made a face, but did not protest when he turned to speak to Aunt Agatha, who sat down next to the bed. "I had it cleaned and polished, but you will have to have Mrs. Boothe help you find the right blankets to soften the cradle for Jane," he said.

"Thank you, my lord, you are a dear." Aunt Agatha suddenly stood as if an idea struck her. "Actually, I have the very thing, but it is in my chamber. I shall return directly."

Aunt Agatha bustled out of the room, leaving the door wide open. It was an obvious, but sweet attempt to give them some time alone. She smiled at the thought of how much her aunt had changed toward Sheldrake.

They remained silent a moment, and she looked up at him, still standing. "You may sit down if you wish." But he remained where he was, looking hesitant.

"I can stay only a moment—you need your rest." But he did not make a move to leave.

She wanted to keep him with her as long as she could. "Will your mother recover fully, do you think?"

"Yes, she seems to be fine. She has regained her memory." He paused, looking uncomfortable, then he continued, "And she appears to be sound of mind. Pedley said she needs only time to heal completely."

"I am glad." She knew he was thinking of her father, and an uneasiness invaded her newly found peace. Would the cruelty of her father give Sheldrake pause in marrying her?

Perhaps he felt differently toward her now that he knew who had sired her.

It was not the right time for them to discuss the portrait, even though she knew it must weigh heavily on his thoughts. "I must apologize for causing such an uproar," she said quietly. "Not a very good time to have a baby."

"Olivia." He knelt by her bedside. "Do not dare apologize."

The earnest look in his eyes gave her hope, so she reached out and he took her hand in his. "Thank you for staying with me. I was so afraid."

"You were very brave and strong." He started to chuckle. "I thought you would break my hand, you gripped it that hard."

She laughed in return. "It hurt like the very devil," she whispered.

"I cannot even begin to imagine, but at least I understand."

She squeezed his hand gently and stared deeply into his eyes. "You always understand, do you not?"

"What do you mean?" His gaze clouded over.

"You are the most understanding and kind man I have ever met, Lord Sheldrake."

He actually flushed at her compliment. "You do me a great honor, Lady Beresford."

"Olivia," she whispered. She did not wish to be considered Robbie's wife by him calling her thus.

"Then you must call me Richard," he said.

"I will. Always."

He brought her hand, which still rested in his, to his lips. And then he turned her hand over and placed a soft kiss upon her palm. "I would hear my name from your lips," he murmured.

Her heart skipped a beat at the look in his eyes. "Richard," she said softly.

He leaned forward, and she knew he was about to kiss her. She responded in kind, but Jane decided against it and chose that moment to wake with a gurgled cry. Olivia leaned back and pulled the bundled infant into her arms and rocked her. She looked up at Sheldrake, who now stood, looking ready to leave and almost relieved for the interruption.

"It is late. We had best say our good nights."

"Yes," she said distractedly as Jane nuzzled against her, seeking nourishment.

"Rest well, and we shall talk more when you are recovered."

Understanding that he meant they would talk about her father, she nodded. It was not something she looked forward to, but knew that it had to be dealt with before they could make plans for their future together. Jane grew more insistent, and Sheldrake retreated to the door.

He turned and smiled at her though. "Good night."

"Good night," she answered. And then he was gone.

Sheldrake walked away with a heavy heart. He wished they could go on as they were, but he knew that he owed her the truth about her father's death—a truth that could shatter her desire to make Sheldrake Hall her home.

How would she face his mother once she knew the truth? Would he have to choose between them if Olivia held her father's death against his mother? He knew he had to tell her the truth and not try to protect himself or his mother with anything other than the actual events of that night. But he was scared to the soles of his boots of her reaction.

But for now he realized she had to rest and recover. And he wanted to bask in the pride he felt for her. She was strong and even more beautiful to him than he ever thought possible. And he loved her, which made it all the more difficult to let her go if he must.

Chapter Fifteen

"Godspeed to your bride," Sheldrake said to Peter as he mounted his horse.

"Thank you. I hope to bring Winnie here to meet you and Olivia one day."

He merely nodded. He was too tired from a sleepless night to argue the point that he and Olivia might not marry.

"Take care Shel." Peter tipped his hat, then spurred the horse to a trot.

Sheldrake watched his friend disappear down the long drive, and then he finally returned to the Hall. He chewed the inside of his lip and decided he may as well work on his ledgers in his study. He knew it would give him no relief, no respite from the bitter longing and heartache, but it was better to stay busy than remain idle.

He had to let her go. When Olivia was fully recovered, he would tell her the rest of the sordid tale of Abbott's death and then let her go.

Later, he sat in his study, twirling the pen quills in his fingers. He could not concentrate on his accounts. He kept reliving the previous day in his mind—from the time Olivia had first laid eyes upon the portrait to Jane's miraculous arrival.

Pride still swelled in his breast when he thought of how hard Olivia had worked bearing little Jane. And he had felt a tug at his heart, a draw toward the babe as if she had been his own, as if Jane had been theirs. He closed his eyes in pain.

He closed his account books with a snap and rose from his desk. Perhaps it was not too early to seek his gardener.

Entering the greenhouse beyond the stables, he found him. "Lawrence," he called out.

"Yes, my lord?" the gardener answered.

"I would like you to accompany me into town today."

"Yes, sir."

"We shall purchase roses. I think it high time we planted more roses."

"Aye, my lord."

Two days had passed, and Olivia was at last able to get up from her bed. She sat upon the couch in her chamber, leaning against a bevy of pillows. A fire burned bright in the hearth, and Jane lay sleeping in Sheldrake's cradle.

They had seen little of each other since Jane had been born. Olivia had slept most of the first day after bearing Jane. She woke only to feed her. The second day was filled with visits from the doctor and her aunt and sister and even Lady Evelyn. But Sheldrake had looked in on her only briefly.

The shadows behind his eyes had been more pronounced, and she knew that his heart was heavy. Before she could encourage him to talk to her, he had been called away by a servant. She had made considerable peace with his mother. Lady Evelyn had assured her that she harbored no ill-feelings toward her for being the daughter of the man who had caused her such pain. But even Lady Evelyn's eyes held shadows of doubt when she had said she would allow Richard to tell her the truth of her father's death and then they could talk more.

Olivia knew it would be difficult, but was strengthened by the way Lady Evelyn had hugged her and whispered that everything would work itself out in time. They would get through this. She needed only to make sure that Sheldrake believed it as well. She planned on seeking him out if he did not come to her first. She heard a light knock at the door, and a rush of anxiety filled her.

"Come in," she called. She sat straighter and put down her

needlework when Sheldrake entered the room. He looked so handsome in his buff breeches and dark blue coat that she was grateful to Bonnie for washing and styling her hair. He closed the door. He seemed terribly somber, and she knew the time for *talking* had come.

"Good morning, Richard. Did you sleep well?" she asked nervously.

"Not well enough, I am afraid."

"I am sorry. Jane did wake a couple of times through the night."

"It was not Jane." His expression was guarded, but his blue eyes were sorrowful and so her heart twisted. He had worried himself wretched.

She watched him shift his weight from foot to foot, clenching his hands. "You wish to speak of what happened that night, with Abbott." She felt more comfortable calling her father thus.

"Yes, but first I wish to address the manner of our engagement." He came closer and leaned against the arm of the sofa. "Olivia, I care for you deeply and hold you in the highest regard. Under the circumstances of accepting my offer, I think you may have felt pressured to do so in order to keep me from leaving." He stopped for a moment, then added, "I release you."

She stared at him. He stood with his gaze locked to hers, waiting for her response. Did he regret that she accepted his proposal? No, she could not believe that. Then she understood fully. He thought that she must want out of the betrothal because Abbott was her father, that she could not marry him because of it.

What made matters worse was that she had not announced their engagement. She knew that until they had come to terms about Abbott being her father, she could not announce such a thing. He may have taken her silence as reluctance or regret. Mrs. Boothe and Doctor Pedley had not said a word to anyone either. And so, he stood tall and proud, waiting for her to release him. She knew how much it cost him to stand there waiting for her to refuse him.

Anger toward her father burned anew within her. Sheldrake expected to be rejected by yet another woman because of her father, and that made her heart break for him. She reached out and took hold of his clenched fist. He looked surprised when she pulled his fist to her face. She opened his curled fingers and placed a light kiss in the center of his palm.

He dropped to his knees next to her, his expression one of awe. "You do not even know what happened to your father, and yet you trusted me." His hand reached up to stroke her cheek.

"I know what sort of man you are, Richard. You are gentle and kind and just. I know that whatever happened the night my father died was justified. My father was cruel and heartless. I cannot pretend feelings of warmth for him that are not present. I wish only that it had been different, that he had been different." She covered his hand with her own. "When I said I would marry you, I meant it with all my heart."

"I do not deserve you, my love."

There was only one way to answer him. She bent toward him to meet his lips with her own. His fingers thread through her hair, messing its already loose knot. His mouth moved slowly over hers as he cradled her neck with his palm. When his tongue teased her lips, she opened to him and the kiss deepened instantly. She felt dizzy when they finally pulled back.

"I love you," he whispered.

"And I love you."

He smoothed the tendrils of hair that had escaped from her knot and tucked a stray curl behind her ear. "I must tell you all of it."

"Yes." She tensed. She suddenly did not wish to know. After all this time trying to find out the truth, she found she was not eager to hear it.

"Olivia, this is hard for me. Knowing that Abbott was your father." He stood and paced the room.

"I know, but you must. We cannot have any secrets between us now."

"You are right, of course. What was his real name?"

"Charles Lacey. He was banished from England for dueling when I was seven, but it appears that he did not leave. He merely changed his name."

He took a deep breath and let it back out, then said, "The truth of the matter is that I came upon Abbott in the conservatory. My mother stood much as she did at dinner, clutching her hair, screaming, a still smoking pistol at her feet."

"My goodness, your mother shot him?" She would never have guessed such a thing, and yet it made perfect sense. She shuddered when she thought of how horrible it must have been for her, for them all.

"Peter and I had been out late that night. He was down for a visit as he does every year. Had we not come home when we did, the entire household would have found my mother. The scandal would have been incredible. We heard the commotion and rushed in.

"Peter had been the quick one. He had me gather my mother up and take her to my study. He managed to put everything together to look like an accident. He explained to the staff that Abbott, drunk, had shot himself while he was cleaning his pistol.

"Pedley was called. We had to tell him the truth. Not wanting my mother to end up in an asylum, since the law is not on a woman's side in matters such as these, he stuck to our story as well. The constable was satisfied."

"But why did your mother shoot him?" She could think of many obvious reasons, but needed to know what event caused Lady Evelyn to do such a thing.

"As I started to tell you before, Abbott raised his hand to my mother on occasion. After my threatening him, I can only assume that he was careful not to let the other marks show. My mother never told me, but I pieced it together with the help of her abigail, Sally, that night. Bonnie, the maid assigned to you—her mother was my mother's abigail. Sally is a beautiful woman, and Abbott had been pursuing her, much to Sally's distress. That night Abbott had cornered Sally in the conservatory and forced his attentions upon her. When my mother found them, she tried to make Abbott stop, but he would not. He struck my mother and threatened to kill her if she interfered." He took a deep breath.

Olivia sat stunned. It was a horrible story, but so like her father's actions toward her own mother. She shuddered. "Go on."

"My mother went to my study and retrieved a pistol. It was loaded. She returned to the conservatory and warned him again. He did not heed her, and to save her maid from being ravished, she shot him."

"So that is why Bonnie's mother was sent to London," she said.

"Yes. My mother lost all memory of what had happened. She did not speak a single word for a week. She merely sat and stared out of the window. I was so afraid she had lost her sanity that I dared not allow a reminder like Sally to remain here."

"That is truly terrible. I am so sorry." She reached out to him.

He took her hand. "You may still release me. I will understand if you do not wish to marry into such a family."

"You forget that my own father is the one who has caused you and your mother such pain. Perhaps I will be a sad reminder to you. Do you want me to release you?" She held her breath, waiting for his answer. If he said yes, she knew she could not bear it.

He caressed her cheek and sat down next to her. "I want you as my wife more than anything."

"Then your wife I shall be."

"But what of my mother, how will you . . ."

She laid a finger upon his lips. "Your mother and I have already spoken about my father. She said that we would discuss the situation more after you had told me the whole story. I cannot blame her for what she did. She suffered as my own mother had under my father's cruelty. I will let her know that I forgive her, that I understand completely. I only hope that I can help her with it somehow. Will I be a reminder of my father to your mother, do you think?"

"Olivia, she loves you. You may be what she needs to accept what has happened, to finally come to terms with it."

"She is fortunate to have a son like you," she whispered.

"I should have protected her." His hands balled into fists.

"Do not blame yourself. You did not know—how could you? It is over now." She took his hands in her own again and brought them to her lips for a reverent kiss.

"What is that for?"

"For being noble."

He protested.

"Richard, you are a noble soul. Please allow yourself to be human—a human who is very much loved."

He smiled and bent his lips to hers again. His sweet kiss held the promise of happiness for both of them. "Thank you. Thank you for coming into my home, turning it on its ear and bringing healing to my heart."

She could have cried. She flung her arms about his neck. She too had come full circle. She felt the ache of never having had a decent father and the neglect from Robbie finally ebb away from her. Their memory would remain, but the pain was no longer present.

She pulled back, gazing deeply into his eyes, and her heart was full. She trusted this man she had come to love with more than just her heart. She trusted him with her life, her child's life, and her very happiness. And he had trusted her with the truth.

They sat for some time entwined in each other's arms. They whispered words of apology and forgiveness for the sins of their parents. Finally, there were no more secrets between them, and their future lay shining before them.

Epilogue

Olivia turned around before the full-length mirror. Her bride's dress, a gift from Lady Evelyn, was the most beautiful gown she had ever seen. It was made of the softest peach silk with an overdress of exquisite ivory lace covered in seed pearls. In her hair a simple arrangement of white roses from Sheldrake's newest hothouse strain hugged her dusky curls. Her mother's pearls encircled her throat.

"You look like a fairy princess," Susannah said.

"I do, don't I." She twirled again and smiled.

"And to think, only last summer I suggested we take the turn to drive by Sheldrake Hall. I believe you have me to thank for this day." Her sister rocked a sleeping Jane in her arms.

Olivia bowed toward her sister with mock gratitude. Their eight-month betrothal had been a long one, and she had waited patiently. After her confinement, she and her sister had returned to their aunt's cottage a half day's ride north of Sheldrake Hall.

Sheldrake had visited often, but it had been agony to be apart from each other. He had insisted it was best for them to wait until she could officially put off her mourning clothes before the banns were read. And so, they had waited to be wed, and no lack of propriety could be found by anyone.

"Come, my dear. It is time." Aunt Agatha stood in the doorway, beaming with pride.

Olivia breathed deeply to tame the excitement bubbling

within her. She feared she would shout aloud her happiness at any moment. But she followed her aunt demurely into the April sunshine, where a carriage waited to take them to the church.

When they pulled into the churchyard, Olivia could see Sheldrake standing at the open door, greeting the guests. She smiled and waved as he looked up. He waved back and ran forward to meet them.

"You look radiant," he said.

She took his hand and nearly flew from the carriage. "And you are very handsome."

He brought her hand to his lips and let his kiss linger. "Are you ready, madam?"

"Very much so." She slanted him what she hoped was a seductive look.

"Impatient wench," he whispered in her ear.

She shivered with pleasure.

"Hey, enough of that until you are safely wed," Peter Blessing called out from the steps. He stood next to his smiling wife, Winifred, who was beginning to show that she was in the family way.

Sheldrake laughed, then tucked Olivia's hand in the crook of his elbow. "Shall we?"

"Yes, we most certainly shall," she agreed, and they walked into the chapel draped with flowers and filled with happy faces. But nothing surrounding her could compete with the love shining from Sheldrake's eyes, so she concentrated solely on him. When the parson announced them as Lord and Lady Sheldrake, Olivia wasted no time in kissing her new husband, senseless to the cheers of their many guests.

His eyes darkened. "I am tempted to skirt you off to our inn and forget all about our bridal breakfast."

She knew her cheeks were pink, but she felt exactly the same way. "Perhaps we can leave early," she whispered as they made their way to the back of the church.

"Perhaps, but we should savor every moment of this day.

It has been a long time coming and one we deserve." He brushed her lips lightly with his own.

"True, very true. Besides, we have our whole life together."

"Together, forever, amen." He brought her hand to his lips for a reverent kiss.

"Amen," she whispered. Filled with gratitude, she cast her eyes heavenward and silently whispered her thanks.